What They Are Saying About Jessica James' Books

"A riveting piece of historical fiction, very much highly recommended reading."
– Midwest Book Review

"It is a book that I think could have the impact of a 'one With the Wind."
– Jonathan A. Noyalas, Assistant Professor of History and Director for Civil War Studies, Lord Fairfax Community College

"Explores the War Between the States in a way that will touch you like no other work of fiction." – The Book Connection

"I think it is the best Civil War fiction book since Cold Mountain."
– James D. Bibb, Sons of Confederate Veterans, Trimble Camp 1836

"Not since reading Gone With the Wind have I enjoyed a book so much!"
– Sarah Winch

"This is what epic stores are made of. I will not get rid of this one. It is a keeper that I will read time and time again." – T. Weatherby

"A beautiful story with a timeless message. It touched my heart and soul."
– Catherine Bennett

Above and Beyond

A Novel of Love and Redemption
During the American Civil War

By Jessica James

Patriot Press
Gettysburg, Pa..

PUBLISHED BY PATRIOT PRESS

Gettysburg, Pa.

www.PatriotPressBooks.com

ISBN 978-0-9796000-9-8

Library of Congress Control Number: 2013935634

July 2013

Other novels by Jessica James

NOBLE CAUSE: A Novel of Love and War

SHADES OF GRAY: A Novel of the Civil War in Virginia

FROM THE HEART: Love Stories and Letters from the Civil War

Awards

2012 Foreword Magazine Bronze winner Book of the Year in Romance
2011 John Esten Cooke Award for Southern Fiction
2011 USA "Best Books 2011" Finalist in Historical Fiction
2011 Next Generation Indie Award for Best Regional Fiction
2011 Next Generation Indie Finalist in Romance category
2011 Next Generation Indie Finalist in Historical Fiction category
2011 NABE Pinnacle Book Achievement Award
2010 Stars and Flags: Second place for Historical Fiction
2009 HOLT Medallion Finalist for Best Southern Theme
2008 Indie Next Generation Award for Best Regional Fiction
2008 Indie Next Generation Finalist for Best Historical Fiction
2008 IPPY Award for Best Regional Fiction
2008 ForeWord Magazine Finalist for Book of the Year in Romance

Chapter 1

Looks like the innocent flower, but be the serpent under it.
—Shakespeare, MacBeth (Act I, Scene V)

June 1862

Major Douglas Benton rode in front of his men, his straight, broad back giving no indication of the hard-fought battles through which he had recently passed. To anyone watching, he appeared the epitome of rugged masculinity and imposing power, yet beneath the stalwart exterior of muscle and strength rode a man with straying thoughts.

With the fighting well over and the enemy long gone, Benton's wandering mind had turned to more peaceful pursuits. He was day-dreaming—mostly about things like shade and a cool draught of water but also of kindly succor at the hands of a beautiful maiden. It was a dream that had little chance of becoming reality, dusty and dirty and disheveled as he was. But it was his to dream nonetheless as he and his horse, with his staff and troop behind him, plodded wearily down an overgrown bridle path.

Two days and nights in the saddle is enough to dull most men's thoughts of women, but Major Benton found that fatigue did little to diminish his appreciation for the opposite sex. Recently entrusted with his own command, Benton's orders had kept him engaged in tracking and harassing the enemy for the past few weeks, which had resulted in an unusually long isolation from feminine society. So hot as it was and as parched as he was, Benton still dreamed of warm smiles and womanly charms, deciding he would gladly forego the water and shade if only for a few minutes diversion with a female face and form.

"Sir?"

"Yes, Lieutenant, what is it?" Benton's voice betrayed his annoyance when the young officer interrupted his daydream. He knew only the name and rank of some of those he now commanded—and not even that for others.

"Sir, I don't think…"

"There's a house up ahead, Major," another one of his men interrupted.

"Yes, finally." Benton's weary gaze fell upon a well-tended home sitting amidst a clump of old oaks. *Aha, the trees prove evidence of bountiful shade, and the stone well in the yard testifies to the existence of water. Now all that is needed—*

The lieutenant interrupted again just as Major Benton began turning his horse off the path to the wagon track toward the house. ""Sir…as I was saying…"

"It will have to wait, Lieutenant." Benton stuck spurs to his horse to ride in advance of his men. He'd already noticed the place itself was a thing of singular beauty, offering the added advantage of remoteness and isolation. He had only another quarter mile to dream about who might inhabit it.

* * *

The yard smelled of roses and appeared carpeted with velvety grass. The sun fairly gleamed from the broad, white bosom of the majestic ivy-covered house, making it appear almost celestial in nature. As he drew close, the slight hint of a breeze caressed Benton's brow; he felt like he was part of a dream.

As Benton tugged on the reins to slow his anxious horse, his gaze fell upon a womanly form sitting on a garden bench with her head bent intently over a book. He pulled his horse to a halt and took in the scene, then reached down to open the latch of the gate. It was then that she stood and turned her face toward him, and it was then that Benton's movements were for a moment arrested. Even a dream could not equal the perfection of beauty that stood before him. Astonished, Benton moved his horse forward and removed his hat, bowing low over his saddle. "Pardon the intrusion, miss. My men are tired and thirsty and would be much obliged for a place to rest."

Benton was close enough now to see two blue eyes regarding him unemotionally from above the high collar of a drab, black mourning dress. Although he thought he had caught a glimmer of welcome at first glance, he could not help notice now the straight, authoritarian bearing of her stance, a trait he tended to find disagreeable in women. His gaze drifted down to the book she held in one hand, and its scuffed and tattered cover. As black as her dress, it reflected hard usage, but he could still read the title in barely recognizable gold letters: Holy Bible.

"Conscience compels me to decline the honor." She spoke softly yet firmly, never removing her eyes from him as she slowly let the Bible drop to the bench behind her.

"We wish you no ill, miss." Benton leaned on the pommel with negligent grace, confident of his effect on women. "Surely you are aware there is no refreshment more delicious than that afforded by shade." He nodded toward the large canopy of trees to his right as he spoke, yet it took no intimate knowledge of his character or familiarity with his dream to know that shade was not necessarily the refreshment he was seeking.

The young woman's eyes swept across his uniform, then over his shoulder to the approaching horsemen. The suspicion in them turned to intolerance. "I have offered you no invitation, sir," she said in a cold voice.

Benton laughed as much from amusement as from surprise at her tone and examined her in such a way as to surely make her feel he knew her better than he possibly could. He continued to sit erect and poised, full of manly strength and confidence. "I see you are in mourning, and offer my condolences for your loss. But you are mistaken if you think we mean you harm." He loosened his reins, making preparations to dismount.

"I have made no mistake." The woman's voice turned clearly hostile as she lifted an ancient shotgun from the folds of her skirt. In another

3

instant, the gun was locked expertly between her side and elbow and was pointed straight at his chest. "But if one of your boots dares touch this soil, *you* may claim the responsibility for making one."

"But I am Major Douglas Benton—" He stopped short when he saw the look that radiated from her eyes.

"Yes, I gathered that." Her gaze remained locked on his. "I am no stranger to your character and reputation."

The words were said in such a tone that it was clear she believed his character and reputation were not features to be proud of. Benton looked at her incredulously. In her expression, he could behold no friendliness or affection, yet the voice was distinctly Southern, gentle and drawling.

"Surely you do not mean to deny water to the soldiers defending you."

She spoke unemotionally, not deigning to lower the gun. "I can deny water to those who are trespassing on my property."

Benton looked down at her now with blank astonishment and then back toward his men still some twenty yards away. He saw out of the corner of his eye that she shifted her gaze to the east with a look of grave concern, but by the time he turned back around, her full attention was once again upon him.

"Come, my dear, where is your loyalty to Virginia?" Benton knew his tone revealed his agitation and made an attempt to sound less surly.

"I am loyal to the only authority I recognize," she snapped, loud enough now for his approaching men to hear.

Benton let his breath escape him in a loud sigh of exasperation as he thought of the many battles he had fought to achieve his renowned reputation as a fighter. Yet not quite knowing what to do or say, he stared at the foe before him. "You intend to deny shade and water to these men?" He purposely asked the question in such a way as to indicate he did not think he had heard her correctly the first time, and wanted to give her another chance.

Her reply was simple. "I intend to defend my property. If you do not wish me to bestow the contents of this gun upon you, I suggest you urge your men to move on."

In the heat of the moment, Benton completely forgot his dream. "And I urge *you*, miss, to put down that gun!"

Although he possessed a voice of easy command, Benton knew he was in a situation in which he was losing control. Indeed, if eyes possessed the power to kill, he knew he would be departing the earth for good, because her gaze, like the two barrels of her shotgun, remained locked on his heart.

"You may have the power to make that request, Major Benton—but most assuredly not the authority."

"Madam, I did not request you. I *ordered* you!"

Benton looked from the gun to her face and saw no sign of fear or compromise. Then his agitation became obvious. His face kindled with the fire that was wont to burn there when on the battlefield. "I beg your pardon, young lady, for seeing the necessity of giving advice," he said from between tightly clenched teeth, "but as we are men worthy of respect, I must insist that you drop that weapon."

The woman remained unflappable. "As you have kindly begged my pardon for giving me this advice, I must beg yours for not taking it. To be frank, sir, you ought to have more prudence about where you request hospitality."

Benton sat back on his horse as if having suffered a physical blow. Staring at his opponent with a look of intense annoyance, he dropped the focus of his gaze to the muzzle of the gun, which he noticed had begun to lower ever so slightly. Lifting his eyes to hers, he saw they had softened considerably as she followed the approach of a horse and rider behind him.

"Major, this isn't a place you want to stop." The soldier urged his mount forward and then drew rein beside Benton. "It's the home of a traitor."

The woman's cheek twitched slightly at the words, like the spontaneous quiver of a horse's hide when touched by a fly.

"You are acquainted?" Benton scrutinized the same lieutenant who had attempted to stop him earlier from turning down the lane.

"Sir, I have the unfortunate duty to report that this is my sister. Well, that is… *was* my sister."

"I am still your sister, Jake," the woman said softly, all the callousness gone from her voice. "The war cannot change that."

The lieutenant did not answer her, just turned his head and spit into the dust as if that was a sufficient response. Then he addressed Benton again. "As I tried to tell you earlier, sir, there is a loyal family only another mile down the pike."

Benton looked from one to the other for a moment and then decided to take his lieutenant's advice. For a moment, he considered warning the woman about her unpopular stance in the region and the possible danger to her welfare, but one more look into those fearless, ice blue eyes changed his mind on the necessity. "Lead the way, Lieutenant."

Riding at a swift pace, it did not take long for the band of warriors to put the house called Waverly behind them. As they trotted up a small rise, a scout came galloping out of the tree line and pulled his horse to a sliding stop in front of Benton. "Found this in the old tree, sir."

Benton opened the communication and scanned the missive quickly. Turning his horse back toward the east, he scanned the landscape a moment and looked over at his next in command. "You see anything suspicious out there, Captain Connelly?"

Connelly squinted against the late-afternoon sun and then pulled a spyglass from his saddle. "Yea, looks like something's kickin' up some dust down there." He handed the spyglass to Benton. "Might even be heading to Waverly from the direction they're heading."

Benton stared through the lens briefly then closed it in disgust with a loud snap.

"If that's from Sid, looks like he's right again." Connelly nodded toward the piece of paper Benton still held.

Benton merely grunted in reply as he leaned over his pommel and studied the horizon with a scowl. "Whoever *Sid* is," he said at length. "He seems to know every movement the Union army makes in this region—and I don't even know who he is."

The two officers sat silently and assessed the situation as the moving cloud of dust slowly transformed into a small band of cavalry wearing blue uniforms.

"Well, I reckon it's a good thing we didn't hang around Waverly." Connelly shifted his weight in the saddle. "Looks like nothin' but a small scouting party, but they could have caused some headaches."

Benton took one more look, and then turned his horse back around. "Well they are welcome to Waverly—and its inhospitable occupant as far as I'm concerned."

"Speaking of which, what do you reckin' we should do with that one?" Connelly tilted his head back toward the house from which they had come.

Benton sighed heavily, trying to erase the image of those brilliant blue eyes filled with hostility, and attempted instead to imagine them shining with the devotion with which he was accustomed. "Frankly, I'm inclined to cut off the tail and hope it dies when the sun goes down," Benton muttered as he tried to reconstruct the dream that had been ruined by the only woman he'd ever met immune to his charms.

Chapter 2

The best soldiers are not always warlike.
—Chinese proverb

Major Benton paced the foyer of Confederate president Jefferson Davis's home, silently rehearsing his proposal. He had no idea why he had been summoned to Richmond, but he intended to use the opportunity to introduce a matter that had been a source of vexation since the day he'd been given his own command.

Agitated as he was, Benton tried to calm his restless nerves. It would do little good to start a heated discussion with the president. He intended to lay out the facts and convince the president of the necessity of knowing the identities of the spies and scouts that operated in his territory. The fact that he had not been entrusted with that information already was an insult, though he consoled himself with the thought that it was a simple oversight.

Pausing for a moment, Benton strained his ears at the sound of voices floating down the staircase from the second floor office. Although Spencer, the president's butler, had informed him that Davis was concluding a meeting with General Lee, one of the voices from above sounded decidedly feminine. Spencer had since disappeared, so it was impossible to question him about the source.

Impossible. To think that a woman would be granted an interview with the president in that all-important war room upstairs was ridiculous. To suppose that General Lee could spare time from his schedule to be in attendance was simply absurd.

It was only moments more before Benton heard voices moving closer, followed by the distinct sound of rustling silk descending the stairs. He stood erect with anticipation, waiting now for the source of the feminine attire to become visible to him. As the figure descended the final step, he saw her turn to continue a conversation with President Davis. Dressed all in black, complete with a mourning veil pulled back from her face, she smiled over her shoulder as if she and the president had just shared a private joke. General Lee stood at the bottom of the stairs, and took her hand to assist her into the foyer. Turning to acknowledge Lee's courtesy, the woman caught sight of Benton. The smile disappeared utterly.

"Major Benton! What a pleasant surprise!" General Lee said, following her gaze.

Benton did not hear the general. His eyes were intent on the woman. "*You!*"

President Davis entered the room and looked grimly from one to the other. "Yes, I understand you've met."

"The only thing I've *met*," Benton said loudly, "is the end of a shotgun that means business!"

With great effort he released his gaze from the young woman's impassive, upturned face and turned his attention to President Davis. "Do you know, sir, who this woman is?"

"Why, yes, I was just getting around to that. Allow me to formally introduce you. Major Benton, I have the honor to present *Sarah... Irene... Duvall.*"

Benton noticed the obvious and elaborate pause in Davis's voice between each word of her name and repeated them to himself. Little by little, his befuddled mind began to comprehend the meaning in the woman's initials.

His eyes shot to President Davis, and then to General Lee, who stood quietly beside the woman. Then his face reddened as annoyance blinded his eye to all things save his anger. "Why was I not told of this sooner? This is an outrage!"

"I know. I apologize. It was an oversight. Sid is here on precisely the same subject."

"An oversight?" Benton's eyes targeted the woman whom he now knew had been providing intelligence to him through messages left in a hollow oak tree for the past two months. "*She* had ample opportunity to inform me!"

Sarah Duvall, meanwhile, stood arrow straight, staring into space as if she realized the encounter was unavoidable but was not one she had been looking forward to. Her expression seemed to convey that she was neither surprised or the least bit concerned about the unexpected encounter with the man whose life she had threatened to end.

General Lee stepped forward. "Those were not her orders, Major. She was told to allow no one to know her true allegiance without written authorization."

Benton sighed angrily. "Well then, I can assure you she followed her orders precisely!" He threw his hands up in disgust and then addressed General Lee. "You expect me to entrust myself and my men to *her*?"

Lee responded quickly to the intended insult. "Has she not done a commendable job thus far?"

"That is not my point!"

"What exactly *is* your point, Major?"

"She is a *woman*!"

"How very observant of you." Lee smiled broadly while the one about whom they spoke remained silent, raising only a remote, unperturbed eye toward Benton for a moment before gazing over his shoulder again. She seemed completely composed, though she continued to stare at the door as if anxious for the moment she could walk through it.

Benton turned toward General Lee in an obvious effort to ignore her very presence. "Sir, I mean no disrespect, but how can she be expected to understand military tactics and keep secrets?"

Lee blinked, apparently not quite seeing his point. "I can assure you she's done a commendable job of secrecy thus far. And at great detriment to her own good name, I might add."

"But this is not woman's work! You cannot expect me to accept communications from a *female*. The sex is without stability!"

General Lee glanced heavenward for a moment. "Would you accept them from an officer?" His tone revealed his agitation.

"Of course I would." Benton's brow furrowed, insulted by the question.

President Davis nodded toward Lee, who pulled a pad from his coat pocket and began to write. He handed the finished product to the president, who signed it as well.

"I guess it is official," Davis said, handing it to Sarah.

She glanced at the missive and then began shaking her head. "Sir, I have no desire for such an endorsement."

She handed it back to Lee, who smiled and handed it to Benton. "Despite Sarah's misgivings, she is your newest recruit. See that she is treated with the respect and honor she deserves as an officer in your command."

Benton looked down at the paper and scanned it quickly.

In light of her conduct and attention to her country's interests, Sarah Irene Duvall is hereby promoted to a lieutenancy in the command of Major Douglas A. Benton, a position she shall hold as long as the Confederate states are in need of her services.

"This is preposterous!"

"It is done. I suggest you shake hands and make up." President Davis's tone was grave and serious.

Benton sighed heavily, as he gazed incredulously at the two men in the room. Without bothering to hide a look of complete indignation, he reluctantly offered his hand to the woman standing between them. When Sarah Duvall hesitantly accepted, Benton took note of her small and delicate fingers, the type that indicate the prospect of a gentle, tender touch. Yet he knew the woman's distant, noncommittal attitude provided a more genuine indication of the catlike hostility that represented her true character.

"There are now only four people who know Sarah's true allegiance, and they are standing in this room," Lee said soberly. "I need not tell you the necessity of keeping it that way."

Benton's eyes went to Sarah's as he thought back upon the unexpected meeting with her brother. It appeared she was thinking the same thing, for the blue in them turned a mournful gray, the color of a desolate cemetery stone. Otherwise, her dark, secretive face was set with, what he was beginning to learn, was her normal state of detached calm. She was indeed as unyielding and emotionless as a piece of granite.

Disregarding the look, Benton released her hand and turned again to President Davis. "She is paid handsomely, I presume." His tone and his expression indicated he thought the money could be better used in other pursuits, but he soon found out that gold was not on par with her patriotism.

Sarah Duvall drew back at his words and spoke to him for the first time. "I render a service, sir. I do not *sell* it! Her cheeks flamed now. "And I am sorry that you are so little acquainted with my character as to suppose my honor is for sale at any price."

"Not all soldiers carry arms." General Lee interrupted in a low, stern voice, indicating he thought Benton had gone far enough. "Information found and received is worth one thousand slain."

Benton sighed heavily as he looked at the faces in the room. It appeared nothing could be gained by continuing to argue with this foe—any more than could be gained by arguing with any woman for that matter. "Despite my better judgment, it appears I will have to accept the circumstances thrust upon me." He shifted his scowling gaze to the woman standing before him. "But I will accept this charade only so long as the information remains reliable."

President Davis and General Lee exhaled simultaneously at the comment, while Sarah's cheeks glowed again. "Thank you, Major." Her clenched teeth and trembling voice revealed for the first time how hard she was trying to keep her composure in front of a man she knew would never think of her as anything more than an object with which to flirt. "And now that we have been officially introduced, I hope we can continue to keep our distance."

Turning to the president and General Lee, she nodded. "I'm afraid I have a train to catch. Good evening, *gentlemen*." She lowered her veil to cover her face and then turned to acknowledge Benton. "And Major Benton."

Benton did not know if she was paying him a complement by singling him out for special attention or insulting him by not including him with the gentlemen—and so he followed her to the door to find out. "If I am to be your commanding officer, I must insist on some degree of respect." He looked at her hard, making it clear she was not part of his unit with his consent, let alone his approval.

"And shall you give that which you request to receive?" When he did not answer, she moved a step closer and talked in a low voice. "Let us understand each other, Major. I am not here to express insincere salutations of politeness or false professions of friendship. I am here to perform a duty, however unpleasant that duty may be."

Again, Benton could not tell from her expressionless face if the duty itself or the person with whom she was conversing caused the unpleasantness. "It appears we've gotten off on the wrong foot." Benton studied her face as he talked and made an effort to sound conciliatory, though he knew his countenance probably did not hide the fact that he thought the whole affair entirely her fault.

Sarah spoke while casually adjusting her veil. "I find that first impressions are seldom erroneous. Good day, sir."

As Spencer appeared and opened the door, Benton grabbed her arm. He was not one to let a mere woman have the last word or appear to get the upper hand. He grinned flirtatiously, knowing well the effect of his smile on the opposite sex. "May I have the honor of saying before you depart that I have no doubt you will perform your duties admirably. In fact, your superb acting skills almost lead me to believe that you dislike me intensely." He laughed softly at the idea of a woman disliking him.

Sarah flashed a smile as well, and looked him directly in the eye. "You exaggerate my abilities, Major, and would therefore perhaps be surprised to know how very little *acting* is involved. Good day."

* * *

"It appears she is immune to your charms, Major Benton," General Lee said when Benton returned.

"My charms have no effect on stone." Benton, surprised and confused by the actions of one Sarah Duvall, turned and stared sullenly out the window. It annoyed him that despite his best efforts to enchant her, she had remained either serenely unconscious of the endeavor—or supremely indifferent.

"I believe you judge her wrongly," Lee continued. "You know as well as anyone that traveling through that section of Virginia is more dangerous than ever now. She lives friendless in an enemy land at the peril of her own life. You must do what you can to protect her without divulging her true allegiance."

"An unpleasant proposition for both of us," Benton muttered.

"My heavens, man!" President Davis said. "You can't deny how much her information has benefited your reputation! Scarcely is a campaign designed or a strategy conceived within the Federal ranks when it not borne to you. You are probably better informed than Lincoln himself on the enemy's plans for movement in that region!"

"I don't see why you continue to resist," Lee said, continuing the conversation. "It is not hard to trace the source of the majority of your victories back to the intelligence she provided you."

"I resist for the obvious reason," Benton interrupted. "She is a *woman*."

Davis gave Benton an inscrutable stare. "You may as well accept the circumstances as they are, Major. You were given an independent command, the envy of every Confederate officer on the field, as a means to provide protection in that region."

Benton whirled around. "I was given my own command because of *her*?

"You have your orders, Major Benton," Lee said, bringing an end to the conversation. "You are to continue harassing the enemy as you have been doing, but every attempt must be made to afford Mrs. Duvall protection. She can be a great asset to you."

"*Mrs.* Duvall?"

"You may have judged from her dress that Mrs. Duvall is a widow," Lee answered abruptly. "The circumstances of her matrimonial state will no doubt be revealed to you in time. For now, you have a command to which you need to return. I assume your visit has been settled to your approval."

"Yes, of course," Benton said, though his tone reflected no such endorsement. Replacing the hat on his head, he bowed to both men and disappeared out the door.

* * *

General Lee signed heavily as he paced. "I hope we've made the right decision."

President Davis stared out the window at the light rain that had begun to fall, and considered the statement. He knew what Lee meant. Benton was not like most officers—or most men, for that matter. Young for an officer of his rank, he was a great favorite among the ladies—especially, but not limited to, those who were seeking a husband. With his splendid height and rugged good looks, he was recognized wherever he went, and his gift of charm made him welcome.

Yet the man had another side that was equally as remarkable. Within mere months of starting his military career, he had been acknowledged as a true leader by General J. E. B. Stuart and had been given his own command. The fact that he was just twenty-nine years of age enhanced the value of the compliment and had won him unbounded admiration.

Seizing on the opportunity, Benton had taken a group of common citizens and soldiers, and turned them into one of the most feared cavalry units in the Confederacy. No one planned their battles more judiciously, and no individual could bear upon the enemy the terror now wrought by Benton's name. When he chose the ground for a fight, one could be sure his men could hold it as long as they cared to and could withdraw safely whenever they liked. He had collected a trail of successful exploits that more than proved his courage and alacrity on the field, so that within less than a year, he had come to be pursued by two groups of men: those who wanted to serve under him—and those who wanted to kill him.

But could he be reined in enough to use the valuable services of Sarah Duvall? In her own quiet way, Sarah was as stubborn and unyielding as he—a fact made obvious by their brief meeting today. Davis could recall nothing to indicate concession or compromise in either's tone or manner.

General Lee smiled and patted Davis on the back as if reading his mind. "Don't worry. He has yet to discover the strength and spirit she possesses."

"Yes, I know," Davis replied thoughtfully. "And it may prove interesting to watch him bow to someone other than himself."

Chapter 3

Joan of Arc with fierce intent,
Has oft o'er southern saddle bent,
To guide the hero o'er the plain,
And help to victory with her rein.
— *"Dedication," a poem by General J. E. B. Stuart, 1864*

November 1862

Dusty from hard riding and weary with fatigue, Benton loosened the collar of his shirt and unbuttoned his coat the moment he entered his chamber. Although he'd been back at his post for almost four months now, the news that he'd been given an independent command primarily for the purpose of protecting a woman continued to consume his thoughts and annoy him. He cringed at the thought of his men discovering this fact, and though he was familiar enough with the integrity of the president and General Lee to know they would not divulge the truth, the same could not be said of Sarah Duvall.

He removed his coat with a violent shrug and carelessly threw the garment across a chair. As grateful as he was for the appointment to his own command, the new responsibility was now as much a burden as an honor.

"'Scuse, me. Sir?

Benton turned at the sound of his aide's voice. "Yes, Hancock, what is it? Make it quick. I know it's early, but don't let anyone disturb me until sunup."

"Well, sir, there's someone here to see you—"

"Tell him I'll see him first thing in the morning."

"Sir, he says it's imperative that he speaks to you…uh, now."

Benton took a step forward, and the aide took a step back. "All right, send him in! I'll get rid of him myself!" He turned his back to the door and proceeded to unclasp his shirt. Just as he was getting ready to kick off his boots, he heard the door open and close.

"Perhaps you could wait to do that until our interview is complete," someone with a hushed, familiar voice said from behind him.

Whirling around, Benton stared into the same blue eyes he had last seen in Richmond. For a moment, he was so stunned to see her that he forgot his state of undress, but when he saw long lashes touching the top of her crimson cheeks, he began re-clasping his shirt.

"Major, I beg forgiveness for the unannounced visit." She finally raised her gaze. "But I do bring urgent news. There was no other way to deliver it."

Partly confused, partly suspicious, Benton stared at her with a forbidding look intended to warn her that whatever she wanted was out of the question. Dressed as a man, she wore boots obviously not designed for her and that appeared painfully too large. Even more noticeable was the mud with which she was covered from the knees down, and splattered with from the waist up. The depth of mire she had traveled through to reach him was clearly visible by the amount of it she still carried upon her.

"Have you no horse?" His gaze lifted from her mud-coated boots to her eyes. Although her beautiful face seemed out of accord with her ragged and dirty clothes, she somehow appeared attractive and alluring.

For the first time she looked uncomfortable and slightly unnerved as she looked down at her soiled attire. "I was forced to travel most of the way on foot," she said. "My horse is old and lame."

"Yes, so it appears." Benton tried to keep the humor from showing in his eyes. Never before had he met a woman who valued her patriotism over outward appearance and clean clothes. Yet even in her state of disarray, he had to admit she possessed a poise and grace that were slightly unnerving. He turned his back to her a moment to light a cigar, waiting until the end glowed red to speak. "Out with it. What brings you?"

"They are taking to the torch, sir. The plan is already in motion."

He spun back around to face her, puzzled by her calm composure. Her tone indicated neither excitement nor fright, and her frank gaze confirmed she felt neither. She seemed to be offering the information candidly, without giving him the impression he was obligated to accept it. "I have received no intelligence that would show or even suggest that attempt." He studied her closely, looking for any sign of hesitation or uncertainty.

"Nevertheless, it is true. The plan was conceived and put into action in my parlor not four hours ago."

"Are you sure?" His voice was tinged with suspicion. "You will have to excuse me. I am not accustomed to consulting with women on the status of the field."

"I have traveled a great distance and at great peril."

"Show me." Benton took her by the arm, suddenly forgetting his reluctance to work with a woman, and pointed to a map on a table.

"Most of the Union troops will be vacating Glenville." She pointed immediately to the small town that had been in Union hands for months. "Captain Daniels moves here, to torch barns and granaries. Major Pittman is here, to the east, to do the same. Others will fan out in this direction to begin the destruction of Newton. They know these families are assisting you. They are to leave nothing for them to subsist upon."

Benton rubbed his hand across two days growth of beard as he paced back and forth. "I've not the men to go after them all," he said as if to himself. "And the ones I have are worn from two days riding." He paused and faced her. "But if they have abandoned Glenville, it should be occupied by us at any cost."

"Colonel Beckham is here, is he not?" Sarah pointed to a remote spot on the map.

"Yes, but I've no men to spare to alert him. And a lot of good he will do me with no direct roads between us."

"I know the way," Sarah said. "If you give me a horse, I'm certain he can be in Glenville by first light."

Benton failed to suppress a laugh, as he shot her a look of patient tolerance. "Please do not take my hesitation personally, but I do not feel that a battlefield is any place for a lady."

She nodded and gazed over his shoulder. "Yes, I'm familiar enough with your reputation to know where you believe a lady's place to be."

There was no sarcasm in her voice, only disappointment, but Benton's temper got the best of him. He walked up to her and shook his finger in her face. "Allow me to assure you, I am *not* going to send a woman into that countryside alone!"

"And why aren't you?" She stared straight into his eyes, unblinking.

Benton lowered his cigar for a moment and favored her with a martial stare. "We have rules here. Be they unwritten, they are no less binding."

She tilted her head curiously. "And what are these rules of which you speak?"

"*Gentlemen* do not ask *ladies* to send for reinforcements alone."

She smiled politely. "But, Major Benton, you need not *ask*. I just volunteered."

Benton's temper erupted at her calm and composed persistence. "Why you tormenting, headstrong little pest! Must I tell you that if you are caught in those clothes, you will be tried as a spy?"

He didn't say "hanged as a spy" because he knew it was not necessary. They both understood what the ultimate outcome would be.

"That is of little concern to me," she responded simply. "I do not stand here asking if you will let me, but only that you will not stop me."

Benton began pacing in front of her, the ashes from his cigar falling unnoticed to the floor as he silently assessed the danger and the need. "The main roads are picketed and the minor ones patrolled." He stopped right in front of her. "How would you get through?"

She seemed to take the question as full acceptance of the venture rather than reluctant approval to consider it. "I have lived here all my life and am familiar enough with the land."

He cocked his head and studied her. "But I wonder if a woman is capable," he murmured under his breath.

"You may wonder all you wish," she snapped, apparently tired of his stalling tactics. "But do not *doubt* it."

Although the words were spoken softly enough, Benton took issue with her tone. He took a step toward her and did not even attempt to keep the condescension out of his own tone. "Are you sure you know your way?"

For the first time he saw the usually composed countenance flash with anger. "Major Benton, I would not be here nor request the service if I did not know the way. Cast aside your reservations for the sake of the local citizens!"

Now it was his turn to voice anger. "Look here, Mrs....*Sid*." He stood and shook his finger at her again. "I never asked for your service, nor requested your assistance!"

He watched her take a deep breath. "You have little choice." Her voice was calm. "You forget, perhaps, that I *am* a lieutenant in your command."

Benton sat down and squeezed his temples—not sure if he should be angry or appreciative for the help. "Does Colonel Beckham know you?"

She looked down and fumbled with her coat sleeve. "No, of course not."

"That will never do. He won't believe you for a moment, and I won't risk writing anything down."

He stood and started pacing again, then turned to face her.

"Here, take this. We graduated from the Point together. He'll recognize it."

She looked at the ring he held in his outstretched hand and nodded. "Very well."

Benton strode to the door and called to an orderly, turning his head toward her after doing so. "You can ride a strong horse?" Benton didn't know why he asked. He instinctively knew she could handle any animal, if not with those small hands, then with the strength of her will. Before she could answer, a young soldier entered the room. "Private Jenkins, I need you to saddle Sultan for this boy."

The man nodded, saluted, and turned to leave, but Benton stopped him. "And when he returns, I want you to instruct Lieutenant Haines to give him his choice of the remounts. Do you understand?"

Jenkins looked for a moment at Sarah and then nodded again. "Yes, sir. I'll tell Lieutenant Haines your orders."

When the door closed behind him, Benton sat on the edge of his desk and brushed the end of his cigar against a small bowl. "Spare not your speed, yet take no unnecessary risks. Do you understand?" He didn't wait for an answer, but strode to the door and opened it for her. "I'll send one of my men to help you through the pickets. You'll be on your own after that."

"Yes, I understand. Have no fear. Beckham will be in possession of Glenville no later than dawn."

* * *

Despite his fatigue, Benton called together his officers, dispatching his freshest toward the hamlet of Newton and reserving others to fan out as the Union troops had reportedly done. Taking a small detachment, he hurried toward Kingston, knowing the granary there would not go untouched by the enemy's vile torches.

The fast ride in the cool night air did Benton good, but he could not help but question his judgment in permitting his unasked-for recruit to ride for reinforcements alone. The Virginia countryside was a maze of unmapped roads and trails, and as such, even he had to rely on the guides in his command. He could not spare his best from the perilous business that lay before him. Misgivings and second thoughts began to creep into his mind, despite the animosity he felt toward his newest officer. He found it hard to repel the remote, stealthy fear that crept into his wandering mind—what if something happened to her?

The pungent odor of burning wood dragged him from his thoughts, and a feeling of vengeance welled in his breast. He heard the first yells of his advance guard, soon followed by the sound of gunfire as they came upon a small group of the enemy's torches. These were not army stores being destroyed by fire, but the homes and barns of citizens he was sworn to defend.

The discovery of the enemy and the attack by his men occurred within an instant of one another. Benton's heart pounded with anger and vengeance as he whipped his horse into the fray, both guns blazing.

* * *

Major Benton rode into Glenville, exhausted beyond measure, but wearing a large smile of satisfaction. Hundreds of residents lined the streets and ladies of every age and shape waved their handkerchiefs in appreciation. It was obvious they deemed Benton the author of the victorious affair that had freed their town from the invading forces—and at the moment, he had no thought of dispelling that partial truth.

"This is the house, sir." One of his aides nodded toward a stately mansion to his right. "Colonel Beckham is waiting inside."

"Benton, you old cuss, it's about time you get here," Colonel Beckham boomed, hailing him before he had even dismounted.

Benton smiled and grabbed his friend's hand. "Much obliged for the help. I was spread a little thin to do it all myself."

"Indeed!" Beckham laughed. "By God, you're going to make Colonel for this, Benton. Wait 'til you see my report."

"My thanks for the endorsement, but you're the one that took back the town. It's been in Yankee hands for far too long now."

"Bah. We both know I had the easy part." Beckham paused to retrieve something from his coat pocket. "That reminds me. I have something of yours."

When Beckham handed him the ring, Benton stared at it a long moment before placing it back on his finger. True to her word but perhaps contrary to his expectations, she had succeeded in her mission. "Is the boy still here?" Benton looked up at the crowd of men on the porch as if she would be among them.

"My, no. Never even took a rest. Said he was in a hurry to get back to wherever he came from." Beckham began walking toward the house, talking over his shoulder as he proceeded up the steps. "Glad you gave him that ring, though. Not sure I would have believed the dirty rascal without it."

Benton nodded thoughtfully as he pushed away the foreign feeling of regret. Knowing that she had recognized and accepted a veiled role that would never allow her name to be praised made Benton pause. "Excuse me, Beck. I need to talk to one of my men a moment."

Making his way to the picket line of horses, Benton finally found the face he sought. "Lieutenant Haines, did a boy find you looking for a remount?" Benton scanned the horses on the picket line.

"Why, yessir. Private Jenkins said it was by your order."

"Yes, yes, it was by my order. Which horse did he take?"

Haines laughed. "Funny thing. You know that high-strung, Roman-nosed bag of bones you told us not to bother with?"

Again, Benton's eyes scanned the line. "You let him take that good-for-nothing colt?"

"Well you didn't want him, sir. Thought you'd be happy to be rid of him."

"Why didn't you suggest one of the others? The boy needed a good mount."

"Oh, I tried, Major." Lieutenant Haines put his hands on his hips and shook his head. "He went over each horse inch by inch. Said he wanted that one."

Benton walked over and laid his hand on the rump of a large bay. "What could possibly be wrong with this horse?" he growled, not really expecting an answer.

"On that one, suh, he pointed out that old low bow on the right fore."

Benton's gaze went down to the slight swelling on the leg that indicated a tendon had been damaged. The blemish was barely recognizable, though the condition would leave the horse vulnerable to future injury. "Well what's wrong with this one?" He moved to the next horse.

"Didn't like the high, straight pasterns on that one. Said he'd go lame sure with any kind of hard riding."

Looking over the horse, Benton took in the conformational flaw that only a well-seasoned horseman would notice. "And this one?"

"Well, you can see, suh, he is a little cow-hocked behind."

Benton drew a deep breath. "I still don't know what he saw in that Roman-nosed colt."

"Well, he said there wasn't nothing wrong with him a little food and care wouldn't fix. Said he liked his heavy frame and the spark in his eye."

"Heavy frame? Why he was a bag of bones! Spark in his eye? Why that horse was the commonest piece of horse flesh I've ever had the misfortune to come in contact with!" Benton whirled around and stomped back toward Beckham's headquarters, trying to control the anger that flooded his veins. Was she trying to make him look bad in front of General Lee? Would she tell him she'd been offered an ornery, malnourished mule for a mount?

He looked at his own sleek warhorse that was a living legend for his sense on the battlefield and swift and powerful gaits. Benton depended on him for both companionship and his natural abilities, and could not fathom what the blue-eyed spy had seen in the wild-eyed colt she'd taken. Although malnourished, he had been a handful even for the best of his veteran horsemen to ride and had been discarded as an unsuitable mount for the cavalry. Surely he would require a more powerful arm than hers to keep him under control.

Then again, the girl had succeeded in riding Sultan to Glennville and back—no easy task even for a man. Perhaps he had underestimated her abilities—and overestimated his ability to read them. Perhaps he'd been wrong about her all along.

Chapter 4

Mystery, mystery is the secret of success.
—General Thomas Jonathon "Stonewall" Jackson

M ajor Benton stumbled out onto the porch, squinting against the bright sunlight, and trying to ignore the thumping in his head. After enjoying a long night of revelry and celebration over the great victory he and his men had achieved, it was time to get back to business.

"Majah Benton! What a nice surprise!"

Benton wheeled at the feminine voice. He recognized it as familiar, but could not place where he had heard it last or to whom it belonged.

"The girls told me you were in town, but I didn't darah believe it!"

"Mrs. Grimes." Benton bowed as recognition set in. "A sight for sore eyes, indeed." The words were a lie, but he said them convincingly enough.

The woman apparently did not see the need for formality and wrapped her arms around his neck. "Come now, Douglas, away with all this ceremony. When last we met, you called me Isabella."

Benton cleared his throat nervously at the display of public affection, but could not deny the encounter. "I was a much younger man then, Mrs. Grimes," he said, firmly peeling her hands from his neck. "I was not a soldier. And you were not a wife."

The sound of loud voices reached his ears just then, but it was not so much the noise that drew his attention, as the straight-backed figure sitting in a wagon surrounded by armed men. His eyes narrowed at the sight of the familiar drab, black attire, and his jaw stiffened at the realization of what was occurring.

"My pardon, Mrs. Grimes. There is something that needs my attention."

With long strides, Benton closed the distance to the wagon, wondering as he walked how much of the affectionate scene the woman in the wagon had witnessed. At the moment, her gaze was focused straight ahead. She appeared as indifferent to the tumult of a bustling headquarters and the commotion of surrounding spectators as if she were in her own parlor.

"Colonel Beckham," Benton said loudly with a jovial grin upon his face. "What have we here?" By this time, a large crowd had gathered, and many were jeering and taunting the wagon's lone occupant.

Beckham nodded for the provost guard to step forward and take the lady inside before answering. "She's the widow of a Yankee."

"That so?" Benton pulled a cigar out of his pocket unconcernedly, though he was somewhat surprised by the announcement. "I will have to be more vigilant in the future. I did not realize being a widow was a crime."

"It may not be," Beckham replied, walking toward the provost's office, "but the locals wanted her brought in. Said she might have played a part in the burnings."

"Interesting." Benton controlled the urge to glance in her direction. He knew without looking that he would be able to tell nothing from her expression and even less from her eyes. "Mind if I accompany you?"

"Not at all." Beckham motioned him inside. "Your input will be welcome."

It took a moment for Benton's eyes to grow accustomed to the dim light within and discern Sarah Duvall sitting on a chair in an arrow-straight pose of heroic solitude. If she had seen him outside or was aware he had entered, she gave no sign of it. Benton dropped his gaze to her hands that were wrapped firmly around a book she held in her lap. It did not take him long to discern it was the same family Bible he had seen at their first meeting. He leaned back casually against a table near the door, crossing his arms as he listened to the interrogation that had already begun.

"Mrs. Duvall, I think you know why you are here," Colonel Beckham said. "Have you anything to say?"

"I will be glad to answer any questions you have, Colonel Beckham, but otherwise, no, I have nothing to say."

Benton noticed she had a way of talking cordially, but at the same time with coldness and formality. She was all rigid composure and decency.

"Very well, Mrs. Duvall. Let's start at the beginning, with your loyalties. Where do they lie?"

"I make no secret of my loyalties." Her tone was calm and purposeful and showed no hint of fear. "They lie with my country."

"Which is?"

For the first time she turned her gaze upon the colonel. "Until a year ago this was part of the United States, and as far as I'm concerned, it still is—until proved otherwise."

Benton tried to keep his face as unemotional as hers, but inwardly he was wondering if this charade was worth the possible cost.

Beckham bowed slightly at her remark. "We intend to prove otherwise, do we not Major Benton?"

Benton nodded, but noticed she did not look in his direction. Her blue eyes remained focused on the space in front of her, and although they had appeared expressive upon first glance, he could now see that they concealed rather than revealed anything she was thinking. The woman sitting in front of him possessed a grace and a calm dignity that seemed out of place in the dark, dingy room.

Colonel Beckham came out from behind the desk and paced slowly back and forth in front of her. "I might caution you to contain your tongue when conversing with those who are in control of this territory. I don't mean to make personal accusations, but certainly you are aware by now that your name is being associated with those who exhibit a conduct that the Confederacy finds objectionable."

"As I said, I do not pretend to be neutral in thought or spirit, but I am neutral in action." Her voice was soft, but forceful.

Beckham stopped and studied her intently. "At the moment, I accuse you only of opportunity. But since, as you admit, you are in league with our enemies, I must ask if you took part in the recent intentional burning of citizens' houses, barns and granaries."

"I did not say I was in league with them," she said, correcting him. "And if you have any evidence of such an accusation, I would like to know it."

"The evidence against you is this: the Yankees were at your home on the morning of the fifteenth, the burnings began that night, and your home, Waverly, is one of the only houses untouched. *Now* have you anything to say?"

"I cannot deny those facts. I…" Sarah looked down at her hands and did not continue.

"Perhaps you can understand my concern, Mrs. Duvall," Colonel

Beckham said. "The evidence is great against you, and you have admitted to Union loyalties."

Sarah regained her composure. "I do not see what my loyalties have to do with my opinion on the matter of arson."

"Which is?"

"I detest it."

"Very admirable indeed. But tell me this, Mrs. Duvall..." The colonel leaned down with his hands flat on the table so his eyes were level with hers. "Where were you the evening of the fifteenth? One of your neighbors has written testimony that he rode to Waverly and you were absent from the property."

Before she had time answer, but not before all the color drained from her face, Benton began laughing heartily.

Colonel Beckham turned around. "What is so amusing, Major Benton?"

"I apologize, Colonel," Benton said, still laughing. "I just find it amusing that we have come to this."

"Come to what? Out with it, man."

"Interrogating a mere woman for Heaven's sake! Look at her! Do you really feel she is capable of the atrocities of which she has been accused?"

Colonel Beckham stared at her a moment as if not quite sure. "Think back, Colonel, to the night of the fourteenth. Do you remember it?"

The colonel growled. "Of course, I remember. It rained cats and dogs!"

"Indeed it did," Benton said, "leaving quite a sea of muck for a few days as I recall. What *woman* would venture out under such conditions?" He laughed again as he watched Colonel Beckham's gaze travel across the woman who sat ramrod straight. Her dress was neat as a pin; her hair coiled neatly in a bun at the base of her neck. She appeared utterly feminine, if not a little fragile.

"Well, if she did not assist with the plan, neither did she do anything to *prevent* it," Beckham said. "Surely she knew their intent!"

Benton turned to Sarah. "Do you condone the burning of civilian's homes?"

She gazed up at him, a hint of surprise in her eyes. "Never. By either army."

"And if you were a man, and were therefore *capable*, would you do everything in your power to stop it?"

The delay in her response was marked by the rapid blinking of her eyes. Benton noticed she swallowed hard, as if physically swallowing her pride, and nodded. "I do not condone the torch. Therefore, of course, if I were a man and *capable*, I would have done all in my power to prevent it."

Benton clapped his hands together. "You see, Colonel? She may be guilty of sympathizing with the enemy, but she is certainly not capable of assisting them. I believe she had no ill intent toward her neighbors and would have assisted them if not for the unfortunate hindrance of being female. We must not be overly cautious at the cost of common sense and sound reasoning!"

"You may be right," Beckham said, "but she still has not divulged where she was on the night of the fifteenth."

Benton turned to Sarah but could think of nothing more to say to defend her, while the image of the mud-covered figure determined to save her neighbors' homes at any cost appeared vividly before his eyes. He stared now at her proud, erect stance, and marveled at her ability to display and maintain that calm exterior. She had a splendor about her, a grand sophistication that seemed almost unworldly.

"I have given my word I did not aid, assist, or support the Federals in their malicious attack." Sarah stood and looked Colonel Beckham directly in the eye. "There was a time when a lady's word was sufficient."

Her look of rebuke upon the colonel, who considered himself a man of honor, was indeed sufficient to bring the ordeal to a conclusion.

"Indeed." The colonel looked sincerely apologetic. "Much as I hate to admit it, I have no real evidence against you, so I am forced to concur with Major Benton that a woman of your stature is incapable of the crimes of which you have been accused."

Sarah kept her unflinching gaze upon the colonel. "Then I presume I am free to go."

"Yes, of course." Beckham cleared his throat. "But, Mrs. Duvall, I would like to make it clear that if you were to change your course, as it were, you would certainly find yourself in a much more advantageous position."

Benton saw a nerve twitch in the woman's cheek, but otherwise, she displayed no emotion. "Thank you, Colonel Beckham. But I'm sure you understand that allegiances do not change merely because of certain advantages." Her gaze drifted to Benton and then to someplace over his shoulder.

As Colonel Beckham opened the door and motioned for one of his men, Major Benton took the opportunity to speak quietly to Sarah. "I would be glad to accompany you back to Waverly."

"I am sure that will not be necessary," she said curtly.

"In offering to accompany you I was in no way inferring that it was nec—"

Colonel Beckham turned back around and motioned for Sarah. "There's a wagon waiting for you, ma'am. My men will see that you are escorted safely home."

Colonel Beckham stepped back inside and pulled an envelope from his coat. "Major Benton, before you get away, I have something for you." He pushed the document toward him. "It's from the commanding general. A copy has been forwarded to Richmond."

Benton opened the envelope and quickly read the missive.

In the past two days, Major Douglas A. Benton has displayed great courage and enterprise in gathering intelligence of the enemy's movements, organizing an offensive and halting their abuses on local citizens. The victory affords additional proof of Major Benton's merits as commander and adds fresh laurels to his intrepid command so signalized for valor already.

It is for these reasons that I recommend him for a promotion to the rank of Colonel.

Rather than elation, Benton felt a twinge of guilt. "The trust in my abilities is humbling, although I'm not sure I deserve such an honor."

"Folly. The position is well nigh overdue if you ask me. Now then, my men will see that Mrs. Duvall is delivered safely to her home."

Benton looked out the door, and though he didn't know what he would have said or how he would have possibly said it, he was disappointed to see she was already seated in the wagon. Her straight back and proud stance gave no sign of the humiliation she must have been feeling, but the color in her cheeks and her somber eyes revealed it to him all too clearly.

He saw her look down once to the ragged book she held in her hands and sigh heavily, but the action was fleeting. When she lifted her head again, it was as if a new force flowed within her. Despite the abuse and insults to her character by friends and neighbors, she maintained the poise of an all enduring and invincible soldier, exhibiting the type of courage that is not only physical—but moral and spiritual as well.

As the wagon pulled away, a few of the passersby standing along the street began hurling new and offensive epithets upon her. Benton felt in his heart that he would rather die than witness the degradation of one so patently loyal, and he knew that whether he lived a day or a decade more, he would never forget the mask of composure she wore upon her brave face as she faded from his view.

Chapter 5

Our brightest blazes of gladness are commonly kindled by unexpected sparks.
—Samuel Johnson

March 1863

Colonel Benton accepted the report from his scout with a nod, glanced at the massing dark clouds overhead, and turned in his saddle toward Connelly. "Send Blake and Martin ahead to announce to the widow at Waverly we will be stopping for forage for the horses and a meal for the men." He turned back and had already urged his horse forward when his officer questioned the order.

"*Waverly*, sir?"

"You heard me, Major." Benton drew back on his reins and looked over at Connelly. "It is the closest dwelling, and I'm not going to get a soaking in this storm just to avoid the hostility of a noncombatant." Urging his horse forward again as if the matter were inconsequential, he spoke over his shoulder. "We have avoided the widow at the expense of others in the neighborhood long enough. If Mrs. Duvall is able to provide food and forage for her Federal friends, she can certainly offer equal rations to us."

As Connelly saluted and spurred his horse forward to carry out the order, Benton tried to convince himself that sending the two privates ahead had been military protocol, not a way to alleviate his discomfort at being the one to inform Sarah Duvall he was coming to dinner after the unfortunate circumstances that had last brought them together.

As they rode out of the tree line, Benton glanced at the sky. A low vanguard of clouds crouched in the distance, and mutterings and grumblings on the horizon accompanied the lightning flickering like battle flares in the distance. Leaves trembled and twisted on the trees, waving their early spring finery as if making a show of defiant splendor before disaster.

When the house came into view, Benton's heart began beating at a more frantic pace than it had when facing the enemy some hours earlier. Although she had behaved respectfully when last they had met, he had no doubt she would greet him now with anything other than an impenetrable cold shoulder at his unexpected visit. She was beyond a doubt the most aloof, unapproachable female he had ever met, and he had no illusions about a congenial greeting upon his arrival. In fact, the weather seemed somehow emblematic of the turbulence yet to come. Benton put his head down against the rising wind and spattering of rain and prepared for battle as he neared his destination.

He was surprised when one of the men he had sent ahead met him at the gate. "Mrs. Duvall says she can only take five officers in the house. The rest will have to go to the barn to eat and wait out the storm."

Benton nodded and breathed a sigh of relief that at least she wasn't going to greet him with the shotgun.

"And, Colonel Benton, she won't put down that blasted gun."

Benton frowned and dismounted, handing over his reins. "Very well. Go get comfortable in the barn for now."

As Benton made his way to the house, he saw no sign of the widow or any indication that his troops or horses were going to be fed. With his head bent down against what was now an onslaught of rain, he bounded up the steps of the house, almost running into its owner, who appeared out of nowhere and seemed not to notice the wind tearing at her skirts or the rain soaking her face as she scrutinized his men riding toward the barn. He watched her eyes find the face she was seeking and the look of reassurance that followed when she saw her brother was alive and well. By the time her eyes met his, the satisfied look was gone, replaced by a glint of petulance. She nodded in his direction, providing the only indication that she knew he was there.

Being a gentleman, Benton removed his hat and bowed low. "I'm glad to see you haven't lost your charm, Mrs. Duvall," he said, trying to sound sincere.

"And I'm sorry to see you haven't found any, Major Benton," she said frostily, turning toward the door with the shotgun clearly visible in her hand. "I am not prepared for guests."

"I am not here for a social call," he said bluntly, as one of his staff came bounding up the steps.

"The horses are being fed and the men are getting comfortable, Colonel."

Benton watched the woman in front of him stop abruptly, look back over her shoulder at the new insignia on his collar, and then continue into the house. The expression on her face when she had met his gaze for a brief moment was unreadable.

"Very well," Benton said, removing his gum blanket and shaking it out on the porch. There was no abatement now in flashes of lightning and the low, steady growl of thunder above the wind. "But don't let them get too comfortable. I have a feeling we will be wearing out our welcome here rather soon."

When Benton entered the large, inviting foyer, he found it not the least bit extravagant, yet it appeared stylish, reflecting striking elegance and sophistication. The woman holding a gun in the middle of the room as the other officers entered did much to spoil the image of enchantment that first greeted his eyes, however. It appeared that the storm he thought he had avoided by stopping here had not been evaded after all.

"You do not look pleased to see us, Mrs. Duvall." Benton spoke with the calm authority of a man in charge, not revealing in the least his pounding heart.

"I'll admit I've been more agreeably surprised," she responded in an annoyed tone. "I cannot pretend a toleration I do not feel."

"I regret that we are compelled to impress food." Benton took a step toward her but watched her warily as if she were a stray animal he feared would bite. "But I trust you will not make the necessity needlessly unpleasant." He moved his gaze from her face to the gun, and then held out his hand for the weapon. Even without words, the action made clear it was not a request but a command, and it was as arrogantly given as if he were a king and she his subject.

She stubbornly held onto the instrument of carnage. "I thought I had made my loyalties clear."

All of the heads in the room turned now toward Benton awaiting his reply.

"That you did, Mrs. Duvall. But by shunning Waverly, I have allowed you to force your neighbors to bear the brunt of providing sustenance to my men and their mounts."

To this, the widow continued to stand her ground with shoulders square, blue eyes unblinking. At long last she took a deep breath of exasperation and shrugged her shoulders. "I can only offer such hospitality as my home affords." She paused and looked up at him steadily. "I hope you do not intend to confuse my kindness for cordiality."

"You can be sure there is no confusion," Benton said, taking the gun gingerly from her hand. "We are gentlemen and will behave as such. But when circumstances require, as they have today, we will not pass Waverly by for the sake of avoiding a confrontation with you." Benton stood calmly before her though the sound of his own heartbeat rang in his ears. He found himself wanting this woman's respect more than her tolerance, but he knew he would have to be grateful for whatever he could get.

After staring at him a moment, she shifted her gaze to the faces of the three other officers who stood awkwardly silent with muddied boots and solemn expressions in her home.

"Mrs. Duvall, I have the pleasure of introducing Major Connelly, Captain Anderson, and Lieutenant Stevens." The three men removed their hats and nodded, while Benton looked around and over his shoulder. "Where is Lieutenant Callahan?"

"Jake said he'd prefer to stay in the barn," Connelly said. "I told him that was understandable, considering…you know…the circumstances."

Benton marked the rise and fall of Sarah's bosom and the look of torment as she stared straight ahead while they spoke of her brother. Not a limb moved, nor did her eyes waver for a few long moments as she battled her emotions while absorbing the news. Then, with a swoosh of her skirt, she turned toward the kitchen and disappeared.

"Maybe I should see if I can help," Connelly said, seeming to have noticed their hostess' distress.

The others laughed. "Don't go trying to be a hero," Captain Anderson said. "You'd have better fortune trying to hug a beehive."

Benton looked at his second in command and gave him a silent nod of approval.

* * *

Sarah was bending over the hearth, blinking back tears when she heard the kitchen door open and close. Looking over her shoulder, she nodded to the tall, dark-haired officer standing in the doorway nervously fingering his hat.

"I came to see if I could be of service, ma'am…considering you're alone."

Sarah forced a smile and continued stirring the pot. "Thank you, Major. I just made bread this morning and have this stew heating. If you'd be so kind, you could bring in the butter from the porch."

Connelly nodded and proceeded to carry out her wish as Sarah hastily wiped the tears from her cheeks. For the first time in her life, she realized that pretending to enjoy the company of her enemies was a simple task compared to this one—pretending to detest the soldiers fighting for the land she loved. Her hands began to tremble at the thought of getting through the next few hours, and for a moment, she considered putting an end to the charade. That Benton had brought his men to eat here—simply to avoid a soaking in the storm—did nothing to make the visit any easier or more agreeable.

"Are you all right, Mrs. Duvall?" Connelly re-appeared and took the tray of bread from her shaking hands. "You look rather pale. Perhaps you should sit down."

Sarah shook her head and forced a smile, but did not trust her voice to speak. She quickly picked up a large wooden spoon and turned back toward the pot warming over the fire.

"It's Jake, isn't it?" Connelly put his hand on her shoulder and squeezed it in a tender, brotherly way. When she turned and looked up into his brown eyes, she got the impression that, despite the grave look he now wore, he was a man who could laugh exuberantly and hard when warranted.

"I am not the first to be separated from loved ones by the cruel hand of war." Sarah stared at the floor as she spoke, her emotions so tightly suppressed that her words came out as a whisper.

"It is a cruel war indeed, Mrs. Duvall, that rips apart even the most sacred ties."

A sudden surge of wind rattled the windows and the clap of thunder that followed brought the conversation to a close. "Sounds like we found dry quarters just in time."

Sarah nodded as she stirred the contents in the large pot once again. "There should be plenty for everyone." She turned back to him, swiping the back of her forearm across her head to push back a lock of hair that had gone astray. "If you'd like to call the other officers, I believe it is ready."

Sarah hastily sat out dishes and silverware in the dining room, trying to ignore the masculine figures that surrounded her table. She had often served just as many Union officers on any one evening and not felt half the discomfort. Men of distinction, both from the army and from civilian life, were her daily guests. Yet never had she felt so overwhelmed than with these four men with their powerful frames and well-meaning smiles. Although they looked like perfect gentlemen at the moment, Sarah knew these soldiers were the cream of the Confederate army, fearless, daring and bold. No other command could achieve the victories these men had over the past ten months. They were as fine a specimen of Southern manhood as could be found, and she was proud her brother was considered worthy to serve with them.

Colonel Benton took the chair at the head of the table, his long legs and broad shoulders seeming to make the room shrink. Considerably over six feet, he towered above most of the other men and emanated an air of authority that even without his size or status would have been immediately evident. Trying to ignore him, yet failing miserably, Sarah decided it wasn't so much his immense, muscular body but rather the vast power and strength that radiated from him. Although she knew he had been in the saddle for days there was no drooping of his formidable frame, no sign of fatigue.

His reputation was that of a man who commanded attention—not only from his men—but from the ladies as well. Sarah had noticed from the beginning how he looked at her—as if he could possess her if he wanted to. But acquainted as she was with the stories of his persuasive powers with women, she could see now that his intrepid, bold deportment made him a favorite among his men as well.

At first she had despised him for his arrogance and kinglike demeanor, but now she could not help admiring his gallant defense of her homeland. His war record, after all, revealed far more about his character than did idle gossip or a few months' acquaintance could impart. Despite his faults, none could say he was not entirely devoted to his country. In his own careless way, he was captivating and intriguing.

As if to make her job more difficult, Benton seemed to be making an attempt at good behavior—although Sarah reminded herself that one can look respectful in church and still be breaking all the commandments. Try as she might to dislike him, something in that dark hair, that kingly bearing, and that intrepid demeanor attracted and bound her to his service. She took a deep breath and squared her shoulders as she prepared for the hardest battle of her life—keeping up the pretense of detesting the very soldiers she most respected and esteemed.

* * *

Colonel Benton ate ravenously, all the while watching how his hostess fought the womanly instinct to wait on his men attentively. Instead, she treated them with civil disregard, as if providing them with nourishment was a chore rather than an honored service. Yet it was obvious she had not spared her pantry, filling the table with oysters and cold ham, fresh stew, and bread slathered with the diner's choice of butter, honey, or jam. Her dignity and grace were unequaled as she moved among them, her manners perfect in their composure, and her face most beautiful, despite the absence of a smile. No, never a smile. Rather, her habitual expression seemed to be a thoughtful almost mournful look—that of someone with little hope and no pleasure.

As she came near him, Benton lifted his eyes to gaze at her proud, cheerless face. Her melancholy eyes haunted him as he thought back to the great deeds she had accomplished on his behalf. He had never before seen someone so full of decency and dignity and could not comprehend the doctrine of sacrifice and devotion she manifested. He felt a faint stir of compassion, but immediately thrust it away. She did not seek his approval—let alone his friendship. He may as well accept it and keep it that way.

"I can see why the Yanks pay such frequent visits to you, Mrs. Duvall," he said sitting back in his chair and patting his full stomach. "Your expertise in the kitchen is unparalleled."

"And I can see why General Lee gave you a command to make yourself a source of great annoyance to the enemy," she replied as she removed his plate.

A chorus of chuckles arose from his men, but Benton was so surprised at the response to his innocent statement that for a moment, he did not know whether he should offer her an apology or demand one. Then he remembered her duty—and his. A ghost of a smile wavered on his stern face before it quickly disappeared.

"I'm sorry if my table manners have provoked you," he said, somewhat sincerely. "I cannot pretend an eloquence I do not possess. I'm afraid my humble knowledge is limited to the setting of cavalry on a field of battle."

"Yes, it appears your record is not silent on the subject," she said more gently now. Despite her distance and apparent displeasure, her words proved that she was not as unmoved as she wished to appear.

Men began pushing themselves away from the table and patting their mid-sections as Benton debated his next move. His stomach was certainly satisfied, but his conscience still was not. He needed to talk to Mrs. Duvall. Alone.

He turned and gazed out the window. "It appears the storm has let up." He stood and bowed to Sarah. "Thank you for your gracious hospitality, Mrs. Duvall."

She nodded, which he knew was a great deal for her to do, and then turned her back to him as she began to clear the table.

As the men retreated from the room, Benton lagged behind. "I'm going to have a word with Mrs. Duvall," he said in a whispered voice to Connelly, who glanced back at the woman noisily crashing dishes together, and nodded.

Benton fingered his hat nervously. Now that the time had come to express his real reason for stopping at Waverly, he could barely find the words to speak. He became uncharacteristically short of breath as he stared at the back of the woman who was mechanically stacking dirty dishes. It did not escape his thoughts that this was the first time they had been together since her interrogation some months ago, and he felt uneasy about being in the presence of someone so inherently courageous and decent. She had accepted hardships that were certainly more painful than were wounds or physical suffering while receiving no glory or even acknowledgment for the sacrifice. He cleared his throat, yet still his voice cracked when he spoke. "I beg your pardon, Mrs. Duvall."

Sarah turned her head around slowly, as if just realizing she was not alone. Her gaze was bright and questioning, yet otherwise unreadable. "Would you like something more to eat?" She tilted her head questioningly and her eyes seemed strangely kind.

"No, ma'am." Benton cleared his throat. "I just wished to say that you have done me a great service, impossible to measure or reward."

He watched her scan the space behind him, as if to be certain they were alone, and then her unflinching gaze bore into his. "But I do not serve you, Colonel Benton. I serve my country."

Benton realized his inability to say what he intended, so hesitated a moment to gather his thoughts. Sarah must have noticed the look. "I only served you today because it was my duty—and I did not wish to appear to fail in hospitality."

He cleared his throat. "I never doubted that I would be received with hospitality—that is refused by no one—but I'll admit I had hoped for a different greeting."

Sarah's eyes narrowed. "You were treated the same as all who walk through my door, be they loyal friends or worthy foes."

Benton took a step closer. "And which am I?"

For the first time Sarah looked at him as if she were flustered and appeared unsure how to respond. "But what I meant is—I do what I do because we are at war."

"*We* are not at war."

Benton could not understand how he so constantly and inadvertently found himself on her bad side. Her barrier of impenetrable reserve apparently did not yield to any expression of friendliness. No matter what the situation, she neither gave nor demanded, nor evidently desired, any sign of emotion. She was the most regal—and unpredictable— creature he had ever laid eyes on.

Sarah gazed thoughtfully over his shoulder. "Yes, of course not," she said at last, "but there is much you do not know about me."

"When will I?"

With lightning speed, her gaze darted up to his and now her expression revealed immense surprise and not a little suspicion—as if she supposed he had used the line on any number of other women. Yet Colonel Benton could not bring to mind a single woman that had not told him more than he wished to know within the first few minutes of their acquaintance. This one, however, remained a mystery after almost a year.

"Your charms would perhaps be better received in other quarters."

Benton waited for her to say more, but she seemed to think the conversation was over and turned back to the table. Benton's jaw tightened at her response. "I am not here to charm you, Mrs. Duvall—*or* cross swords with you." He fumbled in his pocket and pulled out a well-worn envelope. "To be honest, General Lee wished me to deliver this personally, and the weather cooperated in allowing me to deliver it today without raising suspicion."

Sarah turned around slowly and gazed at his extended hand. "From General Lee?" she whispered.

"Yes. For you."

Biting her lip, she took the communication, and with shaking hands opened it and began to read. To Benton's horror, tears began to flow down her cheeks.

"You should not have given me such credit," she said, looking up at him as if embarrassed at the attention. "It was not my intention to gain laurels from the expedition."

Despite her shiny blue eyes, her pouty lips, and her wet cheeks, Benton kept his composure and remained businesslike, knowing she would wish it so. "Mrs. Duvall, it was a brave act that deserved the general's attention. I only commended you in my report as I would the notable acts of any of my other officers. I assumed you would value equal treatment."

All of the animosity drained from her eyes and her cheeks blushed to a rosy hue. "You are very kind, Colonel," she finally said, staring at the floor. "But it was not necessary. The offering of the horse was reward enough."

"Yes, as for the horse, I will not dispute your choice," Benton said, glancing out the window at his men mounting. "But know that another, perhaps more suitable, is available at any time."

"Oh, no, I'm quite pleased with him…"

"Very well." Benton put on his hat and nodded in her direction. "I've said what I came to say. I will not burden you any longer. Good day, Mrs. Duvall."

He turned toward the door, but instantly felt a sudden pressure upon his arm. Benton was so surprised by the action that he stared down at the small hand that rested there.

"Despite your generosity and impeccable charm, Colonel Benton, you do understand you will be treated in the same unkind manner when next we meet?"

Benton moved his gaze from her hand clasping his arm to the up-turned face right before him, and a boyish smile began to spread at the sight of her blue eyes glittering with frank honesty.

"For my country, I will dare your displeasure, Mrs. Duvall," he said somewhat huskily as he tipped his hat, "which I trust will only be temporary and which I hope will only be for the sake of the cause."

The faint smile she rewarded him with rendered her face one of uncommon beauty, and the tone she had used made him feel more like a friend than a foe. He gazed once more into her eyes—the depths of which were both mystifying and perplexing. If he had thought her attractive before in her someberness and gloom, he now beheld her in a new vision.

"It's a pity you must leave so soon," she said, glancing out the window. "I hope you got enough to eat."

Benton reached for the door handle, more for support than for any desire to leave. Never before had she acknowledged that she appreciated his presence, let alone showed that she cared he was leaving. Heaven knows he ought to have departed long since, but he had no way of knowing when he would see her again. Surely he might indulge himself a little longer.

"I fear it will be a test for me to keep my men from imposing on you at mealtimes in the future, Mrs. Duvall." He smiled and winked, but then spoke in a low, serious tone. "As you must know, our visit today was imperative. I can't help but think the Yankees find it suspicious that we spare your pantry at the expense of your neighbors."

"Yes, I can't help but agree." Sarah stared intently out the window. "We must make sure it does not appear—to the enemy or to your men—that you are intentionally avoiding Waverly. You must treat me as you would any other civilian in the region."

Benton followed her gaze, and saw a young lieutenant already mounted and waiting at the edge of the yard as if anxious to leave.

Sarah's eyes were locked on the image. "Colonel Benton, you have been entrusted with the care of my brother." Her words were whispered and serious. "You will keep a close eye on him for me?"

Benton studied the worried expression and eyes that reflected more clearly than words the depth of her concern. "I take the responsibility of the lives of my men seriously." He put a reassuring hand on her shoulder. "I cannot guarantee Jake's safety, but I can assure you I will do all in my power not to place him unnecessarily in harm's way."

Sarah swallowed hard and nodded as she continued to soak in the sight of her brother. "Thank you, Colonel Benton."

After a moment of awkward silence, Benton tipped his hat one last time. "Good day, Mrs. Duvall."

Once outside, he paused a moment on the step contemplating her words and actions. He had never felt respect, let alone affection from her, yet something had just happened that left him feeling lightheaded and strangely out of breath. An inexplicable sensation of elation washed over him, mixed with a feeling of pure bewilderment at the turn of events. Benton tried to remember another instance when a mere conversation had caused such a reaction as he strode toward his horse. Recalling none, he suppressed the urge to smile, and motioned to Connelly to give the order to mount. Within minutes, despite their full stomachs and weary bodies, his men had swung readily into their saddles again and were trotting off through the rain-soaked fields to their next engagement.

Chapter 6

The surest way to win the prize
Of tender glance from beauty's eyes
Is not at ball or festal board,
But in the front with flashing sword.
—Theodora O'Hara

May 1863

Major Michael Connelly stomped his feet on the porch to loosen any clinging mud, then proceeded into the brightly lit mansion to join the rest of his comrades. Although times were tough in Virginia, Colonel Benton insisted the men take a break from the battlefield from time to time to permit the ladies to "pay their respects" for the sacrifice and service of their countrymen.

Benton's hospitality at balls was famous and his love of festivity renowned among the female residents of the region. As a result, the highly esteemed cavaliers of Benton's battalion had become well practiced at spending half the night in the saddle skirmishing with the Yankees and the other half engaged in social skirmishes with members of the opposite sex.

Connelly watched the men whirling their partners around the room with more enthusiasm than grace and then searched the room for Benton. It did not take him long to spot him, standing as a king might among his subjects. His tall, commanding figure stood out from all the others in the room; his hearty laughter echoed even above the sound of the band. By all accounts he was a man as equally receptive to laughter as gunfire.

As if sensing Connelly had entered, Benton looked up and nodded, then turned his attention back to the striking redhead who stood boldly close. Her stance told Connelly that she had declared that Benton was hers for the taking, and it appeared that she intended to preserve neither dignity nor character in her method to obtain him. Her laugh was loud and brazen, and her voice carried with it all of the coquettish witchery of seduction and desire, slurred as it was with liquor and lust. Connelly frowned. He had seen the woman before, though he didn't know her name. What Benton saw in her, he could not fathom and didn't wish to guess. She was older than many of the others present and seemed to exude impropriety.

His thoughts drifted to his own beautiful wife at home, making the idea of spending the evening in a roomful of doting women tedious and wearisome at best. But he knew Benton was different. The colonel enjoyed swinging a member of the opposite sex across the dance floor, yet he had an even greater affinity for smoke and fire and danger and speed.

Making his way across the room, Connelly glanced again at his commander. Although he appeared frolicking and fun-loving right now, he was just as well known for his headlong recklessness and valor. The colonel made decisions instinctively and instantly in moments of danger, which had garnered the respect of all those who served under him.

Connelly knew Benton's flirtations with the opposite sex were, for the most part, innocent maneuvers to dispel the dangers of the battle-field. Yet still, he felt it his duty to stay and keep an eye on his commander. Despite Benton's intuition about military matters, his instincts with women were lacking. It was understandable really. Given so many temptations and so few restrictions, it was difficult for him to say no.

"Sir, may I have a word?" Connelly nodded toward the open door of the balcony and watched Benton remove the lady's possessive hand from his arm. When the two stood alone outside, Connelly gave him the whispered message. "Turk just returned." He pulled a communication from out of his pocket. "Found this in the old tree." He watched Benton scan the missive intently, and tried to discern whether concern or aggravation flashed across his face as he read.

"Very good," Benton said, folding up the note and shoving it into his coat. "According to our friend Sid, we have no reason to expect any surprise visits from the Yanks. Lambert's men are apparently on their way to Clarksburg."

"How does he always know what the Yankees are doing?" Connelly looked over at his commanding officer curiously. "And who is he, I wonder?"

"As long as he gets it right, I don't care." Benton walked over to the railing and leaned out over to see beyond the shrubs. "The horses are causing a raucous on the picket line. Go see what Harris is doing."

Connelly nodded and hurried to follow the order.

* * *

Benton stood alone in the shadows of the veranda for a moment, trying to figure out why any conversation about "Sid" made him uneasy. He had not been there long when a group of women speaking in hushed tones by the door caught his attention. Assuming they were talking about him, he strained his ears to hear the discussion.

"Yes, well everyone knows about Jake Callahan's sister. It's such a shame."

"A shame?" another said. "Why, it's an outright disgrace! Truly she should be run out of the neighborhood on a rail, just like the days of old."

Colonel Benton stepped out of the shadows and approached the group. "Pardon me, ladies, I could not help but overhearing. Were you speaking of Captain Callahan of my command?"

"Why, Colonel Benton—yes, we were," the first lady answered. "But no need for alarm—Jake is as loyal as they come, even if his sister is not."

"And what do you know of his sister's loyalties?"

The group snickered and laughed. "Why, Colonel, don't you know? She went and married a *Yankee*. Nursed him after he was wounded and then married him. As fate would have it he died, so now she's a widow at twenty-one, and there's no one that thinks she don't deserve it."

"That's very young to be a widow." Benton had not realized that the icy figure with whom he had so often conversed was almost ten years his junior. The wisdom—or perhaps the pain—in her eyes had led him to believe she was more advanced in age. His comment elicited quite a hive of buzzing.

"The widow of a Yankee!" Mrs. Oliver said, with obvious loathing. "Living in Virginia and entertaining those creatures every chance she gets! To think those vile wretches should dare come here and be permitted to pollute our dear old home spots with their footsteps. Why it is outright appalling!"

"Well, I suppose we should not be harsh on someone who followed their heart," Benton said, trying to appeal to the group's feminine emotions. "Sometimes such things cannot be helped."

"Cannot be helped?" one of them shrieked. "They met and married and he was gone. All in a week they say, though I'm in no position to know." The woman waved her fan in front of her face as if the whole idea were abhorrent to her.

Another woman, dressed in a light green silk, had her hackles up and chimed in as well. "And look how she continues to aid and abet—everyone knows it. In fact, don't those Yankees just throw that in our faces when we refuse to feed them! 'Why can't you be more like Mrs. Duvall,' they say to us. 'Mrs. Duvall has sense to know who's on the winning side.' Why it's outright treason what she does!"

Colonel Benton said nothing more. There was nothing more to say. He stood staring thoughtfully into the darkness beyond, thinking of the she-devil of Waverly who carried such a heavy burden upon her small shoulders. If he had not realized the depth and breadth of the sacrifice before, it was hitting him squarely in the chest now. Although she carried no gun on a battlefield and would gather no glory for her service, she was giving as much to the Cause as any man in uniform. Nothing meant more to a Virginia-bred woman than did honor and reputation, and Sarah Duvall had surrendered both to her country. Her life was one of misery and solitude, and he could only imagine the agony it caused her.

Benton's mind drifted to the intelligence that had been delivered from her hands, and had to admit her sacrifices were at least not in vain. She supplied information straight from the lips of the officers who had devised the plans, often with complete sketches of their defenses, positions, and numbers. No scout or spy in the army could boast of such enterprises, yet scouts *could* boast of their endeavors and be swathed in laurels at the end of their mission. She, on the other hand, had no one to confide in.

Benton rubbed his chin and began pacing on the porch. As important as the duty was, as eagerly as she had accepted the role, and as successful as she had been at carrying it out, he felt uneasy allowing her to continue. Jake Callahan's sister, Mrs. Sarah Duvall, was an outcast, hated and despised by everyone she had ever known. Right now, they shunned her as they would a rabid dog, but he feared their anger could turn to violence. A light touch on his arm interrupted his musings.

"Colonel Benton?"

"Yes, my dear." Benton gazed into the anxious brown eyes of a girl of no more than eighteen. "What may I do for you, young lady?"

"Colonel Benton, I just wanted to tell you what an honor it is to meet you, sir."

"The pleasure is all mine, Miss…"

"Carter… Lucy Carter. You are welcome to call me Lucy."

"Well, Miss Lucy, are you from Kingston?"

She looked shyly at the floor and then up. "Yes, well…for now I am."

"Ah, so you are planning a move in the near future?"

"Perhaps," she said, looking around as if wishing to speak confidentially. "Actually, one of your men has asked for my hand."

Benton laughed loudly. "Oh, I see! And who is the lucky man?"

Lucy stepped closer and said the name in a quiet voice. "Jake Callahan."

Benton looked deep into her eyes and then smiled knowingly. "A good man. One of my best officers, certainly among my bravest."

"That's kind of you to say," she said, her cheeks turning red.

"Kind? I only speak the truth. Now what is bothering you, my dear?"

"It's just that…" She paused and gazed at the group of women still gabbing nearby.

Benton leaned over to speak confidentially. "You're worried about the effect his sister will have on your reputation?"

Lucy looked up as if startled that he had read her mind. "Is what they say true, do you think? Jake will not speak of it."

"I believe it would be wise," Benton said, taking her arm and leading her farther into the shadows, "to never accept idle gossip as the truth."

"But you have met her, surely." She looked up at him with imploring eyes. "Do you know her well?"

"I have met her, yes." Benton paused and drew some of the cool, night air into his lungs. "As for knowing her well, I have a feeling there are very few who do."

"It's all so confusing," Lucy said, looking up at the night sky. "My father forbids the marriage, and—"

"Your father forbids the marriage? Because of Mrs. Duvall?"

The girl's eyes now brimmed with tears. "Yes. He does not want my name or reputation to be marred by that of a traitor."

Benton took a deep breath of discontent, though he understood her father's position. The most prestigious families in the neighborhood were whispering about the character of one Sarah Duvall. It was only natural he should wish to protect his daughter's standing. "And what does Jake think about all this?"

"Oh, he will not speak of it." Her eyes glistened with tears. "He will not allow her name to be mentioned in his presence."

Benton felt his heart thump hard against his chest. He had never before felt such a strong desire to divulge a military secret as he did at this moment, but he wisely held his tongue. "You must tell Jake not to judge her so harshly," Benton said, trying to sound undisturbed. "Certainly he is not the only one with a close relative on the wrong side of the war."

"But she does flaunt it." Lucy's cheeks flushed with color. "She lives right here among us, and Mrs. Oliver is right. The Yankees use it against us every chance they get."

Benton took a deep breath and turned to stare out into the great expanse of night. "I cannot justify her actions, but neither can I hold them against her. War is a very…complex thing."

Lucy took a step closer to him. "I feel the same way. In fact, I pity her—especially tonight, with all those angry men."

Benton swung around and faced her. "What do you mean? What men?"

Lucy took a step back and seemed to hesitate as if surprised by his reaction. "The Johnson brothers," she said in a whispered voice. "They've gathered some men and are heading to Waverly. They say Colonel Beckham let her go without any punishment after those burnings in the area. I fear they intend to do some of their own."

Chapter 7

Must I be carried to the skies
On flowery beds of ease,
While others fought to win the prize,
And sailed through bloody seas?
—Isaac Watts

From out of the darkness came the sound of hoof beats—not one or two, or even a dozen—but more like those of an entire cavalry troop. The clattering caused Sarah to run to the window in a panic, fearing she had misled Colonel Benton in her last message. She had told him all was clear, and feared for the soldiers she may have put in jeopardy on the strength of her word. When nothing but angry voices greeted her ears, she pressed herself against the wall and watched shadowy figures appear from the bosom of darkness. In moments, the yard was illuminated from the torches being waved wildly in the air.

Quickly extinguishing the candles that were burning, she grabbed the shotgun and stood with her hand on the door latch, nerving herself for the confrontation to come. The violent force gathering outside the door was palpable—she could feel it without even seeing it—and she knew there was no one within miles to protect her. She was utterly alone.

"Come out and face your enemy!" someone yelled.

Sarah took a deep breath and slowly opened the door. Taking a few steps onto the porch, she searched the angry faces of the crowd for any sign of kindness or compassion. Finding none, she tried to alleviate the tension. "I see only faces of neighbors and friends." Her voice was strong at first, but faded in the end. "I see no enemies."

"The hell you don't!" another person responded. "You give aid to the Yankees and let the rest of us bear the brunt of their violence! Some kind of neighborly friend you are!"

"Burn her house down, like they burned my mill!" a man yelled to shouts of agreement.

"Yes, burn it down. Serves her right!"

Sarah watched the crowd surge forward, the torches waving wildly and creating a streak of light against the blackness of the night. She was

49

experienced at reading the signs of drunkenness, but it took no expert analysis to see that these eyes glowed more from frenzied hate than from too much liquor. She continued to hold the gun plainly in one hand, yet made no attempt to use it or to defend herself.

The sound of hoofbeats thundering through the darkness caused the mob to pause and seek their source. A horse soon sailed over the garden gate at a reckless speed, scattering some of the crowd, while the rest parted like a great sea allowing the horse and rider to approach the house. Sarah heard whispers and astonished mutterings, though all she could see at first was that the rider was a magnificent horseman, broad-chested and splendidly proportioned. As he drew closer to a torch, she recognized the figure, calm and unruffled, the very picture of a soldier.

His gaze met hers only briefly in the soft glow of torchlight before he turned back to the crowd, which had stepped back and made room for him in evident respect and regard. Not a man spoke or raised his voice, yet the eyes of all were upon him. The composed tone, the bold stance, and the gallant bearing revealed a man who knew no fear. His very presence shrouded her in comfort, and brought a sense of calm to her pounding heart.

* * *

"What is the meaning of this?" Colonel Benton grabbed a torch from someone's hand and waved it across the heads of the mob as if to light their upturned faces. Although his horse was heaving from its frenzied ride, he continued to pivot and paw the ground apparently sharing his rider's wrath.

"We're doing onto others as they do onto us, Colonel!"

"We do not wage war against women and civilians." Benton sat his prancing horse with casual ease, though his voice revealed his anger. "No matter what low acts our enemies thrust upon us."

"Well, Col'nel, you know what this woman's been up to well as anybody. We're here to give her what she deserves." Rounds of cheers rose up from the crowd as the torches flamed and spit.

"Gentlemen, I have been given orders to keep the peace in this territory, and I demand that you depart." Benton talked slowly and calmly, but his tone did not hide the anger that was evident. "We cannot lower our good standing as a civilized society by perpetuating the same crimes we so ardently detest."

"But the wretches burned down my barn!" one man angrily protested. "And *she* was the cause of it."

All heads turned toward Sarah, who had moved to a corner of the porch to watch the events from the shadows. She swallowed hard, her eyes locked on the stalwart masculine figure who sat with one hand on the reins, the other casually on the back of his saddle, as he turned to face the speaker. He radiated an image of power and strength, mixed with tremendous intensity and composure. She had never beheld such boldness before.

"If you have evidence to support that claim, I've yet to see it," Benton replied sharply. He paused, but only for a moment. "Regardless, the time for discussion has passed. General Lee has better use for his cavalry than to protect the rights of civilians from a mob of marauders. Again, I ask you to disperse."

His tone, demeanor, and reputation were such that, although many mumbled and complained under their breaths, none made an outright protest. In a few minutes time, the yard had cleared and the night had turned black again.

Sarah turned to enter the house and almost immediately heard spurs clanking up the steps behind her. Once inside, she attempted to relight a candle with a shaking hand, but failed until a hand grasped her wrist from behind and held it steady. When the candle finally flared, he removed his hand but made no effort to step away.

"You are very kind," she said, not turning around.

"And you are very brave."

Sarah held onto the back of a chair for support, not wanting him to see her distress. After a moment to restore her frantic nerves, she turned to him, and noticed how pale he appeared in the candlelight.

"I fear for your safety."

He spoke so softly and sincerely that she began to scrutinize him more closely. For a moment she was stunned at the concern that lined his handsome face. She had not considered the possibility that he cared for anyone but himself, yet his countenance revealed a look of anxiety and worry, as if he had been visibly shaken by the experience. Sarah looked down at her hands and clasped them to keep them from trembling. "I do not know how to thank you as you deserve."

"You do not need to thank me, Mrs. Duvall," he said, somewhat coolly now. "I have no hesitation about rendering a service to one who has rendered so much service to me."

"But how did you—"

"How I discovered it is a matter that needs not be told." Benton seemed suddenly uncomfortable and moved to the window where he slid aside the curtain. "I believe they have dispersed, but I am willing to stay or post a few men, as you wish."

"No. That really won't be necessary." Sarah made an effort to smooth her skirt, pretending to be undisturbed. Through these long years of war, she had learned well how to mask her fear, to hide her desperation. "I am sure there will be no more trouble tonight."

Benton gazed at her a moment, seeming to deliberate before being nerved to continue. "If I may be so bold, Mrs. Duvall, I feel I must report to General Lee this duty has become too dangerous."

Sarah took a step toward him. "You cannot! I accept the burden because I know what is at stake." She threw up her hands in exasperation. "I know you did not wish this obligation, but you cannot continue to hold my gender against me."

"It is not that," he said, his brow furrowed. "It is no longer safe."

"A ship in the harbor is safe, but that is not what ships are for." Sarah put her hands on her hips and shook her head. "I have accepted this duty, and I intend to perform it to the best of my abilities."

"Mrs. Duvall, I beg your pardon, but those people out there can start more rumors in a week about you than I could stop in a year."

She shrugged dismissively. "I would rather forfeit popularity forever than deny my countrymen a chance for freedom."

"That is not the point!" His voice grew loud, drowning out the chimes of the mantle clock. "What if I had not arrived when I did?"

Sarah shrugged again, having no answer to his question. "It would be weak and disgraceful for me to say I cannot endure that which is my fate to bear." She looked up at him. "And you, sir, have no right to interfere with fate."

Benton moved away from the window, his face drawn with tenderness for her and with anger for a situation that caused her hurt. "I have no intention of interfering with fate, Mrs. Duvall. It seldom does any good. But neither will I stand by and allow you to place yourself in unnecessary danger."

Again, Sarah had no answer for that and so attempted to change the subject. "You are here at great peril to yourself." She turned and began to light another candle as if dismissing him. "You risk your standing and reputation by being with me. It would be wise for you to go."

"I will not leave until you answer my question." His expression was stern, and his voice carried a tone of anger in it. "What if I had not arrived when I did?"

Sarah turned to face him, and seeing the nerve throbbing near his temple, she began twisting the fabric on the sleeve of her dress. "At worst it would have been my life, and that is worth little to me and nothing to anyone else."

Benton took an abrupt step toward her. "Do not say such things so lightly!" His voice was very low, but there was a strange and frightening edge to it. "Surely you are aware your threat is twofold. At any moment you may die at the end of a rope from one side—or at the hands of an angry mob from the other."

"I must dare to do what my conscience dictates." Her eyes, seemingly of their own accord, fell upon the open Bible lying on the table. "My life is in far wiser hands than my own."

Benton signed in apparent exasperation, his gaze following hers to the mark of rich ribbon that lay across the pages, bearing in silver text the words, *"Be not frightened for the Lord your God is with you wherever you go." – Joshua 1:9.*

Seeming to sense that arguing any further was futile, Benton returned his attention to her and became calm and businesslike again. "Is that your final word, Mrs. Duvall? I will not press the matter further for now if you are certain of your stance."

Sarah forced a smile. "Duty is not an option, Colonel Benton. It is an obligation. That is my final word." She met his gaze for a moment, and then, fearing that her emotions were getting the better of her, she did not venture to speak again. Instead she turned her back to him and waited for him to leave.

"Very well then," she heard him say. "Good evening."

Sarah listened to the creak of the door as it opened behind her and to the familiar click of the latch as it closed. The awful finality of that sound caused loneliness and despair to surge through her again. Unable to suppress her emotions any longer, she buried her face in her hands and let loose a deep, racking sob. She had taken great pains to repress her tears in front of him, but now...

It was not until she felt a hand on her shoulder that she realized Benton had tricked her and never left the room. He had simply opened and closed the door behind her.

"I will end this agony with but a word from you, Mrs. Duvall," he said in a low, gentle voice. "Permit me to tell General Lee."

Sarah had successfully controlled the sorrow she did not wish him to see, but now she indulged in the tears she no longer had the will to restrain. Unable to suppress what she could no longer endure, she wept passionately, the long pent up agony bursting forth with relentless strength. When she did not answer, Benton turned her around and pulled her hesitantly into his arms.

"Please don't cry." His voice trembled. "They have behaved shamefully toward you."

Sarah had little choice but to lay her head against his chest and take comfort in the manly arms that held her. "I understand the feelings that impelled them," she said. "I cannot blame them." Embarrassed at her emotional display, she tried to straighten and move away, but his arms tightened around her tenderly—yet powerfully.

"The trial is heavy to all, particularly so to you," he said softly. "It pains me to watch you suffer so while I reap the glory."

The anguish in his voice made Sarah wish to console him, yet her pounding heart and racing thoughts would not allow her to voice the sentiment. From the first hour of their acquaintance, she had been aware of her fascination with this man. Now, being held in his strong arms, she could barely remember to breathe.

"You must go," she murmured weakly while allowing herself to be comforted by the hard, heavy feel of his encircling arms. When his embrace only increased, she stopped trying to resist his power and strength and rested passively in his eager hold while the blood raged in her head. He smelled of smoke and leather and gunpowder and felt like safety and solace and support.

"Sarah, Sarah," he whispered. "You cannot continue this dangerous game."

His words gave Sarah the will to draw back. She broke away from him and hastily wiped the tears from her eyes with the back of her hand. "Others have suffered as much. Please don't give me more credit than I deserve."

"But you have received no credit, save a commendation from General Lee." His voice grew loud again. "My victories will never be attributed to you or your sacrifices." He paused and stared at her as if not understanding how she could serve her country to the detriment of her own happiness and reputation. "I shall have the honor of dying covered in glory as a soldier—"

"And I with the scorn of a traitor," she finished for him.

When her eyes welled up again, he leaned forward and wiped away a fresh tear as it splashed down her cheek, then pulled a handkerchief from his pocket. She accepted the offering and dabbed her eyes. "I'm sorry to be so weak. I was so made."

"Weak, my dear?" He stared at her with a look that was both admiring and respectful. "Your courage and calmness are unearthly. I equate you with a heavenly being if there is such a thing."

Sarah looked up at him, blinking away her tears. "If there is such a thing?" She did nothing to hide the shock of his admission. "Can you doubt that there is a God who rules our affairs?" Her gaze remained transfixed upon him, as if trying to ascertain his sincerity.

Benton looked at her uneasily. "You do a much better job of communicating with the Almighty than I do," he said softly. "The pure of heart are provided a leg up, I suppose."

"But surely you believe in the protection of the men you send into battle—that they will be rewarded with eternal life."

He chuckled and smiled at her as if to lighten the mood. "My dear, my duties are many and varied, but trying to get my men through the gates of Heaven is not among them."

With furrowed brow, Sarah turned to the table and picked up her Bible. "Here, perhaps this will help you."

The smile faded from Benton's face as he stared thoughtfully at the well-worn book. "I cannot accept such a personal gift from one who has sacrificed so much already." He handed the offering back to her. "But I will take this."

Sarah looked at him questioningly as he took the handkerchief from her hand. He proceeded to unbutton his coat and thrust the damp piece of cloth into his shirt. "I wish to carry your tears close to my heart," he said, learning forward and brushing away another that had wetted her cheek, "so I may be reminded in the heat of battle that courage and sacrifice are not for the soldier alone."

Sarah studied his sincere expression for a moment, and then spoke to the floor, unwilling to gaze into the liquid brown eyes that studied her. "It is kind of you to say."

"Not kind, just the truth." He walked over to her fireplace, poked at the wood a moment until new flames sprang to life, and then turned to her, saying in a relaxed and casual tone, "Hesitate to ask nothing of me if I can be of service to you, Mrs. Duvall."

Sarah nodded and smiled contemplatively. He seemed very much changed from the haughty domineering man she had once thought him to be. Although still arrogantly domineering at times, tonight he had proved capable of displaying genuine warmth and affection. She had to admit he was no longer an irritation to her. He was her only ally in a friendless world—he was strong, calm, consoling comfort.

Benton walked to the door and laid his hand on her shoulder. "And *take care*. That is the only thing the Confederacy asks of you that you do not seem willing to grant."

Before Sarah could think another thought, or say another word, the door clicked shut, and this time, he was really gone.

Chapter 8

Duty is the most sublime word in our language. Do your duty in all things.
You cannot do more. You should never wish to do less.
—Robert E. Lee

Colonel Benton leaned one shoulder against a tree as he read a newspaper article about one of his recent raids. His merriment was interrupted by the sound of one of his scouts spurring his horse furiously up the hill toward him. The soldier reined his mount to a sliding stop in front of the tree and slid off.

"Sir, the pike's blue with Yankees," Lieutenant Matt Kelsey said breathlessly. "They're thick as rattlesnakes in the May-day sun!"

"Is it Snipes?"

"Yessirah."

Benton closed the paper and sighed loudly as if exasperated by the antics of a child. But the sigh was accompanied with a grim flash of the eye that boded no good for the enemy. "That man is trespassing on my territory and my patience."

"According to some townspeople, he is looking for you," the scout reported.

The men that had gathered around to hear the news started laughing, and even Benton could not resist allowing his mouth to turn up into another reckless grin. "Oh yes," he said. "Snipes is looking for *me* about as hard as a sinner seeks God... hoping he does not find Him."

Colonel Snipes was notorious for riding through the territory, informing the residents what harm he was going to inflict on the evil rebels that lived in their midst, generally making his appearance when Benton and his men were out chasing bigger game—and always availing himself of the pretext of not being able to find his sought-after enemy. Although Benton afforded him every opportunity for a trial of combat, the offer was invariably declined.

As far as the neighboring citizens were concerned, Snipes was considered more of a robber than a soldier. He treated them with insult and cruelty and wreaked havoc on their lives by seizing personal property, slaughtering livestock, and destroying crops. A clash with Snipes would have far more importance for its effect on the minds of the inhabitants in the region than for any intrinsic military value to Benton or the Confederacy—yet this was a fight Benton was eager to have. Although it had not been on his agenda for today, he resolved himself to teach Snipes a lesson.

"Where is he now?"

"Should be about at Mason's place."

"How many?"

"Looked like at least four hundred."

The men looked eagerly at Benton—as they always did—for or an instant solution to the dilemma. Although they knew they had but one hundred, their waiting eyes were filled with confidence as they saw battle written clearly on their leader's face. Benton feared no odds and no numbers. He held the advantage of surprise, and he fully comprehended the value of retaining it.

Benton paused once more and rubbed his chin thoughtfully, as if deciding on a chess move, while the willing faces of his men stared at him in anticipation of his next order. They were barely able to restrain themselves at the thought of having another opportunity to prove their valor, appearing as anxious as a group of boys about to be turned loose for a spring holiday after a long, hard winter.

"If Snipes wishes to teach us a lesson, men, we must make it a costly one. Connelly!" Benton turned to his second in command. "Take your men to the church. They should have passed there by now, and prepare to defend the road. I have a feeling Colonel Snipes may be passing back that way sooner than expected."

Connelly smiled and nodded, galloping away with his devil squadron and disappearing into a cloud of dust. All of them appeared perfectly confident, knowing full well that when an able force is led by an accomplished and capable leader, the ultimate victor cannot always be predicted by mere numbers.

"The rest of you men, follow me." Benton gave a light tug on his reins. "After today, I fear Snipes will as soon think of attacking the devil as riding into *our* territory."

Benton dashed off, and like a pack of hungry hounds on a fresh trail, his men followed. Through cornfields and over stone fences, the invincible little band rushed, blindly following their idolized leader. Yet some of them began groaning under their breath as they watched Benton's soldierly form veer and plunge into a tangled, impenetrable thicket off the side of the road, knowing without looking that there would be no perceivable evidence of a trail in front of him.

"There'll be blood spilled sure," one of them mumbled.

Others swore and cursed, nodding their heads in agreement, for their commander had the notorious and immensely unpopular habit of piloting his troops through the fields and streams of Virginia, insisting a rabbit path through a briar patch was a shortcut. The men knew from experience that they would suffer more irritating wounds and lose more blood by following him through the tangled maze of his imaginary path than they would in actual battle. How he always came away without a scratch was a mystery no one had yet solved—especially at the speeds at which he generally tore through the snarled, angry tangle of barbs.

"Why can't he take the blasted road," one of the men grumbled as a vine slashed his leg.

"That'd be wishful thinking, my friend," another responded.

Indeed, not a hundred yards away, lay a road in the same direction. But that would have been too slow and too far out of the way for the usual rapidity of their gallant leader's mind and motions. If he could find a shortcut through hell, his men knew with blessed certainty they'd find themselves breathing smoke and riding through fire.

When the last man came barreling out of the wilderness, Benton again split his force, placing them on opposite sides of the road in cover of an embankment on one side and cedars on the other. He spread them out as far as he could, intending to make a show of force that would deceive the enemy of his true numbers.

Another scout came spurring in from the opposite side of the road to report on the progress of the enemy.

"They are advancing, sir."

The news brought a wry smile to Benton's face. "I predict they will soon be 'advancing' backward," he replied as he stood in his stirrups and stretched his long legs a moment as if just waking up from a nap. It had been Benton's experience over the last year and a half that two fully loaded revolvers, carried in the belts of a few dozen men with the power, skill, and authority to use them had the magical effect of reversing a Yankees' sense of direction.

"Steady men. Don't fire too soon," Benton said casually as he eased himself back into the saddle and picked up his reins. Although he appeared as relaxed as if he were merely giving the command for the start of a horserace, his men knew that within a few minutes he would be fighting with the fire and energy of Mars himself. He never appeared so happy, so completely in his element as when he had his officers and men engaged in a hot contest.

Directing two of the soldiers to follow him, Benton rode forward on the turnpike toward his foe, casually lighting a cigar after a distance of about a hundred yards, just as a sea of blue crested a hill within view. Had anyone looked upon his face, they would have seen his eyes watching the advance of the enemy with all the attention that a groom shows at the approach of his bride. Yet he pretended not to notice his foe's appearance, riding placidly forward with apparent unconcern... inviting attack.

Perhaps Benton did not realize he was in range of their guns as he crested the hill—or perhaps he did not care. In any event, the resultant barrage of lead from the enemy kicked up dust in quite a lively manner on the road around him and his two comrades. Feigning surprise, Benton and his men wheeled their horses as if in panic, and galloped back toward whence they had come, firing a few shots over their shoulders as a derisive salute.

Thinking of nothing but an easy victory over their most reviled enemy, the Union vanguard pursued the fleeing horsemen and rode blindly into the trap without hesitation or suspicion, closely followed by the main body who apparently did not wish to miss out on the fun.

Meanwhile, silence and deep anxiety hung over Benton's men as they waited breathlessly for the signal. There was no movement and no sound, save their pounding hearts and the occasional impatient stamp of a horse's hoof. These were battle-tested veterans who knew what they were doing—and, more importantly, were experienced enough to know of the disaster that would ensue if they started doing it too soon. Possessing the confidence that comes from routine victories, the impending conflict held no fear for these men, despite the unevenness in numbers. Waiting in the close shadows of the thicket, with reins clasped, revolvers drawn, they anxiously awaited the sign that would signal the unclenching of their hungry jaws.

When it finally came, the demoniacal cry that rose from their throats instantly instilled in the Federals the belief that they had substantially miscalculated their enemy's strength. Or perhaps it was that they did not wish to fight the demons who were speeding undismayed into their midst, yelling as they swept forward like a pack of ferocious wolves. Then again, it could have been merely the fear of Benton himself that lent a thousand terrors to the enemy's mind, for they wavered, broke, and fled at the first sight of the fanatical rebel band. Fired to a divine energy and with the majestic madness so common to them, this band of heroic troopers continued to stir the air with their battle cry, making music enough for a battalion though there were now many less than one hundred on hand.

The combined result of fire and shock instantly drove the vanguard back into the main column, which, for the most part, had already turned and begun running back down the pike—directly into the open and waiting arms of Connelly and his men. Benton pulled his horse up on an eminence and watched his men vigorously carry out his order to "make a meal of them."

"Wear them out!" he yelled smiling, knowing they needed no further coaching from him. They performed their duty with a precision and thoroughness that indicated bountiful amounts of previous practice. The outcome, therefore, was as Benton predicted. Snipes had reversed his direction, suddenly more eager for flight than a fight. Benton observed the action with an expression that looked more like impatience than concern and turned his thoughts to the prompt removal of the wounded, prisoners, and horses.

Rubbing his temple thoughtfully, Benton watched his men round up and separate the enemy from their mounts. With at least two hundred of each, it would take a few men to get the horses back to headquarters, and another half dozen to escort the prisoners south. Although it had been a successful afternoon so far, he was losing men and time. This little fray was going to put him hours behind schedule…and as he glanced at the sky, the weather appeared to be inclined to do the same.

"What say you we go stir up some Yankees," Benton said, once his men were reassembled again. He was impatient to get started on the task he had been ordered to perform: harass and delay—if not prohibit—any advance on General Stuart's cavalry.

The sky was turning dark and massing with angry clouds when the group finally headed south in the direction a force of the enemy had been reported. It was not long after that rain began falling in sheets… a situation that was wholly disregarded by Benton.

The sound of an approaching wagon, barely distinguishable in the storm, sent the men scurrying into the cover of trees. All except Benton that is, who stood in the middle of the road, signaling for the wagon to halt. While speaking leisurely with the wagon's occupants on the possible whereabouts of the Federal army, two Union officers rode out from the darkness behind the wagon. Although their sudden appearance no doubt surprised Benton, he conversed casually with them without revealing his identity. After ascertaining they were alone, and finding out where they were heading, he officially introduced himself.

"Heading south?" When they answered in the affirmative, Benton drew his weapon from beneath his coat so quickly it was difficult to see any movement. "Allow my men to escort you."

As usual, the demand for surrender was so strongly stipulated and forcefully requested that compliance was immediate. Benton's words brought instantaneous action from those waiting in the tree line, and the Federal officers were soon on their way to Richmond. The intelligence gained was then hastily copied to a dispatch and forwarded through a courier to Stuart.

"Forward, men," Benton said when that business was completed to his satisfaction. "I believe we shall find some more this way." These words were said in such a lackadaisical way as if to imply he believed nothing more was needed to establish a victory for the Confederacy than to show his men where to find the enemy.

After another three hours of steady, uneventful riding, Benton directed his men into the shelter of a grove of cedars where only an occasional drop of rain could be felt. As was common, the men instantly took advantage of the pause, many of them sliding off their horses and falling asleep before they hit the ground. Major Connelly lay down with his horse's reins wrapped around his hand and, within minutes, heard Benton mount and ride away, no doubt seeking some stimulating enterprise to win his men a return for their endurance of the inclement weather. In another few minutes, Connelly was asleep, despite his soggy bed, only to be awakened about an hour later by the sound of Benton's voice.

"Connelly," he whispered, standing directly over him.

Connelly was awake in an instant.

"Wake up Jake and question these gentlemen for the countersign."

Connelly looked up at the two Yankee privates Benton had on each side of him. Taking charge of the two prisoners, he watched his leader remove his noisy spurs, lay them by a tree and disappear again…this time on foot. If Benton ever slept, Connelly thought, no one witnessed it.

After waking up Jake, Connelly separated the men for their questioning. From his prisoner's story, it did not take long for him to figure the chain of events. Benton had gotten into the enemy's camp, but had apparently found himself in a larger and more heavily guarded outpost than anticipated. To help him get out he had recruited these two unsuspecting privates, who were innocently having a late-night conversation around a campfire. With a soldier in blue on each side, both of whom had been suitably threatened with death, Benton had merely nodded as he rode by the pickets, asking, "Is all quiet? Good! Keep a sharp lookout!"

It was typical Benton, Connelly thought to himself, as he began questioning his prisoner about the countersign. It soon became evident, however, that the private was no longer in the mood to cooperate. Whether he had gained his senses and had taken in the gravity of the situation or he was no longer in the presence of Benton, Connelly could not ascertain. But only with the persuasive use of a pistol to the Yankee's head did he manage to convince the private to divulge the important code.

Putting the prisoner under charge of another man, Connelly went back to Jake to compare notes. They had just discovered that the two prisoners did not seem to agree on the countersign, when Benton came striding unhurriedly back into the camp as if he had been out for a moonlit stroll. Benton's eyes smoldered when Connelly explained the situation, but he did not appear overly alarmed. He had a way of wringing desired facts from even the most reluctant prisoner, and Connelly ascertained no doubt that the two men would cooperate with a little encouragement.

And so it was that the two prisoners were again questioned separately, and again with a gun to their heads—but this time the weapon was in the hand of Benton, and this time the gun was cocked. Apparently this method was a little more convincing and authoritative, for he found the word he was seeking from each and they matched.

"Let's say we go recruit some Yankee horses to the Confederate service, men," Benton said, before turning on his heel and mounting his horse.

And so armed with the countersign and plenty of nerve, the band of Rebels hastily mounted and followed their leader, riding straight into the outpost unmolested. The negligent, slumped position in which they sat their horses and the casual way in which they nodded at the sentries as they passed led the Yankee soldiers to believe they were a returning scouting party of their own men whose presence was duly noted and instantly forgotten.

The men worked quietly in the enemy camp, each knowing his business and doing it without hesitation or fear. Within minutes, the Rebel band had secured another eighty-five horses for the Confederacy without a shot being fired. Before he left, however, Benton made sure the Federal troops knew he had been there by carving his name into a nearby tree. He understood that penetrating the enemy's mind with fear was as important as penetrating a body with lead. Because of this tactic, Benton had become a legend, his reputation so menacing and his character so terrorizing that the mere mention of his name struck fear in the hearts of the enemy.

There was no limit to Benton's audacity in the minds of the enemy—and therefore no end to his success. Consequently, when calamity, misfortune, or disaster struck a Federal camp, no matter what the circumstances or who was responsible for the blow, the cry that echoed up and down the line was universal: Benton.

Union officers were at a loss to explain what made the Confederate leader so often victorious, but Benton's men were not. They knew that his triumphs were partly due to his calm and indomitable courage and partly to his cool and collected bearing when he stood in the midst of crises and chaos. But mostly he won, even against overwhelming forces, due to his pure, stubborn, and fierce refusal to be whipped.

Tireless, relentless and seemingly always in the saddle, Benton functioned as if impervious to danger and fatigue. No matter how many days he had been in the saddle, or how many hours since his last meal, he was capable of handling any challenge and overcoming any obstacle. Never, no matter the odds, did he hesitate or waver when commanding the field. As one of his men once said, "The Colonel's actions follow thought as a bullet follows the bang…so quickly that they seem simultaneous."

Chapter 9

Anguish and grief like darkness and rain can be described, but joy and gladness like the rainbow of promise defy alike the pen and pencil.
—*Frederick Douglas*

November 1863

The summer turned into fall, and the fall to that time of year when cold, blustering nights keep everyone inside and close to the warmth of a fire. Preparing for bed one such night, Sarah barely heard a tap on the door above the sound of the howling wind and sleet hitting the window. Throwing on a wrapper, she descended the stairs in her bare feet, and hesitantly opened the door a crack.

Standing in the dark of the night, his hair glistening white with ice from beneath the rim of his hat, stood Colonel Benton. "Lieutenant Duvall," he said, bowing slightly, "Pardon the lateness of the hour, but General Lee asked that I stop and see with my own two eyes that you are well and to report back to him."

Sarah stared at him a moment. "You needn't have come in such atrocious weather."

He appeared to shiver. "It could not be helped. I'm on my way back to headquarters now."

Sarah peered over his shoulder into the darkness. "You are alone then?"

"Yes, I sent my men on without me."

"Then you must come in and warm yourself." His powerful physique, as forbidding as it once had seemed, no longer intimidated her. She grabbed his arm and pulled him toward the door, but Benton planted his feet. "It should be safe," Sarah said, looking around him into the darkness beyond. "No one in his right mind will be out in this weather."

"But my horse..."

Sarah frowned at the sight of his horse standing with head down against the cold blasts of air. "Put him in the barn. There's plenty of corn and hay. I'll go stir the fire."

* * *

When Benton reentered the house, she was standing by the fire, poking at flames that were coming to life. He paused for a moment at the doorway and watched as she worked. Her hair, which was uncharacteristically loose and unbraided, flowed in soft waves down her back, almost to her waist.

"You needn't go to any trouble," he said, causing her to turn around.

She rose, shook back her long, magnificent locks and approached him. "Oh, it's no trouble. My head has been aching with the monotony of blue cloth—you are a sight for sore eyes."

Benton would have laughed at the statement had he not felt so woozy. He blamed it on the hard ride, the frigid cold, and now, the heat from the fire.

"Really you do not look well, Colonel." Sarah walked toward him and took his hand to pull him into the room. "Come, stand by the fire."

Before he could move, she stopped and clasped both of her hands around his fingers. "It is as I thought," she said, grimly, her gaze going up to meet his. "Cold as ice." She reached up, placed the back of her hand on his forehead, and then her open palm on his cheek. "And hot as a stovepipe."

"Take off your wet coat," she instructed. "Where is your gum blanket?"

"I gave it to one of my men," he said wearily. Fighting hard to keep his teeth from chattering, Benton felt himself being swiftly drained of strength.

"Come, stand by the fire—"

"Really, I should be getting on my way," Benton said. "I only intended to stop for a moment."

"Your men will miss you?"

"No, not exactly. They are accustomed to my..." He looked into her eyes and sighed at what he saw there. Even with her isolation she knew enough, or had guessed perhaps, of his frequent wanderings.

"You owe me no explanation," she said hurriedly. "But surely there is no reason you cannot warm yourself and rest a minute."

Frustrated he could not come up with another excuse, Benton sighed heavily. He felt so cold on the outside and hot on the inside that he could not think.

"Of course, you outrank me, I cannot order it." Sarah nodded toward the weapon leaning against a wall nearby. "But I *could* hold you at gunpoint."

Benton could see that her eyes, for once, were twinkling with something of humor—though her lips still showed no trace of a smile. She seemed strangely kind and motherly, which confused him. Perhaps it would be better to come in and warm up. He desperately needed to sit down—even if just for a moment. And truth be told, when he glanced into her warm, inviting eyes, he felt more of an interest in staying than any desire to go.

"The gun will not be necessary," he said wearily. "I am at your mercy."

She did not hesitate once he acquiesced and began to unbutton his overcoat. "Your uniform has seen hard service."

"As has the wearer," he said tiredly, removing his hat as she continued unclasping his coat.

"Oh my," she exclaimed as she got to the button in the middle of his chest.

Benton looked down at the dented piece of brass that had caused the reaction. "A souvenir from our last engagement," he said. "It appears the bullet was pretty well spent before it hit me, but the button spared me some blood."

Sarah continued to stare at the button and the wide expanse of chest that was its target as if envisioning the bullet and its course—and contemplating the end result. "May I have it?" she finally asked in a low voice.

Surprised, but weak with fatigue, Benton did not question her motives. He hastily tore the button from the coat and handed it to her. "If it will be of some value to you, it is yours."

Sarah stared at it, turned it over in her hands, and then spoke in a low voice. "As you wished to keep the handkerchief, I wish to keep this—to remind me of the potential sacrifice, and pray for the courage to be equally as brave."

Benton was stunned by her compliment of bravery, but the seriousness of her tone gave him pause. "It is not for you to fight and win this war, Mrs. Duvall, nor do I wish to compete with you in the courage department. You have already demonstrated you possess ample supply."

Whether she heard his words or not, he could not say for she showed no sign of it. "Get out of these wet clothes while I go get you some dry. You are about the same size as my husband."

Benton reached for her arm as she turned to leave. "It's true? You were married then?"

For moment, she seemed taken aback, though he did not know if it was by the question or the fact that he had the audacity to ask it. "I am a widow," she snapped. "Surely you knew that."

"No... I mean, yes... I mean, ah, I suppose it's common knowledge..."

She stared at him silently for a moment with a look that appeared to be disappointment. "I hope you do not pay too close attention to things that have been manufactured in the rumor mill, Colonel Benton," she said before disappearing up the staircase.

Sighing loudly, Benton began unclasping his shirt, his cold, stiff fingers barely able to complete the task. How many months had he known this woman now? And yet he knew almost nothing of her. He became surprisingly curious about whom or what had left her so solemnly reclusive. Perhaps she was so accustomed to solitude that she merely shunned companionship and conversation for their strangeness.

"Hang your wet clothes by the fire there." She entered the room as quickly as she had left it, leaving a pile of clothes on a side table as she passed. "I'll fix you something warm to drink."

Benton did as he was told, and when dressed in dry clothes, lowered himself onto the couch by the fire. Too weak now to keep his teeth from chattering, he sat shivering and shaking until she reentered the room.

"Lean forward," she instructed from behind him. When he did as he was told, she placed a warm, thick quilt behind him and, as he leaned back, wrapped it tightly across his shoulders. "There. Feel better? Now drink this. It will help warm you on the inside."

Benton took a long sip of the drink, then leaned his head back and closed his eyes, trying to clear his foggy mind. "So he was a Union officer, then?" Sarah had risen to stir the fire again, and he heard the poking stop as she paused to answer his question.

"Yes, the rumors on that account are true."

After a long silence, she lowered herself in the chair beside him. He opened his eyes briefly to look at her and saw she wore her usual contemplative expression, one, he surmised was due to much communing alone.

"I suppose you are curious as to the circumstances."

Wrapped in warmth and content by the fire, he kept his eyes closed now. "It's none of my business, but I am not immune to curiosity."

The room became quiet, so quiet that the crackling fire, unnoticed before, now dominated all else. When he opened one eye to look at her, he saw she had turned her attention to the flaming logs. She stared at them hard, as if seeing pictures of the past she had not gazed upon for a long time, or upon things she had been trying to forget.

"Colonel William Duvall patrolled this neighborhood regularly."

He heard her shift in her chair and sigh loudly. For moment he thought perhaps she did not wish to continue, or perhaps was not quite sure how to do so, but then she began again.

"When he discovered that I was a young woman, alone, he kindly placed guards here for my protection."

"He was a gentleman, then." Benton lifted the cup and took another sip of the warm drink. Under normal circumstances he would have ended the conversation rather than invade her private thoughts, but he was so dizzy with fever and fatigue, he spoke aloud the words he was thinking.

"Yes, he was very much a gentleman. He began taking meals here occasionally, and then, after a few months, there was rarely a night when he did not visit." Sarah rose and began pacing in front of the fire. "I suppose you are aware that Jake, my brother, served under General Mason for a time as a scout."

Benton was well aware of the fact, as Mason had recommended that Jake join his elite squadron.

"Jake was captured the first summer of the war on his way here for a furlough." Sarah paused and looked over her shoulder at Benton. "He was wearing civilian clothing."

"So they took him as a spy?" Benton began to see the seriousness of the situation.

Sarah sat down again and stared straight into the now-blazing fire. For all Benton knew, her eyes were brimming with tears, but her tone remained impersonal. "Yes. As it happened, Confederate troops had recently hanged a spy—and the Yankees were intent on retaliation."

She stopped and turned to face him. "You must understand, Colonel, that Jake is all I have. He is everything to me!"

Benton followed her movements with his eyes as she stood and began pacing again, her gown and wrapper flowing behind her like moving cloud.

"Much as I hated to do it, I appealed to Colonel Duvall, and he...I don't know how he did it...but he got Jake's status changed to prisoner of war. He was sent to prison and was later exchanged."

"Jake must be very grateful for what you did for him."

"No, Jake knows nothing of it! I do not wish him to know. You must not tell him!"

"But why?"

Sarah sat down on the couch beside Benton. "He will think that is why I married the Colonel. He will blame himself."

"Is it not?" Benton knew the question was a personal one, but he remained cautiously persistent in his questioning.

She lapsed into a short silence. "Not exactly why. I mean, he asked for my hand soon after. He wished to offer me protection with his name."

Benton looked at her long and hard, but she turned her eyes from him and fixed them on the fire, trying to appear calm. "Even though he knew you were a daughter of the South?" It was obvious to Benton that Colonel Duvall recognized the spirit, courage, and patriotism of the young Southern woman he had befriended.

"Yes, in spite of that fact. God knows I had no thoughts then of the treachery in which I am now inured. But still I resisted..."

Benton watched as she stared at nothing, her eyes full of sorrow and despair. He had often seen her stare wistfully into the darkness or out toward the horizon as if she were looking for someone or something, and he wondered where her thoughts were wondering now, for she seemed unaware of his presence. Then she spoke again.

"I resisted..." Her voice trembled slightly, but she brought it under control after taking a deep breath and starting again. "I resisted until they brought him here wounded."

"Mortally?"

She nodded. "It appeared so. But the doctor said the hope of a brighter future might be enough to pull him through." She paused and took a long, deep breath. "I felt I owed him the happiness and comfort he had provided me by helping my brother. I could not let him die such a death if I held the power to in some way prevent it!"

Again, she took a long, shaky breath that was almost a sob. "He lived only a few days more."

"Still, it was a great gift that you gave him."

"He was the one who gave a gift!" She stood, blinking back the tears that brimmed the edges of her lashes. "As fate would have it, a gift far greater to my cause then the lifeblood he spilled for his own!"

Benton's heart pounded at the emotional, despairing tone of her voice. There had always been more determination than despair in her face and manner, but now her whole attitude spoke unerringly of a heavy grief he was powerless to help her banish.

She lowered herself to the couch beside him. "It hurts me...deeply"—she put one hand on his arm, the other on her heart—"to use his name as I am now, even for such a good cause."

Colonel Benton thought about the advantage of trust she had gained by being the widow of a Union officer, and understood her dismay. The fact that she had not planned this path of treachery made it no less painful to her.

"Believe me, it was not until my friends and neighbors turned against me because of the marriage that I considered using the relationship for the good of the South. It seemed I had nothing to lose."

"He knew your loyalties," Benton said, trying to comfort her. "You must not think he would think ill of you."

With her face in her hands as if to shield her emotions from him, Sarah nodded. "Yes, he knew. But it makes the guilt no less."

Benton stared at the emotion wrought from this vulnerable woman who had suffered so much and been given so little. It was now obvious she had locked her heart away to protect it from future pain, and he suddenly yearned for a small piece of it. "You loved him then."

Sarah was silent for a long moment, and when she spoke, her words were filled with emotion. "I do not believe I loved him." She looked up at Benton with big, sorrowful eyes. "But he is the greatest man I have ever known."

When she got up and placed two more logs on the fire, Benton reflected on what an honor it would be to claim that title—to be regarded as the greatest man this woman had ever known. He remembered watching her delicate yet indomitable figure poke at the logs as he promised himself he would make that achievement his life's endeavor. And then he remembered no more.

* * *

The next morning, Benton awoke to the sound of crackling flames and humming in a distant room. Removing the quilt from across him, he followed the sound into the kitchen. "What was that concoction you made me drink last night?" he said sternly upon seeing her busy at the cook stove.

She looked up as if startled and then smiled. "Good morning, Colonel. It's a pleasure to see you in such a good mood."

"The liquid you made me drink," he said again, rubbing his head. "What was it?"

"Just something my grandmother used to make for me," she said, shrugging. "You slept well, did you not?"

"Yes, I slept well!" he thundered. "That is the point! I intended to get back to my men!"

"But, Colonel, you told me yourself your men would not miss you for one night. And had you tried to ride out of here, you would have passed out within a mile from chill and fever. Now go change into your own clothes while I finish breakfast."

She turned around as if dismissing him, but Benton did not see. He was staring down at his clothes apparently just remembering they were not his own.

"Don't worry, Colonel, you put them on all by yourself," she said, still busy over the stove.

Benton stormed out of the room and returned a short time later fully dressed. Lowering himself into a chair at the table, he watched her pour a steaming cup of coffee. "I suppose I should apologize for my earlier behavior. I did not wake in the best of moods."

"Apology accepted, Colonel. It comes as no surprise me that you are grumpy in the morning."

"And how much time have you spent thinking about what my moods may or may not be first thing in the morning?" he asked inquiringly as he took the cup of coffee she handed him.

The question turned her cheeks crimson. "I have spent no time on it…" She did not finish her thought, but went back to the task of cracking eggs, which became a noisy and violent affair.

Benton's gaze drifted to the gun lying across a chair in the opposite room. It occurred to him that he had never seen it out of her reach—-and rarely out of her hands. "And how did *you* sleep last night, Mrs. Duvall?"

She looked up sharply, and he saw more clearly the weariness in her eyes and the swollen lids that come from lack of rest. "Quite well, thank you." She turned and reached for a plate.

"It's just that I noticed your gun lying across the chair and feared perhaps you stayed up all night on picket duty."

She remained quiet a moment as if assessing the situation and deliberating on an answer. Then she slowly turned to face him. "I suppose I must be honest with you, Colonel. Despite being a mere woman, I do have the ability to comprehend certain things."

"Such as?"

"A colonel, without his command, was asleep in my home behind enemy lines."

He smiled. "That makes it sound like you were worried about my safety. You would grieve for my loss?"

Her answer came with little thought. "It would be the country's loss, not mine." She went back to work, scooping two eggs out of a pan and plopping them onto his plate.

Benton shook his head and took another deep breath. The vein of steel that ran through her was unbreakable and unbendable. Although she was nothing like any of the women he had known in the past, somehow she manifested all the grace and social elegance that makes a woman desirable. He was reminded of his silent pledge the previous night, and the yearning to attain her esteem grew within him.

"Let's be honest," he said softly. "Without the lady's aide, the colonel's value to the country would be greatly diminished."

She must have heard the emotion and respect in his tone, because she raised her gaze to his and blinked. "Nevertheless, I could not sleep." She turned and sat a pitcher down on the table in such a way that he could tell it would be a loss of time to dwell upon the point. "Would the colonel like buttermilk with his breakfast?"

She did not wait for an answer or for an offer to pour it, but swiftly removed her apron and headed for the door. "I have some other chores to do. The colonel may let himself out when he has finished eating."

Benton cringed slightly when the door slammed shut behind him, but he could not stop thinking about the woman who did the slamming. He knew now that the icy exterior was but a shield to hide from view the obvious warmth and compassion that lay hidden within, qualities she kept securely hidden away and disguised beneath a mask of mystery.

* * *

Sarah slipped on her coat and put her head down against the terrible bite of the wind outside. Heading for the barn, her cheeks still red from her conversation with Colonel Benton, she hurriedly threw some grain to his horse, filled water buckets, and continued to the chicken house to gather eggs. When she was sure she had heard him ride away, she went back to the house and found he had stoked the fire to a blaze. Warming her hands for a moment, she decided to clean up the dishes before lying down to get some much-needed sleep.

Standing in the doorway of the kitchen, she paused a moment and pulled out the dented button she had removed from Benton's coat. Closing her eyes, she said a silent prayer and then felt a single teardrop run down her cheek. She did not stop to decipher its cause, but tucked away the dented button that had protected the colonel's heart…and likewise had probably saved her own.

Chapter 10

My heart bleeds at the death of every one of our gallant men.
—Robert E. Lee, in a letter to his wife, December 25, 1862

January 1864

In the dusk of early evening there lay an aura of quiet graciousness about the house called Waverly. It was one of those uncommon evenings in winter when a hint of warmth comes back into the air, bringing with it the comfort and contentment of a springlike night.

Sarah had just lit the lamps when she heard boots on the porch and knew instinctively they were his. No one else moved with such impatience, authority, or strength, and no one else had the power to cause her heart to pound so forcefully. Fighting both the fear and excitement of seeing him again, Sarah restrained the urge to hurry. She wished to appear unaffected by his visit, yet she was so happy to see him that she knew it was impossible to look otherwise.

Reaching the door before he did, she flung it open as he prepared to knock. Her look of welcome faded when she beheld his gloomy countenance, and caused a sinister sensation to creep up her spine. Her gaze drifted over his shoulder to the shaded darkness of the tree line where some of his men waited. The horses stood motionless and the men in the saddles appeared as silent shadows in the gloomy dusk.

"Won't you come in?" She stepped aside for the colonel to enter, and then paused, waiting for Major Connelly who was in the process of tying his horse to the post. Connelly simply removed his hat and swallowed nervously. "I'll wait out here ma'am."

Sarah glanced once more at the men in the shadows, but could make out none of their faces, so deeply were their heads bowed to their chests. Closing the door behind Colonel Benton, she stared at him with heart-wrenching scrutiny, trying to read what the lines on his face foretold. He spoke no words for a few long moments, yet his eyes said everything she needed to know. "You bring bad news?"

Benton gazed at her silently as if mustering strength for a confession. Fingering his hat, he took a deep breath, and with heroic effort kept his voice from cracking. "I fear so. And words cannot convey how deeply I regret the necessity of bearing it."

Sarah took a choking breath as she stepped forward, her fingers digging reflexively into his arm. "Jake?" Her eyes brimmed with tears, yet somehow none breached the lids.

"He was wounded two days ago in that engagement at Bailey's Farm." Benton seemed to be trying to make his voice sound unemotional, but he blinked twice to control an apparent sudden rush of moisture. "He passed this morning."

Sarah nodded, her chest rising and falling as she absorbed the dreadful news. Normally calm and collected, she now trembled, yet her head remained held high as she gazed mournfully into vacancy.

"I had no reason to believe that I would be exempted from the loss that so many others have endured," she murmured, knowing full well there was no house, high or low in the length and breadth of Virginia, had not mourned some lost father or brother or son.

"I took the liberty of telling Jake about your…situation before he died," Benton said, his tone more grave than reassuring. "He wished your forgiveness, and I told him I knew you well enough to know it was freely given."

Sarah nodded in acknowledgment that she had heard him, but her chin trembled at the effort of suppressing her emotions. "It's very kind of you to deliver the news personally, Colonel. You come at great risk."

"He was one of my best officers, Mrs. Duvall." Benton's glistening eyes told Sarah more than his words. "I know this is a great loss to you, but it must give you some measure of consolation to know he died bravely in defense of his country."

Sarah nodded, and then turned to the door to let him out. She was surprised by the light touch of Benton's hand when he laid it upon her shoulder to stop her.

"Wait. There is something else."

She turned slowly. "Yes?"

"Jake's wife came to his side as soon as she heard he'd been wounded."

"His wife?" Sarah cocked her head and stared at him, her voice and countenance giving away her surprise.

"Yes, and I have no means to convey her safely back through the lines now. I know it would be an inconvenience, but—"

"Does she know?"

"No, I did not feel it my place to tell her. If Jake didn't, then she believes you are a—"

"Traitor." Sarah finished for him.

Benton lowered his head and nodded. "Yes. But she is weak right now. I do not wish to risk her traveling any farther, and Jake requested that she come here."

"Very well. Where is she?"

Benton nodded toward the door, where the sound of the creaking wheels of a wagon could now be heard. "Her name is Lucy. Mrs. Lucy Callahan."

Without hesitation, Sarah opened the door and descended noiselessly down the steps. Greeting Lucy solemnly and taking her hand like she was an old friend, Sarah helped her down from the conveyance, and pretended not to be surprised when she saw the young girl was with child.

Benton cleared his throat and walked toward the two women. "Lucy, despite Mrs. Duvall's politics, I believe you will be safe here until other arrangements can be made."

Teary-eyed with emotion, Lucy merely nodded. Sarah wrapped her arm around the girl and helped her up the steps to the door. Letting her inside, she paused and turned when Benton spoke.

"I don't know when I'll be back, Mrs. Duvall. It may not be safe for Lucy to travel for some time."

"She will be safe here. I will see to that."

"Yes, I knew you would." Colonel Benton handed Sarah a bag of Lucy's belongings and went to untie his horse before turning to her one last time. "Your brother wished to be interred here. I can have a burial party detached tonight if it is acceptable to you."

"Near the old oak." Sarah nodded toward the spreading limbs of the tree that dominated the far side of the yard as if anticipating the question.

Benton nodded and mounted his horse. "If I can serve you in any other way, hesitate to ask nothing of me, Mrs. Duvall."

Sarah looked at Benton with glistening eyes, smiled briefly in appreciation, and then disappeared through the door.

* * *

"Miss Lucy, you must be famished." Sarah closed the door and stared at her sister-in-law in the dim light of the house.

"Not so much hungry as tired, ma'am," the young girl answered shyly. "I'd really like to sleep."

"Yes, you poor dear. Let me show you to your room." Sarah lit a candle and led the way up the stairs. "You must make yourself right at home now. You will, won't you? You won't be afraid to ask for anything you need?"

Lucy nodded as the light from the candle flooded a small room. She paused at the doorway, and turned toward Sarah. "This was Jake's?" she asked in a hushed voice.

"Yes. I thought you might like it."

"Yes, ma'am. I like it very much." Lucy sat on the bed and ran her hand across the pillow where her husband's head had once lain, as a lone tear slid down her cheek.

"I'll bring some water up so you can wash before retiring."

"Thank you, Mrs. Duvall."

Sarah turned. "No more of that. You must call me Sarah."

"Yes, ma'am...I mean yes, Sarah." She cocked her head and stared at Sarah a moment before casting her eyes to the floor.

"What's wrong, child?"

"It's just that, well...you don't seem like what they say."

"And what do they say?"

"Oh, I couldn't repeat it." Lucy lowered her head, but not before her cheeks blazed with color.

Sarah sat down on the bed beside Lucy and took her hand. "If they say I feed and house Union troops, you will soon find that to be true. I will not turn away hungry men fighting for their country."

"But don't you love the South?"

Now it was Sarah's turn to blush. "Of course I do. But war puts us in unusual circumstances, and we must act as we see fit. Do you understand?"

"Not really," Lucy answered. "But Jake told me to trust you."

"He did?"

Lucy nodded, her eyes welling with tears again. "I don't know why. I'm so confused. But right before he died, he told me to forget every-thing I'd heard and to trust you."

Sarah reached out and drew the young widow to her, stroking her hair as she talked. "Yes, Lucy, no matter what happens, no matter what you see or hear, please know that you can trust me."

* * *

Sarah left her sister-in-law to rest and went downstairs to check on the stew she had been cooking. Too tired to sleep, she sat up knitting and heard the sound of shovels clanking outside around midnight. True to Benton's word, his men had carried her brother's dead body to his home in the dark of night, not ten miles from where he'd been slain, and laid it to rest where he had been born only twenty years earlier. About an hour later, Sarah heard a tentative knock on the door and opened it slightly.

The young private standing the doorway appeared white-faced with fear. "M-M-Mrs. Duvall, I'm sorry to bother you so late, but I saw the light still burning."

"That's quite all right." She opened the door wider and saw the shadowy forms of the others already mounted on their horses. "Is there something wrong?"

"N-no, ma'am, well yes... maybe," the young man stammered. "It's just that Jake and I were good friends. And I'm, well, I'm sorry for your loss."

Sarah nodded. "Thank you. That's very kind of you, Private..."

"Private Matson, ma'am."

"I appreciate your condolences, Private Matson." She paused for a moment when he did not move. "Is that all?"

"Well...no, ma'am. Not exactly." He took a deep breath and stared at the floor as he spoke. "Jake told me you had a way with horses."

Sarah nodded. "Yes, I suppose I do."

"Well, ma'am, Colonel Benton's horse, Invincible—he calls him Vince—well, he was hurt real bad in that fight that killed Jake."

"Oh?" Sarah again lifted her eyes toward the darkness behind him, but could see nothing.

"Yes, ma'am, and the colonel...well, the colonel ordered me to... to..."

Sarah finally understood what had given the young man the courage to knock on her door. "He ordered you to put him out of his misery?"

The soldier let out a sigh of relief. "Yes. But I thought... I thought maybe you could do something for him. The colonel puts a lot of stock in that horse, ma'am. I mean he and that horse are mighty close, and I hate the thought of..."

"I understand," Sarah said. "But it seems a rather big thing to go against the colonel's direct order."

The boy's face turned red. "We... I mean, *I* thought about that. The colonel don't need to know. I mean, if you think he won't make it then I'll do what the colonel ordered. And if he does make it, well maybe the colonel won't be so mad that I disobeyed."

Sarah shook her head as she realized how thoroughly the men had thought out their plan and how much they revered their commander. Yet she wondered whether it was wise to take on such an enterprise, especially considering the new ward now under her care. Weary beyond measure, Sarah continued to hesitate at the thought of going behind Colonel Benton's back.

But thinking about the magnificent animal she had seen him riding, she decided there would be no harm in looking. Perhaps she owed him that much anyway. Benton had, after all, stood before her steadfast and strong to inform her personally of Jake's death, never giving the slightest indication he had suffered a loss as well. The least she could do was take a look.

"I fear it's too dark to make that sort of decision tonight," she said after another moment's thought. "Put him in the barn. I'll see what I can do in the morning."

The young man smiled shyly for the first time. "He's already there, ma'am. Jake told me you would never let a horse die like that." He tipped his hat, backed off the porch, and disappeared into the night.

Chapter 11

Nothing is there to come and nothing past, But an eternal Now does always last.
—Abraham Cowley

C olonel Benton gazed absently into the fire, his mind wandering to scenes of recent battles, and to the faces of the men and families affected by them. The soft, warm glow of the flames upon his face did nothing to alleviate the stab of pain he felt when his thoughts invariably led to Waverly. The image of that solitary, unmarked grave in the yard always made him shiver and left him with a vague yearning to provide comfort to the friendless occupant of the home.

The sound of voices and footsteps in the foyer interrupted Benton's gloomy thoughts. When his aide entered and announced the arrival of two visitors, Benton readily approved their admittance, hoping the company would thrust the melancholy thoughts from his mind. But when he saw the plump older woman push her young daughter boldly into the room, he wished he had not been so hasty. This was not the type of diversion he'd envisioned. Reluctant to be rude however, he took a deep breath, greeting them with courteous formality as he invited them into the cavernous room he used as headquarters.

"To what do I owe the pleasure?" He bowed to the duo, which caused the young girl to shake and the mother to laugh flirtatiously.

"Colonel, forgive my boldness, but I wanted to introduce my daughter, Melissa, to you before the ball tomorrow night. I know how busy you get during those affairs."

Colonel Benton looked over at the rather plump, blushing young lady, took in her obvious youth in a glance, and turned back to the mother. "And what makes you assume I shall be attending the festivities tomorrow night?" He walked over to the fireplace as he talked and poked at the logs as if they were not already fully ablaze.

"Oh, Colonel Benton." She laughed as if he were merely making a joke. "It would be a mockery to have a party without you in attendance. And besides, we know you never miss such affairs!"

She was right, of course, he thought to himself. There was a time when his afternoon and evenings, when not otherwise engaged, were spent entirely in female society. He wondered why he no longer possessed the inclination. A knock on the door and the entrance of Benton's aide temporarily halted the conversation.

"Sir, one of the pickets just rode in with a message."

"Is there trouble?" Benton strode toward the door, relieved at the interruption.

"No, sir. He said there's no trouble. Just needs to talk to you."

"You will have to excuse me, ladies." Benton pointed them toward the door as he motioned for the soldier to enter. A year ago, he would have enjoyed the bold ministrations of the mother and the endless chatter he would have endured for the next hour. Tonight, though, he wanted nothing more than to take advantage of this convenient interruption and free himself from this disagreeable duty. As soon as the mother and daughter had cleared the doorway, Benton pulled the soldier into the room. "What do you have, young man?"

"Sir, there's a boy here to see you. Said it's urgent."

Benton looked over the man's shoulder. "Where is he? Send him in."

"He's still down with the pickets, sir. Said he didn't wish to come any farther."

Something about the strangeness of the situation caused Benton to reject the thought of sending a subordinate to investigate the request. He motioned for his aide to get his horse and on impulse added another order. "Don't bother gathering the staff. I'm just riding down to the pickets."

The horse was presented in an instant, and after making his apologies again to the mother and daughter who had been waiting impatiently in the foyer for him to finish his business, Benton mounted and rode out into the night. Although guided only by starlight, he rode none too slowly, his horse seeming to sense his urgency. Even the withered leaves on the trees joined in, rustling noisily as if applauding his decision to leave the warm confines of his office.

Benton dismounted at the picket line and stood silently for a moment watching a figure walk a horse in the shadow of some trees about twenty yards away. Both horse and rider were so overheated that steam rose from them in the cool night air. Benton recognized the slim form at once but could not determine which he felt more strongly: anger at the risk she had taken by coming or the burning desire to talk to her again.

With a brief moment of wonder at the woman's inhuman composure, he returned the salute of the young soldier standing at the head of his horse and handed him his reins.

* * *

Sarah heard the hoofbeats of a horse galloping into the picket camp, but dared not look up. She knew the colonel would be upset at her coming, and she practically shook with anticipation when she heard spurred boots moving toward her with that long, not-to-be-imitated stride of his.

Taking a deep breath, she raised her gaze and watched spellbound as his commanding and formidable figure approached her. He stopped a few feet away; but even in the dim light and distance, his figure appeared imposing to her. She could practically feel his bold eyes upon her and could sense the immense strength that emanated from them.

"What is the news? I know you would not come if it were not urgent." He spoke in a lowered voice, even though it was apparent they were quite alone.

Sarah was so dumbfounded by his calm and gentle tone that she was, for a moment, speechless. While debating what to say and how to say it, she noticed the colonel's gaze had traveled to her still-steaming horse. She read the puzzled look on his brow and watched it change to recognition. The flea-bitten gray he had given her many months ago had transformed into a horse the color of dark polished steel. Ribs once prominent now bulged with muscle and flesh. Benton's eyes moved from one end of the horse to the other, apparently absorbing its powerful build and ability for speed.

Sarah ignored the scrutiny and turned to her saddle, carefully sliding a piece of paper from a slit beneath the seat. "They are preparing for a major move," she said as she handed him the document. She paused to watch his reaction as his eyes scanned the missive and thought how very desirable he looked. Standing half in moonlight and half in shadow, his large form appeared almost celestial in appearance.

"You're sure this is accurate? It's unusual for this time of year."

"Yes. I had the opportunity to overhear the writing of the dispatch and took it down word for word."

Sarah waited as he read again the information which included the object of an upcoming expedition, where it was going, by what route, and how many troops would be engaged. "I assumed you and General Lee would wish to know immediately," she added. "Considering you're in winter quarters."

Benton sighed deeply. "Yes. It is important he see this without delay. Excuse me a moment."

The colonel went back to the men standing by the fire and gave an order to one of them that sent him running for his horse. After a few more minutes of hushed conversation he strode back toward Sarah, his gallant, soldierly figure creating a giant shadow that marched along beside him. She watched him closely as he moved toward her, trying to appraise him as if seeing him for the first time. His features, highlighted by deep, dark eyes, were handsome enough, but there was also an air of power and authority about him that conveyed an attitude of fearlessness and audacity. It sent a slight chill down her spine, and made her glad she fought with him—not against him.

"How is Miss Lucy?" Benton threw his hand casually over her horse's neck now that business had been taken care of and talked as if conversing with an old friend. Sarah searched her memory for when they had moved from being strangers—and foes—to speaking on such equal terms.

"She's the mother of a son now. Jake Douglas Callahan." Sarah watched a smile twitch at the corner of Benton's mouth as he took in the news and the significance of the middle name. Then his smile faded as he seemed to reflect upon the loss of the brother, husband, and father. He alluded no further to the subject that Sarah suspected engaged his thoughts, as much as her own, on a daily basis.

"I would be glad to escort you back through the lines." When he took a step closer and gazed down at her, Sarah became magnetized. His eyes seemed to hold her in place with a strange power that left her breathless. Conscious of a sudden, strange attraction for him, she felt awkward and unsure of herself. She wished to flee—yet wanted nothing more than to stay.

"That will not be necessary." She turned to tighten her horse's girth in an effort to find something to do to keep her busy. Try as she might to dislike this man, she found that resisting him when they were standing

85

face-to-face, nearly impossible. "I know the way."

"By offering to escort you I was in no way insinuating you did not know the way." The colonel stood directly beside her now as she fumbled with the leather.

"I mean…it would not be safe," she mumbled.

"For you or for me?"

Sarah looked up into a pair of dark, penetrating eyes that seemed to be imploring her to yield. He stood there smiling in a careless manner, yet his tone had been laced with emotion. She was baffled by his demeanor, which suddenly reflected civilized warmth and affection.

"It's just that…that I see you have no staff to escort you." She looked back toward the pickets questioningly.

"Neither do you." His jaw was set square like a man who is accustomed to getting what he wants.

Her gaze jerked back to his. "But I—"

"Are you afraid to be alone with me, Lieutenant Duvall?" His eyes twinkled, but his face showed no sign of humor.

"Of course not." Sarah let the stirrup leather down with an unintended slap and then tried to display a calmness she did not feel. "You outrank me. You are at liberty to escort me if you wish." She mounted and watched him move with catlike grace back up to the pickets.

As her horse pawed the ground impatiently, Sarah observed Benton nodding casually in her direction a few times as he talked to his men. When one of his men brought him his horse, it became clear he had told them a story that would not pass muster in a Sunday school class. After a last salute, he mounted and trotted to where she waited.

"Your escort, madame." He smiled broadly as he bowed over his saddle, and Sarah thought he looked somewhat more like a schoolboy than a commanding officer. Yet the boyish grin did not hide the strength or potency of his features.

She turned her horse and spurred him forward and saw Benton do the same. After riding stirrup to stirrup at a trot for some miles, Sarah drew her horse down to a walk and Benton followed suit. When Sarah looked over at him, she noticed his eyes were upon her with a serious, yet questioning look. "Is something wrong?"

"No." He leaned down and adjusted one of his stirrups as if embarrassed he had been caught staring at her. "It's just that you are unusually quiet for a woman."

Sarah shrugged and looked at him in confusion. "But I have nothing important to say."

The colonel laughed at the comment as if that were an unusual—or at least atypical—reason for a woman not to talk. Normally, Sarah would have been irritated by his arrogance, but tonight she found the amicable man she rode beside charming and appealing. Friendly, considerate, and courteous, he also conveyed authority, power, and strength. It was not hard to understand why women congregated toward him and men idolized him. Sarah's hands trembled on the reins, and she had to look away. She fixed her gaze on the space between her horse's ears for some miles, until she felt his gloved hand upon her arm.

"Your pardon for interrupting your thoughts, but I hear water, and thought your horse could perhaps use a drink." He nodded toward the sound of a swift-flowing stream.

"Yes, let's stop a moment." Embarrassed that she had allowed her thoughts to drift, Sarah veered off the road into a small patch of forest toward the sound of the water. Dismounting, she allowed her horse to take a few sips before pulling him away. "Not too much," she scolded.

"You probably need a drink too," Benton said as he dismounted. "Here, I'll hold him."

"His name is Chance." Sarah handed over the reins, then knelt to splash water upon her face. Cupping her hands she took a long drink of the cold stream water.

"I wouldn't believe it if I didn't see it with my own eyes," she heard Benton say under his breath, as he ran his hand across the horse's powerful rump and down his sturdy leg.

Sarah sat back on her heels. "You doubted my choice of horses, Colonel?"

He paused and looked down at her. "Let's just say I had my reservations."

Sarah stood and wiped her wet hands on her pants. "He just needed a chance to prove himself."

When Benton's gaze went back to the horse, he shook his head as if he still did not believe the certainty of his own eyes. "He was scrawny and hot-tempered and possessed none of the traits I see in him now."

"Then perhaps you have learned something about making a judgment based on preconceived looks and ideas alone." Sarah climbed back up the bank and stood directly before him. The stern, arrogant lines of his face seemed to have softened, and she thought perhaps he was beginning to doubt his harsh judgment of her. "I recall that you didn't wish to take a chance on me either."

Benton remained silent for a moment, but then his entrancing gaze lowered to meet hers. "I didn't know I had one."

Sarah blinked as seconds ticked into eternity. His expression, his tone, his intensity did something to make her insides congeal as she tried to read the look in his penetrating eyes. "A chance is something that must be taken," she said softly. "It is not always granted or bestowed."

Benton stared at her without speaking, as if now he were trying to determine what exactly she meant by the statement—or perhaps he understood her meaning completely but did not know what to say.

Sarah took the opportunity to relieve him of the reins and swiftly mounted her horse. "It is only a little farther for me," she said, sticking her feet into the stirrups. "You'd better get back to your command."

When Benton just nodded, she leaned down until her head was even with his. "You know, Colonel Benton, sometimes you are unusually quiet for a man."

She saluted him, stuck spurs to her horse and galloped away.

Chapter 12

The best and most beautiful things in the world cannot be seen or even touched.
They must be felt with the heart.
—Helen Keller

March 1864

In the yard of Waverly, Colonel Benton sat on his horse, gazing at the beautiful picture it made. It was not yet spring, but the day was exceptionally warm, and already flowers of every hue were raising their bountiful blooms toward the sky. Birds sang joyfully from every limb of every tree as if they too were happy the gloomy days of winter were behind them. Shadows and sunlight mingled here and there on the lawn as the limbs of the oak in the front yard swayed provocatively in the breeze. The gently rustling branches seemed to add another element to the melodious sounds of nature.

Benton urged his horse forward, the soft earth covering the sound of his horse's approach. It was no surprise, therefore, that Lucy appeared shocked at his sudden appearance as she sat on a bench under the spreading oak near where her husband was buried.

"Colonel Benton!" She stood and strode eagerly toward him. "We were not expecting you!"

Dismounting from his large horse, Benton turned to face her. "Does that mean you're not happy to see me?"

Lucy stepped into his open arms, smiling broadly. "Of course not!" But then the smile faded. "Have you come to take me away from Waverly?" She looked straight up into his eyes with a face that revealed every mood and thought that flashed across it.

Benton held her at arm's length. "Yes. Tomorrow morning, Lucy. I'm on my way to headquarters now, and we'll be back through in the morning. Your family has received word of the little one and are anxious to meet him."

Lucy's eyes lit up, but then she bowed her head and stared at the ground. "I'm not sure whether to be terribly excited or horribly upset."

"You like it here then?"

"My, yes." Lucy's eyes were bright. "Miss Sarah has taken wonderful care of me and little Jake—oh, you must come in and see him!"

Benton held out his arm and she accepted it, talking excitedly as they walked toward the house. "Of course, it was difficult with Union soldiers stopping in here so much, but I found they are not so very unlike our own men." She stopped and gave him a puzzled look. "Though they never did get me to understand why they are fighting for such a bad cause."

"Nor have they properly explained it to me," Benton said as they reached the porch. "And where might Miss Sarah be?"

"Most likely in the parlor with little Jake. She spoils him terribly!" Lucy put both hands to her cheeks as if just realizing she would be departing in the morning. "Excuse me, Colonel Benton. I have to pack!" She stepped through the door and started up the stairs, talking over her shoulder as if she had no time to spare. "If she's not in the parlor, then check the back porch! It's such a nice day. She may be sitting in the sunshine."

Colonel Benton removed his hat and stepped into the parlor. Finding it empty, he continued through the house, pausing when he saw Sarah's figure through the open door. She sat in a chair drenched in sun, rocking the child in her arms. The look on her face displayed pure devotion as she whispered words that only the baby could hear.

For a moment, Benton just stood and stared, contemplating the concerned, caring face bent over the child. Never had he seen a stronger picture of love and compassion, and it made his heart pang at the thought of the torment and isolation she endured. He knew of few people strong enough to bear their troubles in silence, and fewer still so virtuous as not to speak a word of blame toward those who did them injury. She was strength clothed in beauty, with the poise and grace of a queen. Afraid he would be discovered, Benton cleared his throat and walked onto the porch. It did his soul good to see her eyes light up at his appearance.

"Colonel Benton. Come in!" Moving the child to her shoulder, she came forward with an eagerly extended hand and a brilliant smile that lighted her usually solemn face. The look revealed a hidden beauty of sweetness and gentleness all the more winning because so rare. "What a surprise!"

"A pleasant one, I hope." Although it was apparent she was alone, through habit or excessive caution, Benton lowered his voice when he spoke to her.

"Of course," she answered. But then, like Lucy, the realization of his duty seemed to hit her and the gleam faded from her countenance. "I suppose you've come to take them away from me."

"I've received word from Lucy's family." He took a seat in the settee next to her and leaned forward. "They have heard about the child and are anxious for her to come home."

Sarah closed her eyes a moment. "That must make Lucy very happy. Have you told her?"

"Yes. I just saw her outside. I'm on my way to headquarters now."

Sarah rocked the baby a few more times before laying him down in a small cradle. "He is such a good boy." Even though she was looking down, Benton could tell her eyes were misty.

"He's lucky to have such an aunt."

Sarah looked up and smiled. "And I was lucky to have had them both with me as long as I did. Thank you." She walked out of the room for a moment into the hallway, talking as she walked. "You are expecting heavy enemy forces in the region then, Colonel?"

"Shortly. We're seeing some movement now that the weather has warmed. I thought it best to relocate Lucy while it is safe."

Sarah reappeared wearing a shawl over her shoulders. She bent down over the child a moment, pulled a blanket over him, and then turned to Benton. "Colonel, I have something of yours that I need to return. Do you have a few minutes to accompany me?"

"Something of mine?" Benton stared at her, thinking she must be mistaken.

Sarah smiled as she saw his confused countenance. "Yes, I'm afraid it was left without your knowledge."

She walked out the door, apparently assuming Benton would follow her. "It's just a short walk," she said, moving so quickly that he had to lengthen his stride to keep up. "I've had to hide it away from the house. Its value to the Yankees was too great to keep here."

They had not traveled far through a barely recognizable path in the woods when Benton heard a horse whinny. He stopped a moment to listen.

"It's not much farther," Sarah said. "I keep Chance back here. He is worth too much in his current condition to keep in the barn."

Benton took a deep breath. "Oh, I see. It's just that the whinny I heard sounded a lot like—"

At that moment, they broke into a small clearing where his horse Vince stood leaning heavily on a haphazard looking fence, raising his head up and down in greeting.

"You'd better go talk to him before he breaks down the fence," Sarah said.

Benton stood rooted in his tracks, not believing his own eyes. "I thought...I mean, he was supposed to be—"

The horse continued nickering and pawing the ground impatiently as if having a one-sided conversation with his owner. Benton finally walked up to him and patted him tentatively on the head, still not believing his own eyes.

"His injuries were very serious, but as you can see he's improving," Sarah said.

Benton looked at the wound, which was still ragged and raw, but appeared to be healing properly. The bullet had torn away a large portion of muscle and tissue, leaving a definite indentation in the flesh of his neck. "How did you..."

"Why must you ask so many questions?" Sarah attached a lead rope to the horse's halter and handed it over to Benton. "He's not ready for a battle, but I think he can be ridden lightly."

Benton ran his hand over the animal in an effort to convince himself he was real, and then turned to follow Sarah back to the house. The two walked in silence for some minutes as Benton attempted to sort out what had occurred. "You know this cannot go unchallenged," he finally said in a grave voice. "I gave a direct order and it was apparently discarded."

Sarah put her hand on Benton's arm and stopped him for a moment. "Yes, you gave a direct order. Do you remember what it was?"

"Of course, I do! I told Private Matson to...to..."

"If I'm not mistaken, your order was to 'take care of him.'" She nodded toward Vince. "And as you can see, the order was followed implicitly."

A slow smile began to spread across Benton's face, and then he laughed out loud. "I suppose Private Matson is waiting for a promotion for this." As they passed by a wild azalea, Benton snapped off a piece of the fragrant blossom and handed it to Sarah. "For the part you played in this," he said, bowing. "My gratitude."

Sarah blushed, and her mouth lifted to a smile again, giving Benton a sign that the woman inside was not entirely immune to the charms of a man. Putting the flower to her nose, she inhaled its perfume before grabbing Benton's arm to steady herself as she walked down the broken path. When she began to laugh softly, Benton marveled at the sound of her mirth finally being let loose from a place where it had been long suppressed. "It's beautiful, Colonel, and all the more cherished because of the sentiment shared." She giggled again like a schoolgirl at the secret she had concealed, all the while keeping her eyes on the rocky, uneven path.

Colonel Benton also kept his eyes on the uneven terrain, a recent rain having washed out deep rivets on the barely marked trail. When he felt Sarah suddenly squeeze his arm and stop, he came to an abrupt halt as well, causing Vince to nearly step on him from behind. Lifting his gaze, he saw Lucy standing a few feet away in the middle of the path, her hands on her hips, a confused look upon her face as she stared at them.

"I-I didn't know where you went." Lucy pointed nervously back toward the house as if to explain. "I heard voices, and I…"

Utter silence reigned for a few long seconds that felt like a week. Sarah slowly removed her hand from Benton's arm as if Lucy would not notice it had been there, and moved the flower to behind her back, letting it drop as if the girl standing right in front of them hadn't already seen it. She swallowed hard. "Colonel Benton is just collecting his horse."

Lucy's gaze shifted to the horse, then to Colonel Benton, and then came to rest back on Sarah. "I don't understand."

"Vince was seriously injured in an engagement," Colonel Benton said casually, starting to walk again as if nothing was out of the ordinary. "Mrs. Duvall has a way with horses and was able to restore him to health."

Lucy continued to look confused, as if the words perhaps made sense but did not match the camaraderie she had just witnessed. She could not have helped hearing Sarah's laughter—something obviously quite rare. It was apparently not adding up that the two of them were not only amicable, but also sociable. Sworn enemies whose attraction to one another was as impractical as it was evident and undeniable.

"I-I didn't realize you two were so well acquainted," Lucy finally said.

Again, silence reigned until at last Benton cleared his throat. "It should not come as a surprise that I've gotten to know the sister of one of my best officers." He looked at Lucy and winked. "Who knows? Perhaps with a little charm I can prevail in getting her to see things our way."

Lucy turned and started walking back toward the house, talking over her shoulder. "Well, if anyone can do it, you can, Colonel Benton."

Sarah walked up and looped her arm around Lucy's. "I wasn't expecting you two to gang up on me. Is that any way to treat your sister-in-law?"

Lucy giggled and put her arm around Sarah's waist. "No, I suppose it's not. You've been wonderful to me and Jake. I can't thank you enough."

"You can thank me by bringing that son of yours back for visits." She looked around at Colonel Benton who was staring at the two of them with a relieved smile on his face. "You will transport her back through the lines if you must, won't you?"

"I will be honored to escort Miss Lucy here for visits—so long as your friends in blue cooperate."

Sarah frowned and then turned back to Lucy. "You see, the colonel and I have agreed to disagree. I suppose that is the best we can do."

Lucy turned around and looked at Benton curiously as if she still questioned what she had just witnessed. "Yes, if you say so. I suppose that is the best you can do."

Chapter 13

*Does He not see every throe of anguish, hear every sigh, count every groan
and know every pain? And yet He permits them all, giving a loose rein to
His creatures, that they may in their madness destroy themselves.*
—*Ellen Harris, 1863*

October 1864

Sarah froze for a moment with her hands in a bucketful of suds, listening. There it was again, louder now and not so very distant. Giving her hands a quick wipe on her apron, she ran to the door, flung it open, and stepped out onto the porch in a single move. The sound of battle, probably on the outskirts of Taylorsville, reached her ears yet again as she leaned over the banister, her ear cocked to the south. This time, the spattering of gunfire sounded more serious and ominous. When the low, violent throb of cannon fire reached her, she began to make preparations for what was to come.

"There will be wounded coming," she muttered to herself as if there was anyone to help or even to hear. The fleeting image of Colonel Benton crossed her mind, but she pushed it away. Although she had no real intelligence to confirm the theory, she instinctively knew he was engaged. Having destroyed a good portion of a wagon train in Midway earlier in the week, she knew the Yankees were intent on retaliation.

After loading her arms with wood, she built a fire in the summer kitchen, all the while listening to the sound of the contest move away and then become extremely loud and fearfully close. After a few hours, the gunfire abated somewhat, although it did not entirely cease. Late in the afternoon, she heard a noise on the porch and rose to investigate.

"Are you alone?" Colonel Benton leaned against the doorframe in a negligent manner despite his face and uniform being begrimed with gunpowder and sweat.

"Yes. For now. But I expect wounded at any moment." Sarah swept her gaze both directions of the house and then reached out for his hand. "It must be important or you would not have come. Step in where it's safer."

Once inside, she continued talking as she made her way up the stairs.

"We'd better talk up here. If we're surprised by visitors, you can get out through the back staircase. Really, I don't know why you would come, Colonel Benton, with the enemy so close." She turned only once, and then just for a moment. "It sounded like quite a large battle. I suppose you were in it?"

"Yes." The single word sounded strained behind her. Other than that, he did not speak, as if in the many weeks since they had last seen one another, he had been on a prolonged furlough.

"I probably shouldn't...have come," he finally whispered, as if not wanting anyone else to hear.

'You're probably right," Sarah replied matter-of-factly. "I've no doubt they will be here soon with their wounded." When Benton did not answer, Sarah turned to him as she entered her bedchamber. For the first time, she noticed how pale he was and how he labored for air. Bathed in sweat, he was panting much harder than the exertion from the stairs warranted.

"Colonel, are you hurt?"

Benton nodded slightly and leaned against the wall behind him as if to catch his breath from the climb. "Yes. I believe so." He didn't say anything else, but the expression on his face made it look like he wanted to as he began sliding down the wall toward the floor, leaving a trail of blood smeared on the wall behind him.

"Colonel!"

Whatever it was he said in return, Sarah could not understand. She knelt beside him, putting his face in her hands, and waited for him to speak. "Colonel, can you hear me?"

He opened his eyes for a moment. "Sarah...forgive me...the trouble," he whispered.

"But you can't do this!" she cried. "They will be here any moment!"

She stared at the unmoving man helplessly, a feeling of complete frantic terror wrenching her to the point of nausea. Her mind raced wildly, but after a few moments of agonized despair, she forced herself to take command and assume control of the situation. Removing his boots, she shoved them under her bed, out of sight. Doing the same with his coat, she gasped at the amount of blood that had soaked into the shirt beneath. Although the distance was but three feet, it took a good bit of

Sarah's strength and ingenuity to get the barely conscious man onto the bed. He revived somewhat during the ordeal, but did not seem conscious of what was passing around him

Once he was safely on her bed, Sarah ran to the window, and scanned the road in both directions before returning to his side. He was still breathing, which gave her little comfort because it was labored and heavy. She knew she had to stop the flow of blood that continued to ooze from a wound just beneath his ribcage. Usually calm in the face of all danger, Sarah struggled to stay composed in this desperate situation. Knowing that Yankee wounded would likely be arriving, she had to work fast. Running down the stairs, she grabbed what supplies she could and a large bucket of water she had sitting over the fire. Back in her bedchamber, she hurriedly washed the wound, packed it with clean strips of cloth, and wrapped it tightly.

Upon hearing the sound of approaching wagons, she took one of the bloodstained dressings she had used to clean up the blood and wrapped Benton's head so he would not be recognizable. While she wiped the blood from the wall and the floor, the rattle of wagons and the shouts of command fell upon her ears. She ran to the window, and suddenly they were everywhere—men and horses—enveloping her home like the impending darkness itself.

* * *

"I'm afraid we've got some injured men here, Mrs. Duvall."

Sarah stood in the doorway trying to appear calm as the Union officer began directing the removal of the wounded from the wagons into her house.

"I hope not too many." Sarah tried to keep her voice from shaking. She was always permitted the sanctity of her bedchamber when Union troops overtook her home, but she hoped to keep the entire second floor from becoming overrun with Yankee soldiers.

"No not too many," the officer said, looking over his shoulder at her curiously. "The worst of them were taken up to Wilson."

"Very well." Sarah turned back to the house. "I'll help however I can."

The next few hours were the most agonizing ones Sarah had ever endured. Although the men being unloaded were not the most seriously injured, they still needed wounds dressed and a place to rest comfortably. Sarah worked instinctively, her thoughts not on her task, but rather what she would find in her bedchamber when she could at last retire. She knew in her soul it would not be a corpse. Strong as Benton was, it would take an eternity to kill him.

After hours of agonizing work, Sarah was finally able to creep up the back staircase with another bucket of water and some fresh linens. Opening the door quietly, she stood motionless waiting to hear the sound of his breathing. It came to her soft and irregular, along with low murmurings as he talked in his sleep.

Lighting a lamp, she stood over the bed and watched his chest slowly rise and fall. With shaking fingers, she unwrapped the bandage around his head and put her hand on his brow. It felt warmer than she'd hoped, though was not hot with signs of fever. Dipping a cloth into the cool water, she wiped his forehead and then proceeded to take a closer look at his wound. As she had suspected earlier, it appeared the bullet had entered the flesh beneath his ribcage and exited from his back. She was relieved there was nothing to attempt to remove, but only time would tell what damage had been done. As she began to rewrap the wound, Benton tossed his head and groaned. Sarah tried to quiet him, bending over him with the wet cloth to cool his fevered brow.

At last, around midnight, Sarah lay down on a pallet beside her bed and tried to get some sleep. Her usually peaceful surroundings were broken by Benton's occasional murmurings, which sent her sitting upright, her heart pounding with fear that someone would hear. Taking deep breaths, she tried to relax again, concentrating on the sound of the sentinels and the muted voices from below. Just when she thought she might be exhausted enough to sleep, the sun began pushing its soft light through the curtain. Re-dressing Benton's wound before she went downstairs, Sarah stared at the pale countenance that she feared now battled an insidious enemy from within. The bleeding had stopped, but that did not lessen her concern that he was in danger. She considered it a miracle that he had survived the night.

When Sarah had a moment to check on Benton in the afternoon, he spoke to her, but his words were not coherent and his eyes were not open. When she asked him a question, he gave her a rambling, nonsensical answer that made her heart double its pace. The situation could not be more precarious. One of the South's most notorious Confederate officers was confined to her bedchamber—within mere feet of the enemy—and he did not know where he was or realize how dire the circumstances.

Whenever it was possible for her to get away, Sarah stole up the back staircase to her room, sometimes long enough to get a few spoonfuls of soup into his mouth and sometimes a few sips of water. By the second evening, his eyes opened when she removed the bandages, but they were glazed and staring, which frightened her more than when they had been closed.

Exhausted from anxiety and mind-numbing work, Sarah stared out the window at the lowering sun and wondered if Benton's men knew he was at Waverly. Under constant scrutiny from the Union officer in charge, she was afraid to attempt to make contact, fearing she would put the colonel's life in more danger than it already was.

Although her nerves were strung almost to the breaking point, Sarah continued her routine, all the while not knowing how long she could keep Benton's presence a secret. On the morning of the fifth day, she found out. She had just finished re-dressing his wound and wrapping his head in a bandage to conceal his face when she heard a knock on the door.

"Yes?" She opened the door but a crack.

"I'm sorry to bother you, Mrs. Duvall." The officer in charge stared at her through the slight opening with an inquisitive eye.

"What may I do for—" From behind her, Sarah heard a deep cough, like someone trying to rid their chest of smoke that was not there.

The officer pushed his way into the room and gazed from Sarah to the man on the bed. "Who is this?" he roared.

Sarah ran to Benton, tears falling unhesitatingly down her cheeks. "I don't know, Colonel. A Confederate surgeon dropped him here before you arrived. He said his wound was mortal. I was only trying to let him die peacefully." Sarah said the words clearly enough, but in her mind, she was thinking that Benton did not appear as mortal at all. Rather, he suggested the vitality of one with strength enough to sustain a thousand bullets.

"So he is a Rebel? You are aiding the enemy?"

"Oh, Colonel, pray have mercy! I am childless, but I have a mother's heart. You cannot send a dying man to prison! The surgeon gave him no hope."

The officer looked at the bloodied rag that surrounded the soldier's head and seemed to concur. "Very well. I'll leave him in your care." He started toward the door, but paused. "For now, Mrs. Duvall. But I came to tell you that we are beginning the process of moving men out. If your patient does not succumb before we have fully vacated, I will be forced to take him along."

When the door slammed shut behind him, Sarah sank to her knees by the bed and wept. Exhausted from her day and night vigil, debilitated from little sleep, she could no longer hold back tears of frustration and despair. She had suffered as he had suffered—perhaps more so—and now she feared her worst nightmare would come true. They would take him to a prison and learn his true identity—or he would die en route. The combination of fear, weariness and utter exhaustion reduced her to a state in which she could no longer think. She curled into a ball on the floor and prayed for strength as she cried tears of utter anguish and despair.

* * *

True to the officer's word, many of the Union soldiers were loaded into wagons the next day, though the army seemed in no hurry to move them all at once. As days continued to pass, Sarah began to breathe a sigh of relief. Perhaps the man had taken pity on her and would allow her to continue with her patient's private care. But her hopes were dashed when he approached her that evening on the porch.

"I am sorry to inform you, Mrs. Duvall, that it's time your patient is moved."

Sarah grabbed the front post for support. "Moved?"

"He'll be treated kindly as a prisoner of war, but we cannot leave him here. I'm sure you understand."

Sarah swallowed hard, her mind racing with frantic fear. She knew it was useless to argue or plea. "When?"

The officer looked around the camp and seemed to be doing figures in his head. "The last of our men should be leaving within two days. I'll leave a few orderlies for his removal."

"I only hope he receives the care he needs," Sarah murmured.

"He will not be mistreated," the officer said somewhat coldly. "I believe I have shown you great courtesy in allowing him to stay this long."

Sarah lowered her head. "Yes, of course, you have. I'll see that he's ready to move."

When the officer began talking to one of his subordinates, Sarah turned and walked mechanically up the stairs. Barely having the energy to close the door, she put her back to the wall, slumping to the floor as Colonel Benton had done, her face in her hands as she sobbed. She had raised her hopes, but it was all for naught. All she had done, all she had endured, the sleepless nights, the pounding heart, the fear of his being discovered—and now he was going to die in the depths of a Yankee prison. Oh, it was not fair!

"Don't ...cry."

Sarah pushed her fallen hair away from her face and looked toward the bed. What she saw made her stop and blink, afraid she was dreaming. His hand was reaching toward her with the bandage in it—and his eyes were open. She looked at him and stared as if to clear her vision.

"Don't...cry," he said again.

Sarah did not speak. She stumbled to her feet and knelt by the bed, putting his face in her hands and staring into his eyes to see if they were clear or burning with fever. When she saw her answer, she laid her head on his chest and sobbed even louder.

Tentatively he put his hand on her head to console her. "You...never did listen...to me," he said weakly.

Sarah's head jerked back up as she stared at him incredulously. "Are you really awake?" She stared down at him with imploring eyes, lines of fatigue marking her face.

He closed his eyes and licked his lips as if to see if they were working properly. "I'm not sure."

"But you are a prisoner! They are moving you in two day's time! Can you ride?"

Sarah did not wait for him to answer. Despite her weariness and exhaustion, she stood and began pacing, trying to formulate a plan. She could not rest now even though she had little reason to hope for a happy outcome. If there was the slightest chance to help him escape, she knew she had to take it. One thing was clear. There were only a handful of men remaining now, and within a day, even fewer would remain to oversee the withdrawal of the remaining patients.

"Where are…my men?"

Sarah stopped pacing and knelt by the bed. "I don't know, Colonel. I've had no contact. No word."

"Can try to make it to Hampstead." He coughed and winched. "Connelly may be there."

"There should be few patrols." Sarah stood again. "I will try to find out, but surely the way is clear to Hampstead."

* * *

Sarah's hand trembled as she reached for the bottle of brandy that had long been hidden in a small compartment in her closet for a special occasion. Knowing she could not overpower the remaining soldiers, she had to use diplomacy and deception as her weapons of choice. The alcohol would help cover Benton's escape while keeping her free from any liability. Wearing a fresh gown and a warm smile, she descended the stairs and saw the three Union soldiers tasked with removing the remaining wounded, playing a game of cards on the front porch.

"Good evening Mrs. Duvall." The men stood courteously as she opened the door.

"Good evening, gentlemen." She put the bottle down on the table. "I understand you'll be leaving in the morning and thought you might enjoy a parting gift."

The men did not attempt to hide their joy or appreciation. They hooted at the sight and patted each other on the back. "Yes, ma'am. That's very kind of you!"

"Enjoy." Sarah turned to go back into the house when one of the man grabbed her by the arm. "Aren't you going to stay and have a drink?"

Sarah's heart beat wildly in her ears. "I have some chores to do right now, but thank you for the invitation."

The men seemed to accept that—or were so eager to have a drink that they didn't care. It wasn't long before Sarah heard tin cups clashing together as the soldiers' voices grew louder and their conversation more boisterous. Deciding it was time to act, Sarah saddled Chance and left him in the shadows of the tree line. She had done everything she could do to prepare. Now it was up to Benton.

A cold north wind was beginning to pick up as Sarah reentered the house, but the men seemed not to notice. They were singing now, and one of them had produced a fiddle. The clapping and stomping emanating from the front porch would surely cover any sounds from inside the house. Trying to appear calm and composed as she went through the house lighting lamps in her usual routine, Sarah then retreated quickly up the back staircase. When she opened the door, her heart plummeted. Benton was sitting up, but his hand was on his wound as if it caused him great pain and his head leaned against the headboard as if that was as much as he could do. She ran to him and took his hand.

"It is time, Colonel. We must move quickly." She threw his arm over her shoulder and struggled to stand under his weight.

"I'm not sure—"

"You can and you will!" Sarah stopped him in mid-sentence. "Come. This is your only chance."

Benton wobbled weakly against her, but she was able to guide him to the staircase, which he descended by leaning on the bannister. Once outside, she leaned him against the outside wall and slipped into the darkness to get Chance. The singers on the front porch had not let up, and she began to breathe a little bit more easily. Perhaps she *could* get him away!

"Mrs. Duvall, what you doing out here?"

Sarah stopped in her tracks, and saw one of the soldiers coming out of some bushes, apparently having just relieved himself. She glanced back toward the house but saw that Benton was invisible in the shadows.

"Just out getting some fresh air," she answered.

"Well, we'd pleased if you'd come join us."

"Yes, of course. I'm planning on it." Sarah watched the man sway as she talked and hoped he wouldn't remember their conversation for long. "I'll be along in a minute."

When the soldier continued toward the house whistling out of tune, Sarah sprinted toward the trees. Already dressed in breeches and boots, she discarded her dress and led Chance toward the back of the house where Benton was waiting. From the front of the house, she heard the songs continue with tireless and terrible improvisations.

It was no easy thing to get Benton into the saddle, but once there, she mounted behind him and spurred Chance into the darkness. At first Benton was able to hold onto the saddle with legs and hands, but as the miles wore on, Sarah felt him getting heavier and heavier against her arms as he leaned lower and lower over the saddle. Closing her eyes against the tremendous weight, she concentrated on her horse's hoof beats. "It's only five miles," she said to herself. "Only three now...Only two now..."

Benton had given her some direction about where Connelly might be found at first, but for the last mile he had been silent. To add to her desperation, a storm had hit with ferocity, soaking her and making the night even darker. She could feel, more so than see the tortured trees being bent this way and that, waving their limbs as if in agony. When she drew rein to get her bearings, she heard the simultaneous click of a few dozen revolvers.

"That's far enough!"

The voice came from in front of her horse's head, and she felt the reins being grabbed from her hands.

"Good Heavens! It's Colonel Benton! Hurry up boys! Bring up Doc!"

"He's been wounded." Sarah tried to be helpful, but rough hands dragged her off her horse and twisted her arm behind her back. Someone shoved a lantern into her face, and she heard a gasp of surprise.

"Well I'll be, look at them eyes," one of the men said. "If it ain't the Yankee widow! I told you when we found Vince so close that she was in on it!"

She heard Benton groaning as if he wanted to speak but was too exhausted to do so. "He was wounded in the engagement at—" Sarah's voice trembled as she caught sight of the angry faces surrounding her, and realized she was at their mercy with no one to vouch her. "I have to get back to Waverly before they suspect anything."

She turned to get her horse, but felt the barrel of a gun sink into her back.

"Sorry, but you ain't going nowhere."

"But you don't understand!" Sarah tried to keep the panic from her voice. "I must get back to Waverly!"

While they had been talking a wagon had been brought up and Benton was already loaded. Sarah saw Major Connelly leaning over the side with a relieved look on his face, his hand on Benton's shoulder. When the major lifted his gaze and made brief eye contact with Sarah, she saw an expression that made her immensely uncomfortable. Here, she could tell, was someone who would not be trifled with…a man who thought deeply and reacted strongly. One who perhaps said little, but missed nothing—an officer who obviously took his position seriously.

Nevertheless, relieved to see a familiar face, Sarah tried to walk toward him—but rough hands stopped her again. As Connelly straightened back up and began to stride toward her, it was clear from his expression that military responsibilities were going to be placed above any former acquaintance or display of compassion.

"You have put me in an awkward position, Mrs. Duvall."

"Colonel Benton will explain everything. You must understand how urgent it is that I return to Waverly…so they do not find out who I am." Sarah talked fast, but not fast enough to keep her teeth from chattering. She knew she must look a mess having barely slept for more than a week, and her hair knotted and stringy from the rain.

"Who is *they*?" Connelly looked at her in such a way as to make it clear he thought she was delirious.

"The Yankees!" The mixture of curiosity and disbelief on his face frightened her. "They cannot discover who I am!"

"And just who are you?" Connelly crossed his arms and gazed at her suspiciously.

"Oh, please, Major Connelly, you must believe me! Colonel Benton will explain everything, but right now I need to get back to Waverly!"

Connelly shook his head apologetically but remained steadfast nonetheless. "In good time perhaps—after I speak to the Colonel." He turned and started to motion for one of the men. "Dressed as you are…" He paused and his eyes swept over her. "And considering the circumstances under which you were found, I cannot allow it tonight."

"No!" Sarah ran toward him. "You don't understand. I *must* get back before they suspect me. Already time is against me!"

"I'm sorry, Mrs. Duvall." He nodded toward two soldiers who grabbed her arms and led her toward a house she had not even seen, hidden as it was behind a stand of trees. Despite kicking, screaming, and fighting with all her might, Sarah found herself being forced up a flight of stairs and into a bedroom. She heard the door close behind her and the sound of a key being turned.

"You don't understand," she sobbed, pounding on the door. "I am under Colonel Benton's sole direction!"

She fell to her knees and continued to pound on the door and the floor. Her courage had been subjected to every kind of test that the mortal soul could be tried. And now, through all the tragedy and trials of war, she could not believe she was meant to falter and fail now.

When no one responded to her, Sarah finally pulled herself into a chair where she remained all night, staring blindly into the darkness. When morning light had just begun to stream through the window, she at last heard a key in the door. Major Connelly and an aide entered, but Sarah did not bother to stand or even look up.

"My sincere apologies for the delay, Mrs. Duvall." She heard him shifting his weight nervously. "Colonel Benton sends his regards and has asked me to escort you to Waverly."

Sarah swallowed hard, but did not lift her gaze. "He is conscious then?"

"Yes. Conscious and anxious to return to the field, I'm afraid. He wished to escort you himself, but the surgeon, fortunately, intervened." Connelly paused a moment and took a deep breath. "He is on the mend, but as you know, is very weak."

"They will suspect me now." Sarah spoke while continuing to gaze straight ahead.

"The colonel is quite insistent that you return to remove personal items and find quarters elsewhere. He agrees it is too dangerous now."

"Elsewhere?" Sarah gazed up at him for the first time. "That is impossible. Waverly is my home."

"Nevertheless, it is not safe. I have been given quite a large detachment as an escort in case there is trouble."

Sarah stood and smoothed her wrinkled clothes. "I will accept the escort, but as for leaving Waverly, I will not go."

The major sighed heavily. "Colonel Benton suspected as much. He has given me the authority to post a guard if I deem it safe and reasonable."

When Sarah bristled again, Connelly put his hand on her arm. "You are tired, Mrs. Duvall, as well you should be. Let's go to Waverly. We can discuss the details later."

Chapter 14

*The consciousness of having discharged that duty which we owe
to our country is superior to all other considerations.*
—George Washington

Major Connelly glanced over at Sarah as they rode side by side, but she remained stone-faced and silent, staring straight ahead. He wondered if her quietness was a result of anger at him for the delay in getting her home, or pure exhaustion from so many long nights without sleep. Although her back was straight and her shoulders did not droop, he could see the weariness in her eyes and the strain in the lines on her face. It was obvious she had suffered a great deal as a result of her devotion to Colonel Benton.

Connelly could only marvel at how one so young and so pure could have taken command of the circumstances thrust upon her, and have so effectively play her part. Although he knew of no other woman that had not succumbed to the charms of Colonel Benton, it appeared their relationship had remained purely businesslike over the months. Somehow Mrs. Sarah Duvall had resisted the magnetism that others could not.

After moving at a trot for some miles, Sarah suddenly urged her horse into a canter when they were about a mile away from Waverly. Connelly nudged his horse forward too with a slight smile on his face. He remembered what it was like to finally be home, and knew well the impatience that drove her. When he broke free from the woods and possessed a clear view of the home, Connelly gasped and drew his horse to a sliding halt beside Sarah, who had sucked in an audible breath that sounded like her last on earth.

The house, which had stood as a family home for more than a century, was gone. Fire still crackled along the blackened wood, and a part of the roof tumbled in as they watched its fiery tongue continue to dissolve the last of the home and all its memories. The destruction was immense—the loss to the one who gazed silently upon it, immeasurable.

As Connelly stared at the ruins, Sarah rode slowly forward and then dismounted, gazing at the rubble with a calmness that seemed unnatural.

When she looked back at him though, Connelly felt his heart twist in its cage. Nothing could lessen the heartbreak of seeing the dancing flames reflected in her clear, blue eyes.

As the rest of the escort rode up, they gathered around the pile of debris and stared angrily at the devastation. Connelly heard their uttering low sounds of shock and fury as their focus was led inevitably to the place where the pillared house had once sat so regally beneath the spreading boughs of the oak. The men sat in rigid but dismayed discipline as they stared at the smoking remains and waited for orders.

Connelly too sat in controlled silence as he watched Sarah take a few steps toward the smoking debris and drop to her knees. With her cheek on the ground and her eyes tightly closed, she clutched blades of grass, her lips moving silently as if saying good-bye to the land of her birth. She rose then and turned back toward the men.

"We'd better go." Her gaze lifted to meet Connelly's, and he saw it was stamped with firm resolve. "They're probably watching."

As if on cue, the thundering of hoofbeats could be heard rushing toward them from the edge of the tree line. Connelly ushered his men toward a path pointed out by Sarah, and watched her mount her already-moving horse.

Hearing a tremendous *bang* a short time later, he turned his head, long enough to see two Federal soldiers fall from their mounts as if smote by thunderbolts. Following the gazes of the remaining Union soldiers, he saw Sarah sitting on her horse on an embankment that ran parallel to the road. She must have split off from the group as soon as she had shown Connelly the way, and was now taking potshots from a higher location that gave her an advantage.

Although she was shooting from such a distance that her buckshot was probably not lethal, the gun and its effect nonetheless made an impression. The Federals were obviously not sure how many soldiers were up on the ridge because they began slowing down and looking for cover. When Connelly heard the second *bang* and saw another saddle empty, he ordered his men to turn, and they soon routed the pursuing troopers with uncontrolled vigor.

Sarah rejoined the group a short time later with the same solemn silence she had left it, staring straight ahead with the empty shotgun resting negligently on her thigh. Connelly could not help but notice her pale cheek and weary countenance, but there was no sign of tears.

"We'll take you back to headquarters." Connelly reached out and put his hand on her arm as he gazed at her stony countenance. "Do not despair."

"No, I will not despair," she said quietly after a long silence, looking mournfully toward heaven.

Connelly kept a close eye on Sarah once they arrived, and thought she appeared disoriented and unsure of herself. He dismounted and helped her do the same. "Private Jenkins will take care of your horse."

Sarah said nothing, but handed over the reins, her eyes as blank and unblinking as the dead.

"I can have someone take care of this for you." Connelly reached for her gun.

Sarah stared at it a moment and then brought it close to her body. "I'd like to keep it if you don't mind," she said quietly. "It's all I have."

Connelly swallowed hard and nodded. "I'll show you to your quarters. You'd better get some rest."

* * *

Exhausted as she was, Sarah slept only fitfully. Tired of tossing and turning, she wandered restlessly to the window to gaze out at her surroundings and guess the time. A strip of pink clouds lay like a ribbon on the hills of the horizon, showing her that dawn was well on the way.

Sitting perfectly still and contemplating the widening swath of pink as it flamed to a deeper hue, she thought about all that had transpired in the last twenty-four hours. Her musings were interrupted by a hurried knock at the door, followed by a soldier stepping inside before she could even answer. "The colonel requests to see you ma'am."

Sarah twisted around from the window. "The colonel?"

"Yes, ma'am. Right away."

The soldier apparently meant business because he grabbed Sarah by the arm and led her gently, but insistently out the door. It wasn't until Sarah stepped into the hall that she realized what a hub of activity the headquarters had become. There was the shouting of orders, the tramping of feet, orderlies passing on the stairs, and much running to and fro. After taking just a few steps, she heard the unmistakable bark of a cannon. Surprised, she turned to the soldier beside her. "Did you hear that? Do you know what it means?"

The pressure on her arm increased as he led her even more swiftly down the stairs. "Yes ma'am," he said. "There's folks shooting at us."

Before she could rephrase the question for more details, she heard the baritone voice of Colonel Benton giving orders from behind a closed door. In another moment, the door opened and she was shown inside. As if from an unheard order, the men in the room disappeared tactfully out the door. Sarah walked toward the desk where the colonel remained bent over a missive, her heart picking up its pace as she thought how close he had come to perishing. Yet there he sat, wearing the authority of his position with the controlled deadliness of a soldier. She did not think there was a man living who could equal him in stature, character, or courage. He was Zeus, Mars, and Apollo all rolled into one.

Sarah listened to the crackle of the fire to her left and the sound of Benton's pencil scratching across a piece of paper for a few long moments before he seemed to realize there was anyone else in the room. Then he slowly lifted his gaze and carefully rose to his feet—almost in one movement—though the action was done stiffly and with obvious pain. For another moment he did not speak, but there was a gleam of gladness and welcome in the velvety softness of his dark eyes that did not match the businesslike manner of his demeanor.

"Lieutenant, words cannot describe how terribly sorry I am about the loss of Waverly." His voice sounded scratchy, as if talking in such a low tone was hard for him. Yet his eyes were calm, and even detached now, as if trying overly hard not to show any emotion or anything verging toward sentiment. "I hope I can show gratitude for your sacrifice by proving to you I am not unworthy of it."

The crack in his voice was the only indication of emotions repressed, of devotion subdued in respectful obedience to the very letter of command. Sarah felt her cheeks grow warm and lowered her head. "I am not the first to suffer such a loss at the hands of the enemy." When Sarah lifted her eyes again and saw how pale and weary his countenance appeared, she tried to change the subject. "Please sit down, Colonel. You need to rest."

"I am aware of the need," he said grimly, "but it cannot be helped."

He sat back down and began writing briskly again, calling loudly for an orderly as he did so. "It appears Colonel Lawson is finally emboldened to show us more than his back."

"Colonel Lawson? An attack on you?" Sarah's voice betrayed her surprise. The officer was well known to her, and though full of verbal bravado, he was not one to take a fight directly to the enemy. "What would induce him to do such a thing?"

Benton stopped writing and gazed at her a moment as if trying to decide whether or not to answer her question. "We have something he wants," he said before sealing the document and handing it to the aide. "See that Major Streeter gets this posthaste."

The aide nodded and scurried out of the room.

"What might you have that Colonel Lawson wants so badly as to risk an attack? He is not the type to attempt so bold a move." Sarah heard the sound of gunfire again, but was frankly too exhausted to find it very alarming.

Benton cocked his head and stared at her again, but this time, he did not avoid the question. "That would be you, Lieutenant Duvall. We need to get you away from here as quickly as possible."

Sarah blinked in surprise and sat down slowly in the chair in front of his desk. Somehow, without her knowledge or permission, she had become a pawn of value in this inscrutable game of war.

"They apparently found my officer's coat in your bedchamber," Colonel Benton said calmly, "and figured out the rest." He clenched his teeth and closed his eyes a moment as if to control a spasm of pain, then gazed at her as if they were making light conversation over afternoon tea. "Where would you like to go?"

Sarah heard Benton's words along with the distant throb of cannons, which seemed to be coming in waves from a thousand miles away. She tried to concentrate on his voice rather than the roaring in her ears. "I have no place to go but here."

Benton removed an unlit cigar from his mouth only long enough to speak. "What do you mean? Here?"

"With your men. I will follow where you go."

Benton stood, grabbing his side painfully this time, and remained for a moment bent over in agony. "That is impossible," he said after slowing standing erect.

"I fail to see why." Sarah stared into his soldierly face without flinching. "It's plain and simple really."

Benton walked around the desk and stood directly in front of her, his tall, broad form dominating the room. "Yes, plain perhaps." He swallowed hard and dragged his gaze away with obvious difficulty, concentrating instead on the fire. "But not so simple."

"Why not?"

He continued to study on the flames as he spoke in a low tone. "That I should like to have your company is certain." His jaw tightened noticeably. "Whether it would be judicious or wise for either one of us is another question entirely."

Sarah took a deep breath as she stared at his manly features. The light pouring over him through the window and the low glow of the fire gave him an alluring aura that was both alarming and unnerving. Despite the obvious danger, his very presence felt comforting.

"The road of Providence is never certain," she finally said in a calm, even voice that masked her turmoil. "It is uneven and unpredictable, yet we must not veer from it."

"Neither must we tempt fate by placing you in harm's way," he responded, walking back to his desk. He moved slowly and stiffly, the pain from his wound noticeable. "Your horse should be saddled and waiting outside, along with an escort. I'm sending you out of harm's way." As if on cue more gunfire erupted, this time closer and sounding more ominous than before. "I regret there is not more time to discuss this, but my decision has been made."

"Have I no say?" Sarah put her hands on his desk and leaned forward. "I know I ask a favor sought by many and granted to few, but have I not earned a place here?"

Benton did not look surprised at her reaction, but sat down and tapped his pencil on the desk impatiently. Despite his weakened condition, he still exhibited immense physical strength.

"Remember what I have suffered." Sarah spoke calmly but firmly, pleading with him to reconsider.

"I am not likely to forget." Benton's eyes softened, but the furrows on his brow appeared plowed with pain. He cleared his throat. "Lieutenant Duvall, once this has blown over, I'll send for you. We can discuss your future then—but I make no promises." He put finishing touches on the missive and leaned forward. "Is that agreeable to you?"

Sarah took a bold step forward. "Of course it's not agreeable to me! You cannot spare any of your men for an escort when there is such serious work ahead." As if to accentuate her words, the roar of cannon fire caused the pictures on the wall to tremble.

Little did Sarah know how correct she was about the current situation. Federal infantry and cavalry were converging in the area, all hastening forth to check the progress of the dauntless rebels and spy who had wreaked havoc on them over the past two years.

"Perhaps you do not understand the urgency of our circumstances," Benton said, his voice losing its gentleness. "The Yankees know who you are—*what* you are. They know how much you know, and they want to eliminate your ability to share it!" Despite his injury, he never looked more menacing. Ferocity gleamed in his eyes, but it was matched by the determination shining in hers.

"I have sacrificed all," Sarah responded, trying to fight the tears she felt welling in her eyes. "*All*! I will not go!"

The private who had escorted Sarah to the office poked his head in the door. "Sir, your staff is ready and waiting outside."

Sarah's eyes grew large with disbelief as she realized the implication. "You are going to the front?"

"I can't very well lead from the back," Benton said matter-of-factly. "I want this matter taken care of once and for all."

Sarah ran to where he stood and grabbed his arm. "But they want *me*! You are injured and weak! If something happens to you, *I* shall feel responsible!"

Benton stared down at her with a face of marble, but his words were full of emotion. "Now you know how *I* feel, Sarah Duvall."

Gunfire sounded louder and closer due to the silence that befell the room as they stood face to face, neither willing to move. Benton seemed to possess the solidarity of a rock as he stared at her, yet Sarah saw only a gentle, manly spirit, the very soul of chivalry and honor.

Finally, Benton broke the spell, walking to the door and yelling for an aide with a tone and manner that spoke of command. By the time the soldier appeared, Benton had scribbled out a note. "Take Lieutenant Duvall to the medical department and introduce her to Doctor Jenson."

"Yes, suh! The lieutenant's horse is saddled and waiting outside."

When he had disappeared, Benton tried to make an effort at lightness, though the circumstances called for anything but. "Since you've proved yourself an effective nurse, your orders are to report to Dr. Jenson and help him with any wounded." He paused a moment. "I hope you don't take it personally if I attempt to make every effort to stay clear of your position, Lieutenant."

Sarah looked up and met his gaze. His attempt to lighten her spirits amazed and astounded her: a tall, stalwart, respected warrior and yet considerate and compassionate to the core. She forced a smile, knowing the coming fight would not be an easy one. A large gun cracked ominously just then, and the sound seemed the voice of doom itself.

"Very well." She swallowed hard as she attempted to drag herself away from him. "I hope you take care, Colonel. I could not carry the weight of your loss."

"No matter what happens, no weight is yours to bear," he responded brusquely, all business and commanding. "Remember that and go now."

Sarah nodded and turned to the door. Although her heart sank and seemed to falter in beating, she refused to look back.

Chapter 15

A gem is not polished without rubbing, nor a man made perfect without trials.
—Chinese proverb

November 1864

It had been a week since Colonel Benton had seen Sarah, two since he had spoken to her—and then only briefly. The last time he had visited the hospital, he'd been surrounded by staff so had not sought her out. When he'd caught a glimpse of her kneeling by the prostate form of one of his men, he'd had to drag his gaze away from the scene to keep from attracting attention.

As Benton trotted along the muddied road en route once again the makeshift hospital, his mind wandered over all that had transpired in the last two-and-a-half years. The woman he had tried so hard to discredit was now an integral part of his command, and everyone who had come into contact with her had fallen under her spell. She seemed to possess an appealing, captivating, endearing *something*, which everyone recognized and felt but which no one could really explain or describe.

Even her work at the hospital revealed that her characteristic fearlessness was infused into everything she did—yet she remained, in every sense of the term, a lady. Scrupulously neat in appearance, she had a way of combining dignity and a tender heart with strength and poise. Everything about her wore the mark of honor.

Benton had overheard enough conversations to know that his men not only accepted her as one of them, but that many also hopelessly, madly adored her. He could not blame them. Not only was she intoxicating to gaze upon, but something in her grace of movement, bearing and poise marked her as "different," a lady who possessed composure and courage and strength of will. Her virtues were emphasized by the power of Christian principles that had sustained her through all her hardships and trials.

The position in which she had been placed in the hospital made her well known to many and seemed to bring a newfound respect and politeness to his ranks. Benton had noticed an obvious change in his men—they were courteous and deferential when in her presence and civil and considerate when not. It was impossible not to notice the influence and authority she wielded. Even those who had only met her briefly could feel her particular brand of magic. Her presence was as familiar to them as one of their battery guns, and they seemed to esteem her courage in equal measure. No one was unaware of her valiant service to the Confederacy or of the sacrifices she had made by doing it covertly.

Benton dismounted in front of the hospital building and waved for his staff to remain outside. Standing in the doorway, he allowed his eyes to adjust to the dim light. When his gaze finally fell upon her, he noticed that her mourning period had apparently ended. The high-necked black day dress she typically wore had been replaced with one of a slightly lighter hue—steel gray, the color of the belly of a rain cloud and every bit as dreary. Still, she wore the plain outfit with a quiet sophistication that somehow brought elegance to a place that reeked of misery and death.

When Benton saw that she was sitting with the same captain she had been nursing the previous week, he felt a sudden pang in his heart. It occurred to him the uncomfortable feeling might be jealousy—but as he had never had the occasion to feel the emotion before, he wasn't quite sure. Sarah leaned forward just then and whispered something that caused the captain's mouth to curl into a smile.

"Captain Gage." Benton strode into the room with a loud clank of boots and spurs. "I'm happy to see you are feeling better."

Sara turned and looked at him, her dark, secretive face never losing its matter-of-fact calm as she beheld his entrance.

The captain, though still weak, made an effort to salute his commanding officer. "Yes, sir. Lieutenant Duvall is seeing to that."

Benton's gaze slid over to Sarah as if seeing her for the first time. With heroic effort, he managed to keep his gaze emotionless and his tone subdued. "Oh, yes, Lieutenant Duvall. There you are. Just the person I've come to speak to…if you can spare a moment."

Sarah turned back to Captain Gage a moment, gave his hand an obvious squeeze, and stood to follow Benton. When she got out onto the sunlit porch, he turned to her. "I see you've taken your duties quite seriously." His tone was a little colder than he had intended.

"I know of no other way." Sarah looked up at him as if confused. "Is that what you wished to talk to me about?"

"No." Benton continued walking to a tree in the yard as he put a match to a cigar and got the end burning red. "I've received new orders and need to talk to you."

"Very well." Sarah crossed her arms and waited.

"Not here." Benton looked at his staff waiting by the horses. "I'd like you to come to headquarters."

Sarah's forehead creased as she turned worriedly and looked through the door of the hospital.

"Surely they can spare you for a few hours," Benton said curtly.

"Colonel, can you send me about a dozen more of these?" A tall, barrel-chested surgeon patted Benton on the back as he walked by, nodding toward Sarah. "Don't know what I'd do without this one."

Benton took a long draw on his cigar and then gazed absently at the tip glowing red. "I'm hoping you can spare her for a few hours, Doc." He flicked some ashes onto the ground. "Need her down at headquarters."

"Sure. Sure." The doctor barely stopped, and continued to talk over his shoulder. "Just be sure you give her back." He gave a wave with his hand before disappearing into the makeshift hospital.

"I guess that's settled," Benton said.

Sarah stood eyeing him, her arms still crossed and her hair mussed and hanging like a frame around her face. "What needs to be said that cannot be said here?"

Benton removed the cigar from his mouth. "It's...complicated," he said in a low tone.

So compelling was his stare and so magnetic was his gaze that Sarah apparently could not refuse him. "I've heard rumblings of a change of orders," she said musingly.

"Is that so?" Benton's irritation got the better of him. He took a step closer. "From whom?"

"Oh, no one in particular," Sarah said, quickly. "Just talk of something afoot."

Benton knew better than to try to get any names out of her. The woman was as loyal to her comrades as she was to her country. He gazed up at the sun. "It's about half-past noon," he said. "I'm heading back to headquarters now."

"Very well." Sarah looked down at her dress and made a half-hearted attempt to smooth out the wrinkles. "But I need to change first."

"I'll leave Benning and Martin here as an escort." Benton nodded toward the two men. "Let them know when you're ready."

He didn't say anything more, just gave his cigar a toss into a nearby mud puddle, mounted and rode away, all the while musing that he was leaving her as he always did—feeling more at peace, and yet more in turmoil—than he'd ever felt before.

* * *

Benton sat down on the couch in front of the fire and stared into its flickering flames. He'd ridden hard to get back to headquarters so he'd have time for a quick wash and change of clothes before Sarah's arrival. He closed his eyes and tried to sort out his thoughts in an attempt to prepare for what lay ahead. He needed to try to predict how she would react to his news and be ready to counter her arguments.

Amid his musings, Benton heard the door behind him open and close. Having heard no horses coming in, he assumed it was his clerk dropping some papers onto his desk. It wasn't until the sound of soft rustling of silk met his ears, followed by the rich scent of a woman, that he looked around.

"Why, Kul-nel. Ah didn't really expect that you'd be all alone."

Mrs. Grimes took a step closer, her bosom heaving as she stared boldly at him, her wide, unflinching gaze sliding from his eyes to his lips, then slowly across the breadth of his shoulders before resting on his hands that lay on his lap. It caused him to stir uncomfortably. He had heard she'd arrived for a visit with the owner of the house he used as headquarters, but couldn't help but wonder if there was some other reason for her sudden appearance—especially amid talk that she was as friendly with Union officers as she was with Confederate.

Although he had not disapproved of her promiscuousness when she was single and much younger, he did not believe it becoming now. He wondered again about her motives, and a shiver of uneasiness ran through him. It could be that she wanted to be seen with a man of his military status—or it could mean she wanted access to his position for another reason entirely. It troubled him that his sense of unease signaled something sinister—an indication it was probably the latter.

When he came to his senses and started to stand, the matronly woman strode hurriedly toward him and gave him a gentle push back down on the couch. "Colonel, no need to rise for an old friend like me." Mrs. Grimes sat down beside him, entwined her arm in his and leaned into him, hard.

Benton dared not look down at her. Instead, he stared straight into the fire, his jaw clamped tightly. "I'm expecting company in a few minutes." His voice cracked, and he labored over the simple words.

"Oh, that should be plenty of time." She took his hand, placed it on her lap, and leaned into him more boldly, gently stroking his cheek suggestively. "If we don't tarry over small talk."

Benton swallowed hard, trying to control his impulses. "The door is not locked."

She laughed with a throaty, infectious sound he knew she used when she wished to get her way. Unfortunately, awareness of that fact did not lessen her power over him, nor free him from the natural desires pulsing through him.

"Indeed. There was a time you would have thought that added to the excitement."

She breathed heavily, so close he could feel the warmth of her breath on his neck. Benton concentrated on the fire as he tried to think of a way to extricate himself from the situation. Yet his mind could not erase the memory of this woman in younger years and the images that it wrought.

"Oh, look, how careless of me." Mrs. Grimes leaned low over his lap. "I believe I've dropped my earring."

Benton heard a short gasping sound behind him, and turned to see Sarah Duvall standing at the door. "I'm sorry…Private M-Manson said to come right in." She pointed to the door and took a step backward as if she was going to disappear through it.

Benton stood in one motion, leaving Mrs. Grimes struggling to regain her balance on the sofa. "That's quite all right." He bounded toward Sarah and pulled her back into the room. "Mrs. Grimes was just leaving."

The agitated Mrs. Grimes stood with a look of indignation and rage that made the color of her face nearly match the redness of her hair. "So this is the visitor you were expecting." Her eyes, still lit with fury and resentment, remained on Colonel Benton, while her tone and expression reflected that she did not think Sarah worth the interruption. "You'll pay for this," she said to no one particular.

Benton took her by the arm and led her toward the entranceway. "Good day, Mrs. Grimes."

But before he could get the door closed, she repeated her ominous words, and this time they were directed at him. "You'll pay for this."

The room fell silent then as Benton turned back to Sarah and tried to think of something appropriate to say. His head ached terribly now, and he suddenly felt sick to his stomach. Beads of sweat began to run down his forehead, though the room was anything but warm. Although he had responded neither by word or movement to the woman's advances, he knew the scene had appeared anything but upright.

"I'm sorry to intrude." Sarah did not meet his gaze as he strode across the room, but stared at something on the wall over his desk as she spoke.

"Your arrival is not an intrusion." Benton went to his desk and opened a folder, staring at it intently a moment as he tried to determine how to start. At last, he decided on a course.

"As I told you at the hospital, there has been a change of plans." He gazed up at her for the first time. "I've received new orders from General Lee." When she responded with nothing more than an inquisitive look, he continued. "I've been ordered with a large detachment to the peninsula. Lee wants the citizens of this region to be free from the strain of feeding man and beast for a few months."

Sarah nodded. "That's understandable. This area has been forced to provide for both armies." She walked slowly to the window and gazed out as a horse and rider came galloping in. "I suppose that leaves you wondering what to do with me."

Benton didn't try to beat around the bush, though he knew those serious eyes could turn turbulent in an instant. "Yes. What do you suggest?"

She looked quickly over her shoulder at him. "I believe I have stated that already."

"But things have changed. We are no longer going into winter quarters here." Benton strode across the room until he stood behind her, his voice low and grave. "The ride to the peninsula will be long, and the weather is turning colder every day. The journey would be quite a severe test of your endurance."

"I comprehend the distance and the tendency of winter weather to be cold," Sarah replied, putting her hands on her hips and turning toward him. "Circumstances may have changed, but my position has not."

Benton had calculated her objections and was not angered by them, but he could not end the conversation without bringing up the greater risk. "There is another consideration." He walked to his desk and sat down, then leaned forward for emphasis. "One that perhaps you have not contemplated."

Sarah gazed at him with questioning eyes.

"I'll put this frankly, as I know of no other way." He took a deep breath as if to proceed, but with her gaze intently upon him, suddenly found himself at a loss for words. Picking up a cigar as if that would give him the nerve he needed, he fumbled slightly with a match until finally the head burned red. "As I said, I'll be frank." He raised his gaze to the beautiful face that looked like chiseled marble. "Your head is esteemed by the Yankees as a valuable piece of anatomy."

She merely shrugged. "That does not mean I wish to run and hide." When he leaned back in his chair and said nothing more, she threw up her hands, knowing she had no say. "I do not intend to beg, Colonel Benton. You have the rank to compel me to obey your command."

He frowned at her. "I'm glad you appreciate my position, although you state it with unnecessary harshness."

"It is the truth that is harsh, not my stating of it," she said in an unemotional voice.

Benton sighed deeply and began to tap the pencil again. "Is it my understanding that you wish to accompany us?"

She took a step forward. "Of course."

"Then I'll consider your request." He picked up a stack of paperwork and began to thumb through it. He raised his gaze then, but not his head. "That will be all."

Sarah remained steadfast. "When will you let me know what you decide?"

He stopped and looked up at her sternly. "When I've made my decision."

"Well, when will you—"

"You are dismissed," he said sternly. He made no further comment, but had Sarah been looking, she would have seen a glint of approval and respect in his eyes.

Chapter 16

The error of one moment becomes the sorrow of a whole life.
—Chinese proverb

December 1864

Colonel Benton had finally given his consent for Sarah to accompany him, though with obvious reservations and deep concern. That had been more than a week ago, and they were now well on their way.

Already they had ridden out of familiar territory and crossed miles of stark and deserted land. Houses grew few and far between, and those they did pass were mostly just shacks, appearing randomly along the side of the road as if tossed in place by the hand of a mighty storm. Trees and shrubbery dotted the landscape here and there too, but even the finery of nature seemed determined to avoid the region.

By the fourth day of riding, as Benton had predicted, the journey grew both toilsome and perilous. Although Sarah had known the distance would be considerable, she had not anticipated the severity of the weather. Golden Indian summer had vanished soon after they'd ridden out, replaced with lashing rain and a blustering wind that, just this morning, had settled into a spell of bone-seeking sleet. The sleet had since turned to a heavy, blinding snow that was just now beginning to taper.

The whistling of the wind through the trees and the occasionally dense snow squalls claimed any warmth the sun could wrought, leaving Sarah feeling gloomy and cold. She rode with her head down, not paying attention to anything but the gentle plodding of her horse's hooves, when suddenly the column came to a halt.

"Why are we stopping?" She turned to the man beside her.

He shrugged and nodded toward a house barely visible through the swirling snow.

Sarah could see now that Benton's staff had halted under some trees. The men were already dismounted and standing at the heads of their horses, apparently just waiting for orders. An ominous feeling overtook Sarah as she thought back to the scene a day and a half earlier. While encamped at a house on the way to the peninsula, she had been surprised to learn that the home was owned by a relative of the disreputable Mrs. Grimes.

Although given no details, Sarah had learned that Benton made a sudden change of course based solely on the intelligence of that home-owner. It concerned her that the colonel's sound judgment may have been impeded by some sort of feminine duplicity—or worse—outright deceit. She hoped Colonel Benton was not so naïve to allow a petticoat to cloud his better judgment, but she knew from her own experience that men often succumbed easily to false information when delivered by a woman.

After the change in course, they had ridden another day and a half with little knowledge of the new terrain. They still remained ignorant of the country and the roads and knew nothing of the enemy's numbers or location—save what the woman had told Benton and insisted was fact. Patrols had been sent out looking for supplies in this desolate land, but success had been minimal, and any relief would surely be slow to arrive.

Even less encouraging were the reports from the scouts. They had spotted Union cavalry where no cavalry was supposed to be. To whom those regiments were attached, and what their intent was, weighed heavily on all who understood the significance. Benton had since ordered his men back out to reconnoiter and told them not to return until they had something of value.

"Lieutenant Duvall."

Sarah shook herself from her reverie. "Yes?"

"We're waiting here until the scouts get back with word." Major Connelly nodded toward the road. "The colonel wants to talk to you. He's about a hundred yards yonder."

Sarah nodded and urged her horse forward. So Benton felt it too. He was unwilling to move his men any further until he knew what was in front of him. At least the short pause would give her an opportunity to talk to him. It would be the first time she saw him face to face since they had started this journey.

Despite the feeling of gloom she could not shake, Sarah felt a rare pounding of excitement in her heart as she rode forward through the darkening twilight. Some divine, mysterious hand had led her here and would continue to lead her until the will of God was done. For that reason and for an instant, she looked almost giddily to the future, certain of one thing—it could hold no trials comparable to those of the past.

The freshly fallen snow sparkled like tiny mirrors in the advancing starlight, and the serene silence of the night made it impossible to believe that anything as ugly as warfare could be near. Sarah's horse made no noise as it plodded along, making strange patterns in the snow along the trail. She spotted the colonel when she was still twenty yards away, sitting with his back to her while appearing to survey and contemplate the long, empty stretch of road ahead.

With so much to do and so much at stake, Sarah suddenly felt the need to lighten the mood. Acting on an impulse, she stopped at a pine tree heavily laden with snow, and when she was close enough, she hurled a well-aimed snowball toward the large target. The missile hit its mark with a soft thud, causing Sarah to laugh with amusement.

"I'm sorry, Colonel," she said, her eyes wide with astonishment and disbelief. "I did not realize I was such a good shot."

When Benton turned around in his saddle, Sarah saw his eyes were lit, first with surprise and then, almost instantly, with revenge. As a result, she reacted on instinct, spurring her horse away from him, fearing the assault to come.

And come it did—but faster and even more furiously than she anticipated. When she saw how quickly he was gaining ground, she laughed again, partly in triumph but mostly from fright, and made the decision to abandon her mount and make for higher ground to gain a tactical advantage. The plan would have been a wise one had her pursuer not been so fleet of foot. He apparently saw her intentions, perhaps before she even knew them, and jumped from his horse in a most athletic dismount, quickly closing the distance as she slipped and slid up the grade. Within moments, he brought her sprawling down to the ground.

Shocked and surprised by both his speed and strength, Sarah struggled and squirmed against his powerful form and soon gained the advantage by sitting on top of him and pinning his arms over his head. It was a position, she surmised with one look at his smiling face, he had intended all along. He appeared youthful and masculine—though it occurred to Sarah that they were both too old for this type of revelry.

"It appears you have the advantage of me," he said mischievously.

The smile slowly faded from Sarah's face as she thought back to that other woman, Mrs. Grimes, and to the scores of other women with whom she knew Benton associated. "One apparently not held by me alone, Colonel Benton." Her tone sounded both wistful and sad.

Benton instantly reversed their positions, his face just inches from hers. "My name is Douglas."

He stared down at her so intently that Sarah felt the urge to squirm. "I know...but I thought I should wait for permission."

"You needn't have." He relaxed slightly, but his eyes still bore into hers. "Surely you know there is no one more highly regarded or esteemed. Whatever I have is yours—including my name."

Sarah was silent to that, but her eyes searched his for a few long moments as she tried to decipher his meaning. "We'd better get back," she finally said, pushing him away half playfully, half hastily.

Benton helped her up and held her hand firmly in his as they turned back to their horses. He seemed quiet and suddenly serious as he led her skillfully through the bramble and snow.

"I'm sorry for acting so childishly." Sarah looked into his warm, dark eyes when he turned around. "It seems the occasion calls for anything but humor." Despite the seriousness of their circumstances, she felt a swift, illogical contentment when she felt the pressure of his hand on hers increase, all the brighter for it being brief and unexpected.

Benton made a gallant effort at a smile. "Yes, but no need for an apology. I will cherish the memory." He walked up to her horse and grabbed the reins before speaking again in a low, grave tone. "I called you forward to apologize for placing you in harm's way. The intelligence so far has done nothing to alleviate the worry."

"Perhaps the scouts will report some good news," Sarah said, trying to sound hopeful as she accepted his assistance in mounting. "Regardless, we must not fret over what we cannot change."

He cocked his head and smiled. "Thank you, Lieutenant Duvall. Your optimistic attitude will set a good example for my men."

Sarah gazed at him curiously, as if his words confused her. "But there is only One who provides a true example." When he started to turn toward his horse, she reached for his shoulder. "Really, Colonel, I wish you would accept Him before you are brought to some crises in your destiny for which you are not prepared."

Benton laughed and patted her hand as a father might a child. "There you go trying to save my soul again—a nigh impossible task." He walked to his horse and mounted without another word.

* * *

They rode back to the command in silence, she staring at the moon and the stars and the thousands of vivid reflections they created on the snow; he staring at her, at the way the moonlight lit her hair and softened her face. It was as if she had been created by magical fairies from fallen snow sparkles and frost gleam so unearthly and glowing did she appear. It warmed Benton's heart to know that with sufficient cause she could laugh—he'd never really thought it in her. To see her so playful tonight, with so much at stake, was like seeing the sun after a cold, long night. It had wrought a dazzling change in her and brought out feelings he had tried desperately to resist.

He had known how dangerous this journey would be, and tonight had revealed why he had gone against his instincts and allowed her to come. She made his lonely heart yearn for things he had never felt before. Until only recently he had not even thought of himself as lonely. The idea seemed preposterous. But the frivolous and shallow antics of the women who usually surrounded him were no longer pleasing or charming. There was only one whose poise, grace, and charm could cause his heart to race.

A thousand thoughts rushed through Benton's head as he rode silently beside her. This feeling of friendly companionship was a far different thing from the casual, skillfully conducted flirtations to which he was accustomed. It was strange and thrilling, and yet frightening and alarming. Thoughts and feelings and emotions surged through him in such a way that it almost made him shudder. He had given himself to many women, but he had never surrendered his heart.

Nevertheless, his conscience warned him to curb his yearnings for her sake, and to still his longings for the sake of the command. It was her respect he wished to win more so than her adoration. But when she leaned over and began to brush snow from his back and shoulder, it nearly unseated him.

"What shall your men think of a commander who lies on his back in a snowbank?" she asked, her voice light and full of laughter again as she swept away the traces of white from his coat.

Benton spoke hastily with his heart, not his mind, as he pulled his horse to a stop. "That he is wildly and passionately in love, perhaps?"

Sarah's hand stilled upon his shoulder, and she froze. Eyes that had been looking down slowly lifted to meet his. She blinked in obvious surprise, yet sat unmoving as if held by an invisible hand. Time seemed suspended as neither moved.

"And is he?" she finally asked, a mixture of astonishment and fear in her voice. "Perhaps?"

He brought his hand up and touched her cheek, softly, as if he were touching a rare treasure he had long admired from afar. His voice trembled ever so slightly, as did his hand. "No," he said hoarsely. "That is... there is no *perhaps* about it. Just wildly. Passionately."

It seemed the very wind held its breath as no sound save the neigh of a distant horse could be heard. Benton remained silent and still waiting for her to answer, his heart beating so tumultuously he felt it in his throat. Surely she could hear it. Yet everything about her seemed to offer encouragement, from her widened eyes and her half-parted lips to the breathless expectancy in the way she gazed at him. And certainly the flush upon her cheeks was not caused by the cold alone.

The night seemed to close in around them, shutting out the world and all its complications. Both seemed to realize they were succumbing to feelings they neither understood nor expected, feelings they had tried to prevent or ignore but now were forced to face. And for two people who prided themselves on discipline and control, the feelings were overwhelming and frightening in their intensity.

At last, Benton leaned toward her, his military bearing gone, and briefly pressed his lips upon hers. She did not pull away, yet neither did she embrace him.

The sound of a horse, galloping hard through the snow in their direction caused them to hastily part. The muffled hoofbeats were soon followed by the strains of a trumpet, its urgency muted by the snow and the distance.

"Sir," Mahony saluted and drew rein beside him in a shower of snow as his horse came to a sudden stop. "Scouts are back."

The colonel waited for something more.

"It's urgent, sir."

Benton's gaze as it rested on Sarah was possessive and concerned. She looked up at him with clear, blue, fearless eyes.

"Go to your men," she said softly. "You must not think of me at all."

Benton nodded and turned his horse, but he knew that was easier said than done, for she was more on his mind than was the enemy, even as he felt them gathering around him.

Chapter 17

'Tis the business of little minds to shrink; but he whose heart is firm,
and whose conscience approves his conduct, will pursue his principles unto death.
—Thomas Paine, The American Crisis, No. 1, 1776

Sarah rode back toward the encampment at a slow trot, her stomach turning in knots out of concern for Colonel Benton and a fear of the unknown. A strange, gloomy light from the moon still shown from above, but it was fitful now through the gathering clouds and cast only straggling gleams that seemed to tease and torment. It occurred to her that these signs in winter portended danger as plainly as heat lightning foretells a storm in the heat of summer.

Although she was only a few minutes behind Colonel Benton, there was already a purposeful activity throughout the camp when she rode in. The rush of movement seemed in contrast to the relaxed attitude of Benton, whom she saw sitting calmly in a tight circle of officers discussing the news from the scouts. The importance of the meeting was something that could be sensed—if not felt—by those who milled about or hurried around carrying out orders that had already been given.

Sarah did not need to hear the words of those who sat around their commander with wrinkled brows and determined looks. It was not hard to guess the basic details of the frightening facts. The enemy was apparently out there, approaching quietly and in strength. Benton had been intentionally deceived and now they were trapped on a slim piece of land that held no escape.

After dismounting, Sarah stood discreetly beneath a tree, trying to blend in with the shadows. She could hear only bits and pieces of the conversation until Benton began to speak again, his clarion voice carrying quite clearly. Bathed in a cocoon of pale yellow light from a fire, he appeared calm and unruffled, the very picture of a soldier as he discussed the necessity of the upcoming conflict.

Sarah knew that Benton was not a man before whom it was ever safe to indulge in mistakes, and the enemy had made one by allowing his scouts to alert him of their presence. He would use that knowledge to calculate, analyze and assess every aspect and detail of the upcoming conflict. Nothing would alarm him, nothing would dismay him, and nothing would daunt him. The more serious the intelligence, the more determined he would become

Sarah watched him with something of awe, and observed a new refinement, a calm composure and quiet dignity that she had failed to see before. Whether it was the stamp of birth and breeding or just a confident authority that had been long practiced, she did not know. But she knew that action—prompt, bold, and decisive—was the breath of life to him.

Her eyes went back to the group and swept over the men, before falling again upon Benton. Although she knew he had slept little in the last three days, he showed no trace of fatigue now, presenting his usual appearance of confidence and conviction. Yet Sarah could tell by the steely color of his eyes that he was concerned. The wrinkle of his brow revealed that his quiet reserve was strained, and his carefree smile was absent.

Of course, everyone in the camp felt the peril, but none carried the burden like Benton. Sarah knew well the responsibilities that weighed upon him and marveled at the man who had been laughing like a schoolboy in the snow less than an hour before. He was all manhood and military genius now, making her wonder how anyone could change so quickly and so much.

Sarah leaned against the strong trunk of the tree behind her and stared into the blackness beyond. The reports of the scouts had apparently only varied in the depth of their gloom. The enemy was close, yet was surprisingly—and suspiciously—quiet. Their silence and deceitful calm most likely covered an important movement. Her mind came back to the present as she heard Benton's voice again. His face was serious, and his tone was grave.

"Gentlemen, the enemy is around us in overwhelming numbers and in irresistible force." He paused and stared into their eyes as he swept his gaze across them. "The points upon which we can be attacked are numerous and their strength unlimited."

Sarah knew Benton's command possessed but one small advantage. The Yankees did not believe the Rebels would put up a fight, let alone attempt to hold their ground against such extraordinary odds. She also knew these men, filled with the desire for battle and inspired by their leader's heroic words, would be nerved to the point that they would cheerfully attack anything in their path.

It was good they trusted him, Sarah thought, as she watched the men look with supreme confidence toward Benton. They would have full need of blind obedience to orders today. If he decided too soon or delayed too long, they would be doomed. Yet Sarah wondered how Benton would devise a scheme that had any hope of success, for he had blundered into land he couldn't defend and from which withdrawal was now impossible. So much had to go right, and so much had already gone wrong, that it seemed the situation was growing more desperate by the minute.

For a moment, she allowed her gaze to shift to the beauty of the world around her. Snow hung each tree, adorning each limb and branch like lace, making her surroundings feel peaceful and calm. How strange that the enemy was out there lurking, silent and ill intentioned. The sound of Benton's calm voice drew her back irresistibly to the present and reality.

"Gentlemen, we must win or die, and as dying can do our country no good, we must win."

The other voices Sarah heard seemed generally to signify assent, making it obvious that the ambition to hold Benton's esteem amounted to passionate devotion. These men would forfeit their lives in emulating the virtues of the leader they so admired.

Sarah looked down and kicked at the white mound at her feet. Murderous, murderous snow. Although the peninsula was wide enough to hide for a while, the snow would render their tracks into the woodlands unmistakable. The men, already fatigued by their long and exhaustive march, were in no condition to make the long march back—even if the way was not blocked by Federal troops. Yet every moment of delay now was precious. Every minute could mean a life; every hour the loss of the battle. And the loss of this battle with *these* men could strike a huge blow to the Southern cause.

Another scout rode in, and Sarah overheard the news. The enemy had found their tracks and was but a day's ride away. Their advance, although not rapid, had apparently been steady. Standing in the shadows, she watched the intelligence being given to Benton. She saw his eyes sweep across the camp again, at the men he had fought with for almost three years, and the sacrifice he knew was imminent. But his composure remained calm and unruffled as the threat was absorbed and the complications assessed with a mere nod of his head. Sarah's heart throbbed in her throat as she gazed at his unemotional face, for it was at this instant that she realized with certainty that death held less consequence for him than dishonor. Even with disaster looming, nothing could subdue his gallant spirit.

Sarah turned her attention to the expressions of the men, and saw concern now, but no panic. One of the men walking by patted her on the back as if for encouragement, and she gave him a lackluster smile. She had been accepted by these men—hesitantly in some cases, but almost universally—and felt like she belonged for the first time in her life.

Feeling Benton's eyes upon her, Sarah looked up and met his gaze, surveying his expression as he surveyed hers. What he saw in her eyes at that moment she would surely never know—what she saw in his was nothing but strength and determination. The look lasted only a moment, but it was a measurement of time she would remember forever.

Benton nodded and turned. As his large, looming figure dissolved into the darkness, Sarah knew that everyone awaited the dawn and whatever the light of day would bring, but no one more so than Colonel Benton.

Chapter 18

Well, if we are to die, let us die like men.
—General Patrick Cleburne, last words, 1864

Colonel Benton stood lost deep in thought as he groomed his horse in the shadows, alone and apart from the others. Although he wasn't sure why, it seemed important that the animal be immaculate in advance of the coming day's fight. He heard the sound of muffled footsteps approaching a few moments before Sarah walked out of the darkness and stood by the head of his horse. Her smile had rewarded him abundantly earlier that day, but he could see in one glance that the feat was not to be renewed. Her expression was serious and grave.

"You intend to fight then?"

Benton did not stop his work. "I do not intend to surrender without a stand." He paused and shot her a look that displayed courteous, intolerable pride. "I am prepared to die, if that is what you mean."

Sarah remained quiet for a few long moments, and when she did finally speak, he noticed she kept her eyes pinned on his horse's forelock as she distractedly ran her fingers through the hair. "Soldiers should always be ready to die, I suppose." She bit her cheek and looked up at him. "But, Colonel, I believe you are worth too much to the country to perish like this here."

Benton paused a moment and looked down, curious about the sound of her voice and the grave tone it bore. "It cannot be helped." He turned back to Vince and resumed his duty. "We must beat them or perish in the struggle."

Sarah sighed heavily and shook her head as if his words were exasperating her. "Considering the unevenness of the numbers, it appears a battle should not be risked except in the last extremity—and hardly even then. Perchance the hand that guides us will open some other door."

Benton brushed away the comment as he continued to brush his horse. "The time for another door to open has passed. It is a consequence of my bad judgment that we are so arraigned. I must do what I must do."

The moon appeared just then, pouring in through the somber shafts of the forest's canopy to cast an eerie glow on the snow and create distinctive shadows beneath the trees. It disappeared just as suddenly, and all was dark and strangely quiet again, as if all heaven had withdrawn to leave them alone for a moment.

"Colonel Benton, I believe you know how perfect my confidence is in you and how deep my affection." Sarah looked down for a moment, seeming to lose her nerve. "But it seems a lesser sacrifice can be made than *your* life."

Benton stopped grooming, though he did not turn to her. "It is an honor to hear you say so." He made a valiant attempt to keep his voice from trembling. "It has long been my hope…that I would someday be held in the same high regard as your late husband."

Sarah touched his arm hesitantly. "I have perfect faith, Colonel Benton, that you will attain your goal…and someday be a very great man."

Benton turned toward her, trying to hide the disappointment from his voice. "I fear Fate will make it necessary to accept who I am now. I only wish to die without an earthly regret." He looked at her with wistful admiration that her downcast eyes failed to see. For a moment, Benton considered revealing the full extent of the promise he'd made to himself that snowy night at Waverly. But as she gazed at the old wound on Vince's neck, it was clear her thoughts were on that joyous spring day many months earlier when the horse had been returned to its owner, and he did not wish to disturb her reflections. He went back to his grooming. "The time for conversation is over," he finally said, bending down to brush Vince's legs. "I will do as I am inclined to do. You know my intentions."

"Yes, I know your intentions," Sarah said mechanically as she gazed on neither sky nor earth. "War to the death, I believe."

Benton stood. "Yes, war to the death."

Sarah laid her cheek against his horse's forehead and closed her eyes as if thinking of a proper response. "Hear me then, Colonel," she said, seeming to finally find the resolve to say what she had come to say. "We are here in God's care and for some wise purpose of His own. I beg of you think of those who you lead, and do not misjudge the opportunities that are placed before you."

"The enemy is between us and the mainland. The only way out is to *fight* our way out." His words were harsh, but anyone could see from his eyes that his heart burst with admiration and high regard for the one to whom he spoke.

Sarah put her hand on his wrist to stop him from grooming. "But if it were *not* the only way out"—she looked straight up into his eyes, refusing to relinquish her hold or his attention—"would you accept it and move on and be at peace with what fate befalls you?"

Benton sighed, deeply confused and exasperated with the whole conversation and went back to grooming his horse. "What are you trying to say?"

"What if the enemy turned and retreated?"

Benton laughed loudly and majestically. "I do not believe even your prayers could accomplish that feat." He looked down into her serious eyes. "Why would they suddenly decide to turn and run when they possess every advantage?"

"What if they received intelligence that the trap they thought they had set for you, was really a trap you have set for them?"

Benton laughed again. "It's a plan that would require more than a little help from Heaven, and I'm not sure I'm in a position to ask for it." His smile faded when he saw the seriousness of her expression. "Anyway, I would never order such a thing. It's too dangerous."

Sarah shrugged. "Any rational possibility of defusing this crisis must be entertained, no matter the source and notwithstanding your orders." She stared up at him as if to see if he understood. "Fate may decree *other* orders—orders from a higher authority, relating to duty here."

"A higher authority than *me*?"

Sarah's tone showed she was beginning to lose her patience, yet she gazed at him intently with wrinkled brow, as if memorizing his features for some future occasion. "Orders that would require equal fortitude and faith in the Almighty as a bloody battle would."

"And just what are these orders?"

She contemplated his question for a moment, then turned away. "That is for Providence to reveal," she said solemnly.

"When will He reveal them?" Benton shook his head. "I hope it's soon because I have a battle to fight."

Sarah blinked as if at a painful wound. Her calm, holy eyes stared beseechingly into his, and the woeful conviction within them caused a shadow like doubt—or perhaps dread—to begin to invade his mind.

She did not lower her eyes, but continued to gaze at him with a look that was straight and frank and fearless. "I beg of you remember, your greatest defense is the Almighty."

"God?" he said, continuing to brush his horse because he didn't know what else to do. "What does he have to do with it?"

"If you do not know, Doug," she said gravely, placing her hand on his as it lay on his horse, and squeezing it gently, "I hope the lesson Providence provides is a kind one. Good night."

She bowed her head and disappeared while Benton stood dazed in the darkness as stunned by the sound of his name on her lips as he was disturbed by the tone of finality in her voice. He stared into the darkness that had swallowed her, and then at his hand where her trembling fingers had pressed, and wondered why he had the feeling she had been saying more to him than the mere words he had heard or understood.

He turned around in desperation and spoke her name, but small foot-prints in the snow were all that remained to give evidence she had ever been there.

Chapter 19

Then two shall be in the field; the one shall be taken and the other left...
Watch therefore: for ye know not what hour your Lord doth come.
—*Matthew 23:40, 42*

Colonel Benton had to fight the impulse to scout the peninsula himself, but knew he had to remain where his orders could reach his subordinates promptly and stay where their reports could find him without delay. He had been planning his tactics all night, but hoped fate would allow him to meet the enemy in the open. The close proximity of the foe seeking to overtake him had awakened a sense of imminent danger among all of the men. For now, the fringe of trees in which they hid was sufficiently thick to screen their movements, and the darkness concealed them—but morning would bring a revealing light that would be merciless and cruel.

When at last he heard the sound of a horse coming in fast, Benton stepped out from beneath a tree to greet the incoming rider. He'd been up all night and there was only about another hour until dawn. Yet he felt little need for sleep as he prepared for what this day would bring. The man pulled his horse to a sliding halt, spraying snow on the colonel, but he seemed not to notice.

"They are moving back, Colonel."

"*Retreating?*" Benton grabbed the horse's rein to steady him, and glared up at the scout as if he could not possibly have heard the man correctly. It was obvious to those who watched that he was more startled by the retreat than he had been at the advance.

"It appears. Martin's forces are almost to the gap. If we move swiftly, we can squeeze by them in the event they change their mind."

"Your duty is not to recommend or advise but to report and obey," Benton snapped, his nerves strung to their limit. "I asked for information—not your opinion of it!"

Benton seldom showed explosive anger, but when he did, it was remembered by all who witnessed it. Nonetheless, his harsh words were promptly forgotten as he agreed with the scout's course of action. Not wishing to waste even a moment of time, he gave the order to mount up. Instantly there could be heard the tramping of feet as men charged toward their horses, followed by the shouting of orders to others further down the line.

"Sir?" A private saluted, and stood waiting nervously amid all of the chaos for a response.

"Yes, what is it?" Benton was already motioning for Connelly to move up for more orders.

"I know she told me not to, but I'd feel better if I hung back and waited for Lieutenant Duvall to return."

Colonel Benton hauled back on the reins to stop his prancing mount. "Return? Return from where?" He looked around and then nodded toward her horse, standing alone now on the picket line. "There stands Chance." The disorder of the night and constant reports from scouts had kept Benton busy. After his short conversation with Sarah, it had never occurred to him to wonder where she was or where she might not be.

"B-u-u-t, she didn't take Chance." The confused soldier stared at the horse as if just realizing something was seriously amiss.

The men already mounted seemed to understand something was awry as well and moved closer to hear the forthcoming explanation. No one seemed able to fully realize the exact nature of what had occurred, but all were conscious of an impending calamity.

"Take him where?" There was a sense of urgency in Benton's voice. "Where is she now?" He turned in his saddle, his severe eagle-like glance scanning the soldiers around him as if expecting to see her face.

"Sir, I was on picket duty. She said she had a dispatch to get through the lines. She was on—" He paused for a moment, then swallowed hard, and finished in a low voice. "Old Ironsides."

Benton gave a grimace of resignation, or perhaps one of regret, as an expression of vague dread spread across his face. Everyone watched the breath go out of him as he stared over the soldier's shoulder into nothing. Ironsides was a horse used primarily for prisoners because no amount of spurring would increase his slow pace. The evidence was therefore accruing that if someone took Old Ironsides while in close proximity to the enemy—they wanted to be caught.

Others seemed to sense the importance of the picket's words too.

Where once there had been clamoring and commotion, all had turned solemn and silent. Lieutenant Duvall had ridden out on Old Ironsides and had not returned. They were not sure what it meant, but they knew the absence of the lieutenant and the departure of the enemy were probably somehow related.

"You did not try to stop her?" Benton's face had grown pale, though he spoke more calmly than from his look one would expect him to speak.

"Sir, I told her I would do the duty, and find someone to take my place on the line," the soldier responded, stammering now. "But she insisted. She said she was the only one who could do it properly."

Benton looked as if he had just suffered a mortal wound, but he did not speak aloud the words he was thinking. *No one of my command could be less spared.*

He swept his gaze around to the faces of his men. Some looked confused as if they did not understand what had happened; others appeared angry, as if they did.

"I did not authorize it," Benton mumbled. "I did not take her seriously."

"Sir?" Major Connelly pulled his horse astride with Benton's and looked at him questioningly.

Benton stared at the rising sun and the eerie mist it created as he spoke. "Last night she suggested we let the enemy find a dispatch that would lead them to believe we have set a trap for them."

"But how would that be accomplished?" Connelly seemed utterly bewildered. "Why would they believe it?"

"They would believe it if it were found on a known spy." Benton's voice was so low and grave, it was hard to understand. He swallowed hard as he pictured the scene. "She would have hidden it—so they would think she did not want it to be found. But find it they would."

"But you can't be sure that is what happened, surely!" Even as he said the words, it was evident Connelly knew in his heart that is exactly what happened. Everyone knew her well enough to know she would make just such a sacrifice. That woman-child with the mysterious wisdom in her eyes would figure out a way that it *could* be done, rather than fret about ways it couldn't.

All eyes moved to the colonel, and it was obvious what they were thinking. He was partly at fault—if not entirely to blame—for the circumstances. He had gotten them into a blunder, and she had gotten them out. The mistake—eternal in its consequences—was his, and it was obvious many were wondering if their escape was worth the price she had paid to grant it.

Connelly looked at Benton and seemed to be reading his mind. "It matters not how we got here. It matters only what we do about it."

"But if we leave now," Benton said quietly, "her fate will be sealed."

"If we don't," Connelly replied, "*ours* will."

Benton thought back to the ominous warning he'd been given by Mrs. Grimes, and the weight of his burden increased. The trap had been meant for him, but his entire command had been caught in the net.

"Sir," the courier offered. "They were moving quickly. There can be no doubt they are in a hurry to get to the mainland."

Again all eyes went to the colonel to see how he would receive the news. His pursed lips revealed how deeply the information affected him, and when he swayed, Connelly put out a hand to steady him. "It is your duty to get these men out," Connelly reminded Benton. 'There is nothing you can do for her now."

Colonel Benton stared blankly into space as the full realization hit him with crushing weight. She had known if there was a chance of rescue he would undertake it—perhaps at the cost of other lives. She also knew—as did he—that her chances of still being alive by the time he discovered her missing were slim.

Again Connelly tried to reason with him. "Sir, it cannot be in the stars of fate that such a sacrifice fail of its reward. We must move these men out. Every minute of delay adds to our danger."

"What would have they done to her?" Benton mouthed the words more so than asked them out loud, yet everyone understood what he said and knew the answer: *They would have hanged her without saying grace.*

Benton, with lifeless, unseeing eyes, stared into the distance, then focused on Connelly. With a nod, Connelly gave the command to move out, the colonel going through the motions as he tried to make sense of the unkind lesson Providence had provided.

* * *

Where men had been preparing for a battle to the death, they now rode mostly unmolested past the most narrow and dangerous part of the peninsula. Frequent halts were called to send scouts ahead to ensure against any surprises on the road, but for the most part, they rode undisturbed. When they were close to the mouth of the peninsula, a few skirmishes erupted in the front, the only sign of the presence of the enemy at all. These were more minor encounters rather than fights, as if the enemy was feeling pressured by the swift progress of Benton's men—not trying to stop their advance.

With their safety practically guaranteed, the command's spirits seemed to lift. No one could really believe or accept the possibility that Lieutenant Duvall could have met with bad fortune. She was too young, too vibrant, and too virtuous—and too impeccably pure.

Even Colonel Benton convinced himself she would return, because he could not accept any other outcome. He still possessed a consciousness of her closeness, of her spirit, and knew she must be near. It was a feeling so elusive he was unable to describe it, yet so powerful he was forced to recognize it. The feeling sustained him, uplifted him, and gave him hope. In fact, scouts were told to be on the lookout and to bring her back—as if she was just lost out there somewhere and was actually coming back. It was a courageous thing for Benton to attempt, and he succeeded very well in maintaining the illusion that the absence of the one upon whom his entire universe revolved was only temporary.

But after a full despairing day with no news, a new general order was issued at the request of Major Connelly: "Pickets are expected to pass without the countersign, and scouts to bring in without delay, anyone with information concerning Sarah I. Duvall—be they friend or foe."

Even with no information forthcoming, Benton refused to allow his mind to ponder the possible implications of her absence or accept the possibility that it was permanent. He had too much to do and too many lives depending on him to consider or contemplate her fate. To dwell for even a moment on Sarah Duvall would render him unfit for duty.

Chapter 20

These things have I written unto you that believe in the name of the
Son of God; that ye may know that ye have eternal life, and that
ye may believe in the name of the son of God.
—1 John 5, 11–13

It was the first full night of sleep for General Benton, and it seemed he had no sooner laid his head upon the pillow when he heard the challenge by the pickets and a horse come galloping in. He sat straight up, and in another instant, he was outside his tent where his eyes were drawn to a strange light that glowed by the road. It seemed odd, because the light was neither of night or day, nor of twilight or dawn. No moon or stars were visible to him, yet it was not dark.

As if by magic, a figure appeared out of nowhere, and in an instant, he knew it was Sarah. She wore a grave expression as if having news of utmost importance to tell him, yet for a long moment, she did not speak. "I had to go," she finally said. "I had to go."

Benton took a hurried step toward her. "But you came back! At last! You've come back!"

Sarah sighed heavily and he noticed that a peculiar aura of light surrounding her seemed to flicker and spark. Her face, soft and angel-like, appeared strange and unearthly, yet when she walked toward him and touched his arm, she felt real. "You know I can't stay, Doug. I only came to say good-bye..."

"No... Sarah—"

He reached for her, but as he did, a sound like a thunder clap fell upon him and a dark curtain dropped, instantly blocking all light and turning the night completely black. He stepped forward, groping in the dark for her—but she was gone.

"Sarah! Don't leave! *Come back!*"

Men from throughout the makeshift camp ran from where they slept to find their leader pale and shaking.

"Did you see her?" Benton pointed into the darkness. "Stop her!" Benton ran out onto the road and looked frantically both ways. "Did you see her?" He turned and scanned the crowd of faces all staring at him with pitiful eyes. "She was right here!" He turned in a circle with both palms facing upward as if he could not understand how she had vanished.

"Sir, I was sitting by that campfire, right there," one of the men finally said. "I didn't see so much as a hoot owl come by."

Benton stood in the darkness, gasping for breath, trying to erase the vision from his mind. Staring up at the stars that now twinkled overhead, he tried to comprehend the finality of what he had seen—or thought he had seen. "The sacrifice," he whispered, "it is too much." He did not realize he had said the words loud enough for anyone to hear until Major Connelly came up behind him and placed his hand on his shoulder. The gesture was a powerful one from this reserved and respected man.

"No." Connelly gave his shoulder a gentle squeeze. "Look around at the faces of these two hundred men, many with wives and children—all with loved ones at home. Think of the sacrifice as a great one, but don't believe for a moment that it was in vain."

Until now, Benton had been solitary in his grief and regrets, but now he felt the urgent need to share his deepest sorrows. He spoke from the heart, for the first time admitting to himself she was not coming back. "It seems impossible that one so holy could die such an inglorious death," he murmured.

Major Connelly merely nodded. It seemed he had already accepted what Benton had been trying to deny. She was gone.

Gone for good.

* * *

For more than a week there had been no word, no sign. Rumors chased each other, always vague and elusive, often contradictory, and always exaggerated. The gaiety and laughter that had once been on everyone's lips was now seldom ever heard. It seemed a vital glow had died out of the campfires and the eyes that once beamed so brightly around them. It was just one long, lifeless day after another. The men continued to try to comfort Benton, telling him that time heals all wounds, but the feeling of loss did not leave him or even diminish. It only deepened like a gaping wound that would not heal. She had filled the camp with her presence, her energy, her strength—and that spirit, that force, had departed with her.

Despite the facts facing him, Benton continued to wait minute by minute as hours turned to days, listening for footsteps that never came, praying for the voice that appeared to be gone from his world forever. Although sometimes when undertaking the duties and responsibilities of war he would become himself again, his mind, for the most part, had become overwhelmed and benumbed by days of accumulated agony.

Even after the camp returned to its normal routine, it was still obvious that something was missing. It was not just Sarah's physical presence that was gone—though Lord knows that hole was big enough. It was also that elusive something that she had conveyed to all she had met—comfort, inspiration, a solemn wisdom that stirred and encouraged each man to do and be more.

Benton had found a new Bible in her saddlebag and had taken to reading it for solace, trying to find the answers she had said were written so clearly there. When he first gazed upon the dented button pinned neatly to a bookmark, he knew in his heart that a special bond had formed between them. That she had put the reminder of him in such a place that she would gaze upon it daily was a thought so sweet that he obsessed on it. But when in his silent moments he thought of her goodness and her courage and grace, it seemed to him it was not so much the will of God that had taken her from this world, but the utter wickedness of man.

Benton began to nurse a futile rage and ever-deepening sorrow that went beyond all hope and past all comfort. Nothing he did could erase her calm, serene face, or her solemn and holy eyes. The last words they spoke were the last words they spoke, and when he remembered the concern in her voice and disappointment in her eyes that night, he knew he would never forget those few precious moments as long as he lived.

He began to analyze every memory, every token of the past, and filled his heart with recollections so that he might never forget the words and inspiration she gave him. It made his heart ache anew to recall how he had missed her all those months between their brief visits. And now their separation was by a much greater barrier than mere distance.

Days began to drag by like a painful dream, making Benton wonder—along with many of the other men of the command—if she would have dealt him this hurt had she known what a tormenting wound it would be.

Chapter 21

*For my part, whatever anguish of spirit it might cost, I am willing to
know the whole truth; to know the worst, and to provide for it.*
—*Patrick Henry*

B ack on the mainland, but still far from where they called home,
Benton's command encamped to rest and await new orders. The
daily routine and monotony of camp life soon returned as the
tedious chores and customary tasks became commonplace once again.
Local citizens opened their doors and offered to provide every comfort
to their hero soldiers, and of course, feminine society was once again
widely accessible.

Most of the men expected Benton to drown himself in liquor to forget the pain of that expedition, or to surround himself with women to
prove his worth, but he did neither. He attended the social gatherings
that required his attendance—but only as long as was necessary to sat-
isfy the hostess. He was still courteously polite to women, but even that
was forced, as if he took no pleasure in it.

Balls and social gatherings, once so celebrated and admired, were
now tributes Colonel Benton endured rather than encouraged or enjoyed. Even his men felt the difference. Events that had once been filled
with boisterous toasts and discordant songs were now quiet and subdued
affairs. Something in the colonel's eyes prevented anyone from refer-
ring to the past, and time had not made it easier.

Benton had turned inward, the gay signs of happiness no longer
reaching his lips, and the haunted look of loss never leaving his eyes. He
smiled only by necessity and laughed not at all. As the hours and days
wore on, he appeared disheveled; the clothes he wore appeared flung
upon him—or perhaps had never been removed. It was disheartening to
watch this man changed so drastically by war. He was a still a warrior,
but a nobler flame and purer spirit animated him now.

His men noticed that Benton spent a great deal of time in front of
his tent, supposedly working on reports, but most of the time, sitting
with pen in hand, forgetting to write, his gaze focused vacantly on the
horizon. He would gaze at whatever was in front of him, motionless and

silent, apparently weighing and contrasting what ought to be with what was. Although unheard of before, it was now quite common to see Benton in the pastor's tent at night, sitting with hands crossed and speaking in low tones by lantern light. A few of the men even claimed to have witnessed him all alone on his knees in the quietness of the morning mist, with his head bowed, his lips moving in fervent prayer.

Tonight, though, with one of the local homes lit from top to bottom and with dozens of young women roaming the halls, Colonel Benton looked tormented and extremely uncomfortable. Although the colonel had always moved at a hurricane pace, eager to flirt and to dance, it now seemed a great exertion for him just to talk and socialize with members of the opposite sex.

Major Connelly watched Benton silently from the doorway and knew there was but one touch, one voice that could sooth the colonel's pain from the past that stalked him. Surrounded now by beautiful women, Benton's eyes remained cast with a look of loneliness, seeming to take more interest in the flames of the fire than the conversation going on around him. Every now and then he nodded, but it was apparent to Connelly he only did so when he thought it called for.

It was the first time in all the years of war that Benton looked defeated or overwhelmed, and there was something painfully touching in the weakness of this strong man.

A white-faced lieutenant suddenly appeared at the door, looking left and right searching for someone. When he saw Connelly, he strode toward him and shoved a piece of paper into his hand. "A communication for Colonel Benton."

"He's right there." Connelly started to hand the piece of paper back as he nodded toward the colonel.

"I think you'd better deliver it, sir." The lieutenant swallowed hard. "They're holding the man they found it on for interrogation. I'll wait outside to escort the colonel." The lieutenant saluted, turned on his heel, and disappeared as quickly as he had appeared.

Connelly glanced down at the unsealed missive merely to see from whom it had come, but he could not stop reading when he saw the scratchy writing of the hastily written note. The major closed his eyes as the breath rushed out of him in an audible groan. When he opened them, he saw Colonel Benton walking toward him with an intent, strained look in his eyes.

"That for me, Major?"

Connelly nodded. "Yes, sir." He paused a moment. "Perhaps you should read it outside. The person who delivered it is being held by the pickets."

Connelly watched Benton's composure crack visibly. His face turned ashen, and his hand noticeably trembled when he took the piece of paper, as if just by touching it he could predict what it said. He did not look at it right away, but took Connelly's advice and stepped out onto the portico. As Benton read the missive, Connelly watched him pass an unsteady hand across his eyes, like one who is awakened abruptly from a deep sleep and doesn't quite understand where he is or what he is doing. Connelly replayed each word in his head as Benton's eyes moved back and forth slowly across the communication as he read and reread each word:

One Sarah I. Duvall, a civilian, was captured and detained upon suspicion of previous duplicity with the enemy. In the subsequent search, she was found to be in possession of a dispatch containing information about the strength and movements of military forces and was therefore accused as a spy.

She was consequently tried as a spy.

She was condemned as a spy.

And you may rest assured, she was hung as a spy.

I have the honor to be Colonel Clayton M. Foxx, U.S. Army

Benton swallowed hard in an obvious effort to suppress the groan that rose from his throat. He trembled with the suppression of emotion, and Connelly felt he could almost see his heart die within him.

"Right this way, sir."

Benton began to walk quietly behind the captain of the pickets as if in a daze. Behind him, news of what was transpiring began to be whispered from one to another in the great hall. In mere moments, the news had spread throughout the room, and in another moment, the entire house was empty of men. No one asked any questions, because the silent tread of their commander told the men everything. As if by an unspoken missive, an aspect of sorrow and silence enveloped the entire camp.

Just as Benton and Connelly stepped into a clearing, the sound of an interrogation already in progress fell upon their ears.

"I didn't have nothing to do with her hanging, I swear!"

Benton stopped in mid-step, and his gaze seemed so bright with such unwavering calm that for a moment, those in attendance wondered if he had heard. But without warning, he lunged toward the man sitting on a log with his hands tied behind him. Grabbing the unsuspecting prisoner by the throat with one hand, Benton's lifted him off the ground, and shook him like a ragdoll. Never did fingers more tenaciously grip a throat.

"What did you say?"

The prisoner, whether from the fact that he had no air, or that he was looking into the raging eyes of Colonel Benton became instantly speechless.

"You lie!" Benton bore the man to the ground in one swoop, placed his knee on his chest, and cocked his revolver behind the man's ear. Inured as he was to danger and accustomed as he was to the horrors of war, it did not appear he could accept the reality before him.

The captain of the pickets came running over and put his hand on the colonel's shoulder to calm him. "Sir, you are doing nothing to help his memory. Have mercy!"

"*God* is for mercy," Benton said in a low, violent tone. "*I* am for justice."

The prisoner, profuse with sweat, trembled and shook so as to be rendered nearly unconscious.

"Colonel Benton." Major Connelly's voice was low and direct behind him. "You will not get the information you seek that way. This man came to us of his own accord."

Benton lifted his eyes, but it was apparent he was not really seeing, not really thinking. A few moments passed before he came to his senses and pushed himself off the man. "Go on then. Speak!"

The prisoner looked hesitantly at the intent faces around him as he struggled to his knees. Connelly helped him back over to the log, where he practically collapsed, his head bent between his legs. "I didn't know they was going to hang her," he said. "I swear!"

"Hang who?" Connelly did the questioning now as Benton stood silently watching, breathing heavily. No one could tell what he suffered. They could only guess from his trembling form and his ashen face that it was overpowering.

"It was the widow woman." The man took a deep heaving breath, seeming to recall the scene. "I don't know her name." The last words were whispered, and he put his head back down between his knees as if to escape the image. "They told me to go fetch her," he finally said. "Everyone else had moved out because they feared an attack. There was only one wagon left."

"Go on." Connelly glanced over at Benton, but his countenance was set in stone.

"Captain Delbert, he tied her hands…and he asked her if she wished to take the oath of allegiance or accept her fate."

Connelly swallowed hard and felt the man beside him lean forward to hear what the prisoner would say next. The rest of the men had been silent through this and remained so now.

"She said—" The man paused and bit his lip.

"Out with it, man!" Colonel Benton, his shoulders square with barely controlled rage, roared.

All who were gathered there knew…feared…what her answer had been. Deep down where the spirit meets the bone, they knew she would not answer the enemy's questions nor submit to their authority by taking the oath—even at the cost of life.

"She said she would accept her fate, that her honor had already been pledged."

A surge of breath was released simultaneously be those who heard the words. Benton turned his back on the man, his chest heaving as he clenched and unclenched his hands, trying to gain control of his emotions.

"Then what happened?" Connelly tried to sound commanding, but his voice was low and grave.

"Then he put a noose around her neck and told her to stand in the back of the wagon. I-I asked what he was doing and he said, 'Rope justice for a damned spy.'" Tears began streaming down the man's face.

"He ordered me into the wagon, and then he slapped the horses...."

The prisoner began rocking back and forth as he recalled the memory. There was nothing for a long moment but the prisoner's sobbing, while grown men with closed eyes tried hard not to imagine a scene they had convinced themselves had not occurred.

"It was dark," he said, staring into space now. "I jumped off the back of the wagon. They didn't see me." His voice got so low the men had to lean forward to hear. "I cut her down. It was only a few minutes, but she was so pale...like a ghost."

"Was she dead?"

"I don't know. She looked dead. But I-I-I didn't have time to see. I had to go back!" He looked up at the faces surrounding him. "I had to go back to the wagon, don't you understand? They would have shot me for desertion!"

The group remained silent, but the man spoke again, mumbling as if talking to himself.

"I just couldn't let her hang there like that," he said, as his shoulders shook with sobs again.

His story had taken only a few minutes to tell, but the grief and suffering it caused would last much longer. On the surface, everything around them was the same—the moon, the stars, the eerie silence of the night—yet everything was completely and irrevocably different.

Benton's voice came out of the darkness, sounding strange and detached like something other than human. "Untie him."

When his men had done as they were told, the prisoner stood quaking visibly before him.

"Take me there."

The prisoner looked up at Benton questioningly.

"To the tree." Benton's eyes drilled into the man, determined, unwavering and unearthly. "Take me there."

Chapter 22

If God has made this world so fair,
Where sin and death abound,
How beautiful beyond compare
Will paradise be found!
—James Montgomery

With grief-blind eyes, Benton rode at the back of his escort so that none could see his face. For weeks he had awakened each morning with a pain in his chest, but now that aching anguish and emptiness had turned to a torturous hurt that threatened to undo him.

As he gazed around him at the crystal dewdrops adorning the trees and listened to the muted conversations of his men, it seemed unnatural that the world could go on spinning, and the clock keep on ticking. Abundant life flowed all around, yet he had no part of it. For him, the black flood of numbing despair and agony encompassed all else in the world.

Benton's mind involuntarily went back to those moments in time when he could have said something or done something to prevent this tragedy—mere seconds that, having said nothing or done nothing, had wrought that which could never be undone.

Just thinking about the long and torturous days to come, about the bleak, endless march of time made Benton cringe. He knew there would forever be a constant gnawing of torment, more deadly and bitter than all the perils of war, because he loved Sarah Duvall with an intensity that could never be repeated in a lifetime. The grief, the utter dread, spread through him like an illness—it did not kill him, but made him wish that it would.

When the group came to a sudden halt, he urged his horse to the front.

"He thinks we're getting close, Colonel," Connelly said. "He's trying to get his bearings now."

The group moved out again, but there was barely a sound now, save the creaking of the saddles, the steady tramping of hooves, and an occasional sneeze from one of the horses. The men appeared impatient, fidgeting in their saddles while Benton sat gazing straight ahead, trying to master his emotions and the situation. After just a few more minutes, the Union soldier drew back on his reins and pointed. "There it is."

All eyes from the staff went to the tree, first to the trunk which seemed too small to carry out such an evil duty, then slowly, in unison, each gaze lifted to the limb above, where a piece of frayed and tangled rope had wrapped itself over and over upon a branch. Where all had been still and eerily quiet, a wind with bone-seeking chill in it suddenly stirred from some invisible place, causing branches to rub together and groan so that even Nature seemed to join in the somber event.

During this time of war, a mangled and torn body would cause only a passing glance and not a moment's thought from battle-hardened soldiers such as these. But this rope, swinging above their heads in its ghastly suspension between heaven and earth, created an overwhelming emotional response from those who gazed upon it. All sat still as death and rested their eyes where last hers had rested. Nothing could lessen the intensity of the heroic and horrific act that had occurred here, or soften the haunting cruelty of the sacrificial scene.

A sudden surge of nausea all but choked Benton as he clung to his horse. He closed his eyes, trying to blot out the picture of her composed, serene face hanging there in the dark. His ears rang. His heart stopped. He couldn't move or breathe. But even putting a hand in front of his tightly closed eyes could not stop the images that continued to appear. Her sweet voice echoed with every beat of his throbbing breast, and he selfishly wished he had died in advance.

Knowing that others watched him, Benton urged his horse forward. After taking a few deep breaths, he dismounted slowly, trying hard to control his emotions—but the calm exterior cost him. He sank to his knees, unable to stand, and touched the bare ground beneath the tree with his hand incredulously. He could not help but picture her with the cold dew on her eyelashes, and her cheeks as pale and cold as death. He had refrained from thinking of her thus, lying with her delicate skin against the damp unforgiving ground, but now, involuntarily, the image formed before him, and he uttered a cry that only those who have heard the roar of a wounded lion can conceive.

Confused, Benton looked around as if expecting to see her body—or perhaps a relic of it—but there was nothing but the rope to testify to the atrocity that had taken place here. Perhaps the enemy had recovered it, or a kind passerby had buried it, but in any case, this was the spot where her spirit had left its earthly bounds, and it was all that remained.

Continuing to stare in confusion at the stark, barren scene, Benton could feel his whole being straining toward something he could neither see nor comprehend; something that hovered above and beyond, out of his reach, yet so near he felt he could almost touch it. He swallowed the bile rising in his throat, wishing he could console himself with the thought that her death had been a swift blotting out as in battle—perhaps *that* he could have accepted. Instead, her last moments had been a ceremony of horror and shame, which unfolded before him now in a scene so despicable and revolting that he shuttered at the thought. She, who had unsparingly doled out spiritual nourishment to his men, whose destiny it had been to protect the fate of so many, and who represented nothing but white-robed Angelic peace, had been taken from this earth by an act repulsive to the senses.

With deliberate effort, Benton stood and, without a word, walked back to his horse. Lifting an ax from his saddle, he strode back to the tree and swung the instrument into the wood. The sound of the ax head burying itself into the bark echoed through the air with an explosive *thud* that seemed to reverberate through the souls of those watching. He swung it again and again, faster now and more furiously.

Connelly dismounted and grabbed his arm. "Take a rest, sir. We can finish it for you."

Benton pushed him away and began swinging the ax again. Slivers of wood flew furiously through the air, and drops of sweat sprayed from his forehead with every motion. His men watched silently as the ax landed time and time again deep into the tree until finally there was a loud crack and it began to give way.

Red-faced and soaked, Benton fell to his knees in exhaustion as the tree groaned and creaked in retaliation before falling with a crash. Steam from the chilly air rose from Benton's heated body and flowed in puffs from his mouth as he panted, creating a ghostly and ghastly image in the dim light of the forest. When Connelly stepped forward with a knife, Benton cut the rope, and closed his eyes as he felt the course piece of hemp scrape against his hand. He had to accept it now—she was one with the sacred dust. "God of mercy," he whispered, "yield me the power to make a sacrifice equally as brave."

Before it had not seemed real, but now there was proof in the harsh, brutal texture of the rope in his hand. Reality washed over him with a peculiar mixture of despair and bewilderment that he had spent that last evening with absolutely no sense of her fate, while what was to come was coming. Try as he might, Benton could recall nothing in her countenance or her demeanor that indicated an awareness of any impending danger or fear. He remembered only a calm, daring, unflinching look of unearthly calm. How could he have not seen death shining from those glorious eyes? And how could she have escaped to heaven before he could adequately tell her what she meant to him?

Colonel Connelly lifted his hands into the air beside him and closed his eyes while the others in the group bowed their heads. "Heavenly Father, we ask for blessings for our comrade Sarah Duvall, whose fortune, honor and life were laid willingly upon the altar of her country in its hour of trial. God grant that the lesson of devotion and loyalty be not lost, and may her beautiful spirit, through the mercy of God, rest in peace." He paused and glanced at Benton. "And Dear Lord we pray that this be our comfort and our consolation: Sarah Duvall is where she deserves to be, and where a merciful Lord wanted her to be. So give us the strength to bear the loss and say, *His will be done.* Amen."

The solemn finality of the prayer left the men's cheeks damp, but the gloomy day made it hard to discern whether the tears were theirs or those of Mother Nature. Connelly lowered his hands and placed one on Benton's shoulder. "Be consoled that Death has placed her soul beyond human malice, and she is in a place where she can forever rejoice with the Savior she so dutifully served."

Benton nodded as he thought of the hardships and tumult she had endured during her short life, and the weight she had carried on her fragile shoulders. If not comforted by the thought that she was now in Heaven, he was at least a little less miserable. But oh, how his hands trembled at the desire to see and touch her once more!

"Yes, she belongs to the ages now," Benton said, his voice trembling, "though I preferred it when she belonged to us." He stared silently another moment at the rope in his hand and then began to walk toward his horse, the tragedy of having no grave at which to grieve settling upon him like a heavy weight.

"Colonel, may I have a word?" Connelly steered Benton away from the other men so they could talk privately.

"Sir, we all understand the depth of your pain. The loss is a blow to us all, but…"

Benton remained unmoving, staring into the nothingness that lay before him. *Did* he know the depth of his pain? Some compelling power or emotion had urged her to the sacrifice, and he had failed to see it, discarding her forewarning for the sake of his own pride and reputation.

Connelly paused a moment apparently unsure how to continue and then blundered right on. "Sir, we must in this time of great peril, *particularly* in this time of great peril, be resolved to forge ahead, to focus solely on the task before us. She would wish it. It is our duty to be worthy of what she gave to us."

When Benton still did not respond, he blurted out what he was trying to say. "What occurred is a tragedy. What *could have* occurred? A catastrophe. She is gone, sir. It is time to forget." Benton reacted by exhaling loudly as if he had just been punched in the stomach, and holding his tightly clenched fists by his side. His breathing came in gasps rather than breaths as he made an obvious effort to control his emotions and his rage. Then, as if she were standing beside him, he heard her voice clearly in his ears. *"Observe what Christ says. Make his conduct your example."*

"Yes, she is gone," Benton said after staring again at the rope he held in his clenched hand for a few long moments. He took a step closer to Connelly, his eyes glistening madly in the early morning light. "For the sake of the men, Major Connelly, I will move on." His voice quivered as he spoke. "But I shall *never* forget!" He swallowed hard, then walked back toward his waiting men. "Parole him," he said, nodding toward the Union soldier with a look of searing agony and regret.

Benton tied the rope onto his saddle and mounted, waiting patiently for the rest of the men to follow. When Connelly was ready, he rode up beside the colonel and leaned toward him. "Sir, I noticed a path to a house a little ways back. Perhaps we should stop there for some nourishment and warmth."

Benton nodded. "Lead the way, Major."

Connelly saluted, but before moving his horse forward, he paused a moment and touched the rope that was tied to Benton's saddle. Without a word, the other men of the detail moved their horses into single file behind Connelly and silently touched the rope as they passed by. Although painful to feel, it served as a way to remove all doubt about the course of events, and cleanse them of burdens held tightly but best let go.

For some, the rope served as a source of inspiration, for others a way to recall a lost comrade—but for most, it was a way to find the courage to continue the fight, and perhaps make a silent pledge to avenge the death of one so brave. The piece of hemp seemed to become a symbol of their unity for the mere fact that they had nothing else of her to see or touch or hold.

Chapter 23

Be thou assured, if words be made of breath,
And breath be made of life, I have no life to breathe.
—Shakespeare, Hamlet (Act 3, Scene 4)

The troop moved silently through the shadows as the sun continued its climb above the treetops. The distance to their destination was only about four miles, but the time, as far as Major Connelly was concerned, was an eternity. The day was raw and cloudy, and whether from the damp air or the deep gloom that surrounded him, he felt chilled to the bone. As he had predicted though, the trail off the road led to a large farmhouse that showed bountiful amounts of smoke pouring forth from the chimney. Before dismounting near a pine tree, Connelly ordered one of the men to knock, which brought an older woman and young girl to the door.

"Pardon the intrusion," Connelly said, leaning forward in his saddle, and lifting his hat. "Could you spare a meal for Colonel Benton and his staff? There are but eight of us."

The woman eyed Connelly suspiciously and then swept her gaze across the group, pausing as she watched Benton dismount wearily from his horse. "I suppose we can feed eight." Her lips held no smile, but her offer seemed genuine. "There's corn in the barn for the horses."

"We're mighty obliged." Connelly replaced his hat and nodded toward the far corner of the yard. "I can see this must be a difficult time for you. Our condolences for your loss."

The woman's gaze darted nervously to the fresh mound of dirt and handmade cross near a small grove of trees. "She ain't no one of ours really." The little girl who sat swinging her legs in a chair from behind the woman spoke up. "Just some stranger we found."

"Hush child!" the woman scolded, as she watched the men who had been unsaddling their horses seem to freeze in place.

"I-I-I beg your pardon?" Connelly said.

"My husband will be home shortly." The woman turned to go into the house as if the conversation were over.

"But, ma'am," Connelly said, dismounting and rushing up the steps with a great rattle of spurs, blocking her path back into the house. "What did she mean *she* was a stranger to you? Whose body lies yonder?"

The woman, obviously flustered now, looked up at the serious face of Connelly and then to the anxious and penetrating eyes of the rest of the group. "It's just what she said. We don't know her…anything about her. She was dead. It's a terrible thing, but she was dead, and my husband buried her."

The woman ended the conversation by going back inside the house. Connelly quickly turned to Benton, who had stopped unsaddling his horse and seemed to have forgotten what he was doing or how to do it. He leaned now upon his mount. It appeared that without the support, he would be unable to stand.

"Sir, Lieutenant Janney will tend to your horse," Connelly offered.

Benton did not answer. Instead, he turned and stared over his shoulder at the mound of dirt as if it were coming in and out of focus. He looked dazed and incoherent, like a man just awakening from a terrible dream. His face, already pallid from weeks of anguish and grief, took on a shade of gray that deepened the ashen hue.

"Sir, your horse," Connelly said, a little louder.

Again, Benton did not respond. Connelly could see he was breathing heavily and the reins in his hand were literally shaking. He continued to lean against Vince, apparently fighting for calm, and passed a hand over his eyes as if to shut out a vision he couldn't bear to see. "Colonel, you are tired. Go in and get some refreshment." Connelly pried the reins from his unresponsive hand. "I'll take care of Vince."

When Benton heaved with a deep sigh, Connelly studied his appearance. His face did not appear like Benton's face had just a few months earlier. It was grim and set like marble. And when he spoke, his voice was strange like his face. "No, I…ah, I don't think I'm hungry. You go on."

Connelly felt sorry for Benton, but knew the colonel had to face letting go of a past that no longer existed—and face it alone. The vacancy she had left was not a thing tucked away in Benton's subconscious, dormant and inactive. It was obviously a thing that controlled his every waking moment, and possessed and tormented him in sleeping ones. Connelly nodded in understanding, and motioned for the others to follow, leaving Benton standing alone in the yard.

* * *

When the men had disappeared into the house and barn, Benton walked hesitantly toward the mound of dirt, the very earth seeming to roil and roll beneath him. No sound reached his ears other than a loud, pulsing thump that he realized was his own heartbeat, pumping his body full of terrible, poisonous despair. Staring at the cold unadorned pile of dirt, he shuddered as he recalled his last glimpse of her—the proud deportment, the defiant chin, the sad yet knowing eyes—all now crushed by the hand of death. "In the name of mercy," he murmured as he sank to his knees, "turn back the hands of time."

He choked as he tried to suppress the strangled hopeless feeling of grief and despair that consumed him. There were times over the past weeks when he had told himself that nothing mattered except that he had known her—hadn't had to die without knowing there was a noble, gracious spirit such as hers in the world. And then came times when life seemed too painful and empty and meaningless to care to go on. Times like this, when he had to think of her as an angel, trailing forever a marble robe.

Tears began to fall, a mixture of sorrow and love mingling down to seep into the dust, causing him to fight the urge to creep into the ground beside her and die. He realized—too late—that of all the women he had known in his life, he had never known a love like this—an eternal love that knew no bounds. Benton dug his fingers into the cold dirt as if he could pull her broken body from the arms of death. But he knew he was powerless to do so, and so he sat in silence with his hands flat upon the mound of dirt as if to feel her. Closing his eyes, he imagined her sleeping in that earthen bed, her spirit rising to be with her Heavenly Father. And then his mind drifted to what lay ahead—for painful as the present was to endure, the future now loomed still darker.

"The only battle I cared to win, I have lost," he murmured, putting his hand on the rugged cross, as he thought ashamedly how he had once valued his own reputation and selfish needs. He swallowed hard and shook his head. *This is not to be borne. I cannot go on.*

"What's the matter, mister?"

Benton looked over his shoulder at the young girl leaning against a tree with her head tilted to one side, studying him intently. He sighed deeply. "The one who sleeps here…was a friend of mine."

"A *friend*?" the girl perked up. "You mean you didn't try to kill her?"

Benton stood and faced the girl. "Of course not. Why would you think such a thing?"

"Well, 'cause, I reckin' she was a spy or somethin'," the girl said. "Grandpa says she musta been. Says that's why they strung her up." She walked over and stared at the mound of dirt. "But he don't know which side done it. That's why he—"

"Louisa! Louisa! Come here this instant!"

The girl's grandmother stood on the porch with her hands on her hips. Benton followed the girl toward the house in a daze, but he paused once and looked back at the mound before continuing on. When he reached the porch, he removed his hat. "If you don't mind, ma'am, we would like to take the body with us…for a proper burial and all."

"No!"

Benton looked at the woman's distressed look in confusion. "Is there a problem, ma'am?"

"I mean… um… that's impossi— it's just that my husband will be here later. I prefer you discuss it with him."

Something suddenly struck Benton as odd, and then something else hit him like the wild kick of a horse. It might have been instinct, or it might have been impulse, but he got down on one knee and grabbed the girl's arms before she started up the steps. "What did you mean *try* to kill her?" He shook her gently but firmly. "Is she not dead? Where is she?"

The girl's grandmother came rushing down and grabbed Benton's shoulder. "Take your hands off her! What are you doing?"

By now, some of the men who were just making their way to the house from the barn, rushed to the woman's aid to help restrain Benton, afraid he had lost his mind. "Your husband found her." Benton's large frame shook them off as if he barely knew they were there. He did not ask a question so much as make a statement, and his tone was severe and measured.

The woman merely nodded. She appeared to have difficulty looking into his eyes.

"And she had been hanged."

"Yes...well, uh...it appeared so." The woman stood twisting the apron she wore with nervous hands.

"And so your husband dug that hole—"

"Yes, he dug the hole and buried her—it was the Christian thing to do! We don't know her; she was nothing to us! Whatever she done... whatever law she broke...she was nothing to us!"

"You're lying!" Benton yelled, lunging up the steps. "She's still alive! I know she is!"

Men who had already entered the house came rushing out and tried again to restrain the colonel, while the woman retreated to the far side of the porch. "No...no," she said, wringing her hands and looking at the questionings stares of the men around her. Her face had drained of its color. She looked as if she were about to faint.

Benton shrugged off the men who held his arms and stood just inches from the woman. He knew now with certainty. Far down in his soul where such things are divined...he knew. "Your husband dug that grave because he recognized whoever hung her would come back looking for the body!"

"No, please, you must wait for my husband. He'll explain." She began sobbing into her apron.

"Your husband wanted you to be able to point to that grave and tell them she was dead!" Benton could feel blood pulsing against his temples, yet his legs felt suddenly weak. "Is there a body in that grave? My men can have it open in ten minutes time."

"Colonel! It is time to bury the past. Leave the grave closed!" Connelly put a restraining hand on his shoulder.

"No, you musn't!" The woman put her face in her hands as if to hide from the intensity of his gaze as she talked. "We were only trying to protect her...poor innocent thing!"

Benton reached out to grab the porch railing to steady himself. "She's here then?" His voice was now hoarse and cracking.

"Yes," she said, taking deep breaths as if trying to gain control. "We thought it best that any strangers we meet think she's dead." She looked up at him with pleading eyes. "It's dangerous out here all alone, you know. We didn't want no trouble for saving her."

"Where is she?" Benton's voice was low and barely audible.

"She's upstairs. But I must warn you…"

Benton didn't hear the rest. He was already halfway up the stairs. Breathing heavily, he pushed open the first door he saw and stared at the form sitting silently in a chair by a blazing fire. For a moment, he just blinked in the dim light, trying to let his mind catch up to the unfolding events.

"Sarah," he finally said. The figure continued to stare straight ahead as if she had not heard him. "Sarah. It's Douglas…Douglas Benton." He walked in and knelt down, lightly touching her arm—more of a way to convince himself she was real than to get her attention.

She turned her head slowly, staring at him curiously as if to recapture some distant, lost memory that could not be brought forth. Although her face was partially in shadow, he could see she now possessed the wide-eyed look of a child rather than the wise and reserved appearance that had been so evident on her countenance before. When he spoke her name yet again, it brought no sign of recognition or response. She continued to stare with unseeing eyes without the slightest evidence that she heard his voice or recognized her name.

Benton gazed into her eyes a few long moments, refusing to believe that the reconciliation that should have been joyful and renewing was not. "Sarah. I'm glad to see you."

She nodded, but exhibited no indication that she understood what he had said. His gloomy eyes drifted to the black-and-blue ring that encircled her neck. Benton stood and turned to Mrs. Ramsey who had entered the room. "I cannot thank you enough for what you have done to protect her." He swallowed hard at the thought that Sarah Duvall had been pulled back to earth by charitable hands, yet she did not appear to be aware of it—and perhaps did not even desire it."I would like my surgeon to look at her."

"Of course. We only wish to help her."

Benton looked back and saw that Sarah still stared at the place where he had knelt beside her, and he wondered if she had actually gazed at him or only at the space he had occupied. In her eyes, he saw nothing of the life she once had lived—only the death she seemed to have already died.

Descending the stairs slowly, Benton avoided looking into the faces of his men. He did not speak, but he did not need to. The tears on his cheeks, mingled with the look of joy and anguish on his countenance, made commentary unnecessary.

Benton pushed through the door and out into the cool, morning air. She was alive, but was she really there? He choked back a sob at the thought of telling his men that the reunion was bittersweet. The one from whom they had parted, the one for whom they had offered up so many prayers, had come back—and yet perhaps really was gone for good.

Chapter 24

I must lose myself in action lest I wither in despair.
—Tennyson

December 1864

With winter underway, Benton made the decision to go into winter quarters and chose the palatial Ramsey house for the grounds. A fine brick house near the home where Sarah had been found, it offered security and comfort at every turn. With a long sloping yard, a grove of trees for firewood, and a view that reached for miles, it was the perfect spot for spending the gloomy months that preceded the spring campaign.

Benton also had chosen the spot because of the quiet quarters it offered Sarah, who was welcomed into the home with open arms by the matron of the household. Between the solace the home provided and the gentle ministrations of Mrs. Ramsey, Benton hoped Sarah could make some sort of recovery. He knew she needed all the help she could get. The girl they had found seemed so detached at first, so frail and weak, that it seemed to him there was hardly enough flesh upon her bones to keep body and soul from parting ways.

But as time passed, her strength began to return little by little, and he saw her walking the grounds more and more often. Despite the fact that she did not talk, the men of his command made every effort to coax a smile or even a laugh from her. She was ever surrounded with a contingent of officers and soldiers who wished to be the first to spark a memory, to see the glint of life sparkle once again from within those blue eyes.

By January, her health had improved steadily, though not as swiftly as Benton would have liked. Other than receiving occasional updates from Mrs. Ramsey, Benton rarely had the opportunity to see Sarah and never made the effort to talk to her. He stayed busy in the outbuilding he used as headquarters or out on short scouts, his guilt and his remorse overcoming him when he thought of the sacrifice she had been willing to make on behalf of his command. The fact she had survived and was gaining in health was a great relief, though it did little to ease his pain or lighten his guilt. She was alive and in a place that afforded him the opportunity to feast his eyes from afar. However, he soon discovered that keeping his distance when she was this close was almost more distressing than even her loss had been.

When he sat by the campfire late at night gazing up at the warm lights of the house, Benton wondered what she must be thinking, sheltered as she was among strangers. If she was in pain, she bore it unflinchingly and uncomplainingly, according to Mrs. Ramsey. He was not surprised. She had never been one to complain about that which she could not change.

The afternoon sun had dipped low in the horizon when Benton spotted Mrs. Ramsey on the front veranda of the house. He urged his horse forward and stopped to say a few words, hoping to get an update on Sarah without asking. Sitting relaxed with one leg crooked over the front of his saddle, he felt his horse lift his head suddenly. From the corner of his eye, Benton noticed the willowy form of Sarah move onto the porch and watched as she took a seat in the shadows.

Benton paused in conversation only slightly when he saw her, but continued to watch her closely without appearing to do so. He noticed she had more color than when last he had seen her, though she still possessed that faraway, lost look in her eyes. Staring straight ahead, she displayed neither attention nor curiosity, interest nor boredom, in the conversation going on in front of her.

Without warning, Benton's horse nickered as if greeting an old friend, and bobbed his head up and down in excitement. "Calm down there, Vince," he said in a soothing tone. "Easy now."

Benton feared the sudden movement would startle or frighten Sarah, but the action seemed to touch a faint faraway chord in her memory. She stood and slowly wiped her brow as if to clear away the mists that obscured her vision. Benton remained quiet, barely daring to breathe as she tentatively walked toward him. His gaze drifted over to Mrs. Ramsey, whose pale face and wide-eyed expression revealed that she too sensed the importance of the moment and wanted to do nothing to interrupt it.

With curious eyes and parted lips, Sarah reached up and lightly touched his horse's scarred neck with her fingertips, then opened her hand and placed it flat upon the indentation of the old wound she had helped to heal. She looked up at Benton with an inquisitive light in her eyes that had not been there before, and then blinked. She seemed to be trying to make out his figure through a shaft of smoke or heavy mist.

"*Hurt.*" She removed her hand quickly, as if the sound of her own voice had startled her.

"Yes, he was hurt," Benton said softly, the music of her sweet voice nearly unraveling him. "You nursed him back to health. Do you remember?"

Sarah stared at the wound intently in an obvious effort to sort the images in her head; then her gaze lifted to the saddle and fell on the piece of rope still tied there. She swallowed hard and touched her throat, a look of deep bewilderment and confusion crossing her countenance. "Hurt," she repeated.

She looked up at him again, and it appeared she wished to say something but was unequal to the task. Turning in apparent exasperation, she disappeared into the house.

Chapter 25

Love does not die easily.
—James Bryden

S arah felt like she was on a wave, ebbing in and out, floating this way and that. It seemed time had taken her back a thousand years and she was no longer herself. Although she caught involuntary visions of angry battles, glimpses of cannons and horses, and the eerie cry of sentinels in the distance, what it all meant she could not discern. As she grew stronger and began to talk, her mind became a storehouse of names without faces to fit them and faces with no names attached. She concentrated on tearing down the invisible doors that shut her in, and slowly felt new life surging through every vein.

Over the coming days and weeks, Sarah began to make order out of the confusion, but while some of the faces became familiar in her memory, others remained dim. The man they called Colonel Benton continued to mystify her. Although she had been told it was he who ensured her every need was met, his manner conveyed only courtesy, never the tenderness that others expressed. He did not seem to try to avoid her, yet neither did he go out of his way to seek her out. In fact, he generally presented an impenetrable cold shoulder whenever they chanced to meet. If he happened to come upon her in the house, he passed her only with that token of recognition that is required, never the type of friendliness that is voluntarily bestowed. His distant manner only made Sarah's curiosity about him grow over the weeks until he had become a wonderful, irresistible mystery. Even though he treated her distantly and visited her not at all, she had begun to imagine that there was more to the man than his withdrawn attitude revealed.

Sarah thought back to the event of a week ago when a number of soldiers and women from the community had been gathered on the yard frolicking. It had been an unusually warm day for the season, and one of the women had suggested it would be nice to have a swing. Within minutes, one of the men had produced a piece of wood, and another, a length of rope. Along with the others, she had watched as the rope was thrown high over an upper limb. From the corner of her eye, she remembered seeing Colonel Benton hand his glass to someone and stride hurriedly toward her. She continued to stare at the tree limb, mesmerized and rapt, when she felt his hand on her elbow.

"Come away, Sarah," he had said in a gentle, low tone. "Follow me."

Sarah tried to turn, to follow his calming voice, but suddenly her vision began to distort. A loud roaring had commenced to take the place of the laughter in her ears, and her body had felt strangely out of control. Slowly, as if in slow motion, she had started to fall, only to be swept up effortlessly in solid, powerful arms. His strength had been immense yet comforting, and she felt herself being carried away with a sense of ease and security. She had wanted to say, "Thank you, Colonel Benton," but somehow it had come out as "Doug," and just as the roiling fog that had been floating above her descended fully, she heard a woman yell, "Give me a rope if that is what it takes to gain the colonel's attention. I shall hang myself to the highest tree!" And then she had heard no more.

* * *

The next thing Sarah remembered was awakening slowly, listening to the sound of the house before actually opening her eyes. She heard Mrs. Ramsey and the doctor conferring together in low voices, and the sound of something else. A constant, vexing *clink, clink, clink*. Opening her eyes, she saw the two speakers come slowly into focus, then, more slowly, the source of the other noise. Colonel Benton could be seen through the window pacing restlessly on the porch in his noisy cavalry boots and spurs. Yet as soon as he had been assured she was awake and resting, he had departed without a word to her, leaving her feeling more unsure and confused than before.

Besides that almost-dreamlike recollection, Sarah had other visions that came frequently and without mercy, independent of any real memory she could recall. When she was awake, she could not escape thoughts of him. When she slept, he intruded upon her dreams. In her mind, he had taken on the image of a chivalrous knight, whose devotion to her she felt rather than remembered, and wished for rather than experienced.

As the weeks progressed, Sarah grew stronger, and began challenging herself to talk to the men of the camp even if she did not remember their names or faces. Major Connelly soon became one of her strongest allies. With his warm, easy smile and patient tutoring, he repeated names and told stories about the command and its members that helped her associate faces with names.

"The men seem to admire their commander very much," Sarah commented one day, as they walked the grounds.

"There is no more noble man on or off the battlefield," Connelly replied, following her gaze toward Benton as he walked along the riverbank in deep conversation with another officer.

"Is he shy around women?"

Major Connelly laughed aloud until he saw the look in her innocent, upturned face and stopped himself abruptly by pretending to cough. "No, not particularly."

"Then I wonder if I have offended him." Sarah did not mean to say the words out loud, but when she did she quickly looked up at Connelly. "I mean, he seems to wish to keep his distance."

"He is a busy man, Sarah." He gazed at her with what appeared to be a look of concern and sympathy. "With many duties and responsibilities."

She forced a smile. "Of course. It's silly of me to seek his attention. It's just that..."

Connelly looked at her closely. "Do you remember something?"

She gazed at him and then over his shoulder. "Sometimes I see images. But they fly by so swiftly and seem so vague, they scarcely seem real."

"You remember nothing about Colonel Benton?"

"No." She shook her head, dismayed at herself that she did not. "But I *feel* it." She put her hand on her heart and looked at him with woeful eyes. "Deep."

Connelly took her arm and led her away from some other soldiers standing nearby. "You must not try so hard to remember," he said, seeming to fear what it would do to her fragile mind if she did. "It's important for you to look forward, not back."

Sarah blinked back tears that rose unbidden to her eyes. "But why? Did I do something to him?" She searched his eyes as if they held all the answers.

"Sarah," he started, then stopped and cleared his throat and stared at his boots a moment. "This is much more complicated than I can possibly...I mean..." Again he stopped. "I wish you would discuss this with the colonel."

Sarah sighed deeply, almost as if she were in physical pain, and then nodded. "Yes, of course, Major. It was very inconsiderate to have asked you." She picked up her skirts and turned away, but not before he had a chance to see the tears she had been unsuccessful in restraining.

"Sarah"—he caught her by the arm—"Sarah, you must understand that Doug...I mean, Colonel Benton...he feels somewhat responsible for your...It's just that he blames himself for the...He does not wish to—"

Sarah put her hand on his arm and forced a smile as she managed to rally her emotions. "I understand, Major...it is *complicated*." She gave him a nod and a teary smile and turned toward the house.

"He regards you highly," Connelly said, in desperation to her back, but she did not stop walking. "Above all others, I believe," he added. But she had already disappeared through the door.

* * *

Major Connelly searched for Benton, and finally found him talking to one of the scouts that had just come in. From a distance it appeared that Benton was back to his old self—yet Connelly knew he was not the same man at all. One had only to spend a few moments in his company to see that all traces of arrogance and vainness had disappeared from his character. He was amiable still, could briefly flash his charming smile, but he was different. And though he made an obvious attempt to avoid Sarah, the strong attraction he felt for her was always apparent in his lingering gaze.

Recalling his conversation with Sarah, Connelly could feel his anger building as he strode toward Benton, and it was evident in his tone of voice when he reached the colonel. With little sign of official military order, Connelly grabbed Benton by the arm and pulled him aside. "Sir, I need to have a word." He did not give the colonel time to speak. "You've got to tell her how you feel."

Although he mentioned no name, the topic was apparently not far astray from Benton's own mind. He pressed his lips more tightly as if enduring some secret torture. "You presume to know how I feel?"

"I know how *she* feels and that you are the only one that can help her."

"I am not worthy of her."

"No one is worthy of her!" Connelly took a deep breath to regain his composure and led Benton into the seclusion of some trees. "There is not a person in this region more honored than she. You could show her some consideration." He paused and stared intently into Benton's eyes. "She has a reliance on you, an attachment *to* you. She feels it, though she doesn't understand it."

"I want her to forget me—"

"*Forget* you? She believes you despise her! Why must you treat her like this?

"I need to suffer as she suffered. I need to sacrifice as she sacrificed."

"But she is *still* suffering!" Connelly threw his hands in the air. "You have been given the luxury few men get—a second chance. And you have somehow managed to mangle it worse than the first!"

"Again you make presumptions," Benton said quietly. "You presume I did not already know that."

"Why can't you just tell her how you feel?"

Benton shrugged and stared into nothing. "I want to do this the *right* way."

"There's no right way to do the *wrong* thing!" Connelly realized how loud his voice had become and spoke the next sentence in a mere whisper. "She does not want your pity. It's your affection she seeks."

Benton appeared detached and unmoved as he looked straight into his friend's eyes. "I killed the first Sarah Duvall," he said in a low, steady tone. "I intend to stay away from this one and do her no harm."

When Benton started to walk away, Connelly noticed he no longer moved like a warrior, but a man carrying a great weight upon his shoulders. Connelly grabbed his arm to stop him. "They are one and the same. Sarah Duvall did not die."

Benton stared at him with a look that was intense and grave. "She is different now. No one can deny it." He lifted his gaze and stared into the distance. "I may as well have put that rope around her neck myself."

Connelly took a step closer and gritted his teeth as he spoke. "Do you believe God gave her back to us so you could torture her with your indifference?"

"God gave her to the world—certainly not to me."

"But she does not blame you! *No one* blames you!"

Benton looked at him hard and forced a laugh. "You are quite wrong on that account, Major." He turned and spoke over his shoulder as he continued to walk away. "*I* blame me."

Chapter 26

In all your ways acknowledge Him and He will make your paths straight.
—Psalms 3:6

Dark clouds amassed overhead as the light of late afternoon began to cast long shadows on the yard. Sarah saw the dim light of a lantern burning in the outbuilding Colonel Benton used as an office, and decided to take Major Connelly's advice to talk to him herself.

A well-known scent greeted her as she stood in the threshold of the door, but it took a moment to recognize that it was the faint aroma of cigar smoke. Gazing contemplatively at the lone occupant in the room, she took a deep breath to calm her nerves before entering. Colonel Benton looked completely unpretentious with his coat off and his sleeves rolled up over his massive forearms, wearing a look of intense concentration upon his face as he leaned over paperwork. The sight of his manly form drove the blood from her heart.

"Colonel Benton?"

Benton came slowly to his feet as his eyes took her in, but he made no real gesture of greeting. He seemed grim and detached, and for an instant Sarah wondered if he even saw or, if seeing, recognized her. His manner appeared so imposingly serious and daunting that his very presence made her cheeks warm and caused her heart to race.

"Colonel, might I have a moment of your time?"

He motioned her in—again with no words—and then turned around to move his coat from the chair on which it lay. "Very nice to see you." He said words with his back to her, and they came out in a cold, raspy tone.

"Colonel Benton, I'm sorry to disturb you." Sarah held her hands at her side, clasping a handful of skirt with each to keep them from shaking. "But there are some things I don't understand. You will pardon me if I ask a personal question?"

Benton faced her, but his gaze was fixed on something over her shoulder, and his jaw appeared set and tense. Sarah waited for him to say something, but he did not move or even look at her. He appeared stiff and uncomfortable, and his cold, distant expression told her nothing of what she wanted to know. She looked down nervously at her hands, almost losing her nerve. "May I speak freely?" She uttered the words in a low, barely controlled voice, no longer sure if she should have come.

Benton glanced down at her and then shifted his gaze to the last rays of daylight thrusting themselves through the windows. "I am not afraid of frankness."

"No, I did not think you would be." Sarah suddenly felt suffocated. He seemed to fill the room to capacity with his mere presence, and his remote behavior almost drove her to speechlessness. Thinking about how foolish she would look simply running from the room, she swallowed hard and began. "One of the men insinuated that you once admired me greatly. Yet…" She took a deep breath in order to get through the sentence. "I see no evidence of that sentiment now."

A look that appeared to be pain crossed Benton's face. He motioned for her to take a seat, never relaxing his distant manner. "My feelings are unchanged on the subject, if that is what you are asking."

His tone was impassive as he reached for a cigar, but she thought she saw his solemn eyes flicker with emotion as he spoke. Sarah sat down in front of his desk and stared thoughtfully into the flame of a lantern as Benton lowered himself into his chair across from her. "It makes me wonder if I returned the sentiment."

The colonel seemed to contemplate the answer as he lit a match and waved it front of the cigar. "You rarely gave me an indication of what you were thinking." He stared thoughtfully at the glowing end a moment. "But if I were to guess, I would say you thought me arrogant and frivolous and overbearing."

She let her gaze drift up to meet his. "And was the opinion justified?"

He shifted his focus to the wall. "Most would say so."

"Yet, again, I see no evidence of those traits now," she said musingly, staring over his shoulder.

"I am a changed man."

The serious tone of his voice drove her gaze back to him. "How so?"

Benton stood and strode to the fireplace, putting his hand on the mantle as he stared at the flame thoughtfully. "I have learned what is important and what is not."

He seemed uncomfortable, yet it appeared that he answered the question sincerely. Sarah nodded as if she understood. "Likewise, I am a changed woman," she said sadly, "perhaps far astray from the one you once admired."

"No, not far at all." Benton turned around, yet still regarded her with detached and indifferent eyes. "And growing more similar every day."

Now it was Sarah's turn to stare blankly at the wall. "Yes, every day I grow stronger." She shook her head to clear her thoughts. "Yet this impenetrable wall remains ever around me. I have no past. No future. Only the present."

Perhaps Benton saw her eyes glistening unnaturally in the glow of firelight, because his voice suddenly softened. "Pray do not take my indifference toward you as unconcern," he said. "I just wish to spare you from—"

"From what?" She stared with sad eyes at his face wrought with emotion. He looked so weary and worn, yet, as always, he conveyed the calm dignity of a soldier.

Instead of answering right away, he walked to the window, drawing aside the curtain for a moment to gaze at the darkness that now pressed its face against the glass. "Whatever else my faults may be, I do not wish to misinterpret or misrepresent that which has occurred in the past."

Sarah was silent as she absorbed his last comment. "You wish me to remember on my own, with no influence from you?" She said the words thoughtfully. "At the risk of thinking ill of you?"

"What you will think of me when your memory returns is not for me to say." He glanced back over his shoulder at her, his dark eyes penetrating but sad. "I regret to say that whatever it is, it will no doubt be justified. I apologize in advance. My faults were unknown to me then."

Sarah put her hand to her temple as if by doing so she could straighten out her thoughts. "You said before I thought you arrogant and overbearing, yet you did not answer my question. Did I return any sentiment you had for me?"

Benton's answer came in an instant. "You risked your life on behalf of me and my men." He kept his back to her as he brought the cigar to his lips, apparently so she would not see his shaking hand. "Yet you never offered me any convincing proof to support my hopes."

"I see." Sarah bit her lip as she contemplated whether or not she should ask the one question that she most wished to know. She looked up at him and took a deep breath. "It's just that I wondered whether you ever thought of me—or wished to be with me—in whatever capacity we shared."

Benton's jaw noticeably tightened, but he stood stalwart and stoical, like a captain on a roiling sea. "The desire was there," he said in a cracking voice. "The opportunity was not." A long silence commenced until he turned his head slightly toward her in an effort, it appeared, to try to change the subject. "Are they taking good care of you?"

Sarah thought she saw a hint of warmth in his eyes for the first time, and it almost robbed her of breath. "A queen would envy my situation. Thank you, Colonel."

He merely nodded politely over his shoulder as he continued his watch out the window. "I am happy to be entrusted with the charge." Then his tone changed as he abruptly ended the conversation. "I hope my answers have been helpful."

Sarah gazed at his broad back, wishing she knew how to cut through the barrier he held between them. "Yes, sir. Most helpful."

She started for the door, but paused for a moment when she passed by him and touched his arm lightly. "I believe you are an honorable man, Colonel," she said. "And you have made at least one thing perfectly clear."

He lifted his head slowly but did not turn around.

"I would have been a fool not to have admired you."

When she crossed the threshold, Sarah gave him one more parting glance, hoping he would soften his stance and call her back, but he was staring out the window again, so she opened the door, stepped out into the night, and left him.

Chapter 27

Better is it that thou shouldest not vow, than that thou shouldest vow and not pay.
—Ecclesiastes 5:5

Benton more or less found his way back to his chair and sat there blindly staring at nothing, trying to erase her image from his mind. There were campaigns to plan and battles to win, with thousands of lives at stake. But when her sullen face flashed before his eyes again, it hit him with brilliant clarity that the only life that had really mattered he had failed to protect. And though he had thought himself possessed of her before, he knew what he had felt back then was nothing to what he felt for her now. She who had so strangely influenced his future was now so intricately entangled with his past and his present that he could not decipher where one stopped and the other began.

Staring contemplatively into space while drumming his fingers against the desktop, Benton came to the conclusion that Connelly was right. He could not continue to hurt her, not when she was so frail and didn't understand why. Surely she would accept his reasoning if he explained himself, and then she could go on living her life as God meant it to be.

Grabbing his coat off of the chair, Benton headed for the tree-covered paths that led down to the river to clear his mind. It was cold—too cold for anyone to be out—and he pulled his great coat around him to shield himself from the chill. With his thoughts churning and his gaze intent on the narrow path before him, Benton almost failed to notice the billowing folds of a skirt directly in front of him until it was too late. He stopped abruptly and slowly lifted his gaze, though he already knew to whom the silken layers belonged. They were standing so close when their eyes met that he took an involuntary step back and lifted his hands in the air as if suddenly finding himself being held at gunpoint.

Sarah smiled shyly at his reaction. "I'm unarmed, Colonel Benton."

Benton swallowed hard. Her eyes, so full of innocence and devotion, aroused and tortured his heart. He had not expected to meet her like this so soon and so close. He sucked in his breath as he tried to prepare for a duty which he had no desire to carry out. "I'm sorry," he said gravely.

"It's just...I thought I was alone."

When he said nothing more, Sarah stared at him intently. "You *can* be if you wish."

Tell her. Tell her all. She stood there, waiting for him to say something, a mixture of confusion and hurt spreading across her countenance. Benton felt robbed of breath as he gazed down at her upturned face, at the wind playing in her hair, and said nothing of what he wished to say. "You came to me earlier to ask a personal question," he finally said in a voice that cracked with emotion. "Might I ask one of my own?"

Sarah gazed up at him, then at the ground. "It would seem rude not to return the favor," she murmured.

Between asking the question and saying the words, Benton forgot what he wished to say entirely and utterly. The lines he had been rehearsing on his walk left him in an instant, and he blurted out something completely different. "The spring campaign is about to begin, and I was wondering if you've thought about where you'd like to go." He paused a moment. "When you're stronger, of course."

Sarah blinked and her cheeks blossomed red. He thought he saw a look of hurt flick across her eyes at his words, but it was so fleeting he could not be sure. "If you wish me to leave, Colonel Benton, you need only ask." She turned with a fling of her head and picked up her skirts, but he grabbed her arm to stop her. With raging eyes, she shook him off. "You seem to dislike being in my presence, Colonel," she said, stepping out of his reach. "Why can you not be grateful that I am sparing you the encounter?"

"You are mistaken." He could feel the beads of sweat gathering on his temple despite the cool temperature. If she only knew the terrible images that burdened his mind. If she only knew that the impulse to love her was stronger than the inclination to push her away and that the things she couldn't remember were things he could never forget. "I believe I told you earlier of my high regard for you, Sarah."

"And I thought you spoke the truth." Her head was bowed, and her lashes sparkled with teardrops. "Yet it is altogether obvious that you abhor me."

Benton stared at her long and hard, desiring to tell her a heartfelt secret, yet unsure of how to do so. Finally he shook his head and took a step toward her. "If I give you that impression, it is only that...that..."

"Yes, I know..." She turned her head away. "It is very complicated."

Even with her back to him and in her obvious weakened state, Benton could see there was something suggestive of defiance and pride in her deportment, just like the Sarah of old. "No!" he said, louder than necessary. He reached out and turned her around, holding her arms and shaking her gently. "No, it is not that!"

He wondered what was reflected in his own countenance as he gazed at the pale, upturned face before him and saw the hopeless, agonized expression that swept over it. He felt his heart breaking at the look of pain, and so with fixed and steady scrutiny he told her. "I regret that what I most desired to say to you has been left unsaid. It is a promise I made. That is all."

"A promise?" Her expression held a look of surprise. "To whom?"

He looked at her face, awash with grief and disappointment, and the tear that had let loose and spilled down her cheek. He longed then and there to draw her in his arms and reassure her, but the thought of his promise made him keep her at arm's length instead. In the time it takes a heart to beat, he rejected and repulsed every expression of his devoted heart. He couldn't bear to see hope kindled in her eyes, not after what he'd done to her.

"I made a promise to God," he said, letting her go and pulling his coat more closely around him to keep his hands occupied. "And as he kept his end of the bargain, I intend to keep mine... though it be the hardest thing I have ever done." The words seemed senseless, even to him, and he could tell that each one he spoke was a rivet of pain driven into the depth of her.

Sarah tentatively raised her hand to her face, and wiped away a tear. "But I don't understand. What does a pact between you and God have to do with me?"

He stared deeply into her eyes. "It is my fault," he whispered, his lips trembling. "All of it."

"It is in the past," Sarah said, repeating words that had been spoken to her. "Why must you recall it?"

He held his hand up to stop her. "I must." He took a deep breath and let it out slowly. "There was a time when I...when *we* believed that it was impossible that you were ever coming back—" He took a short choking sob and turned away, his shoulders heaving as he attempted to regain his self-control.

Sarah placed her hand on his arm. "If you do not wish to tell me…"

He turned at last with measured determination to face her. "No, I shall tell you all. You deserve to know. When it appeared your fate was all but certain, I prayed to God." He looked absently over her shoulder as he spoke. "I pleaded, I begged, I beseeched him to let you live. And in return, I promised to make a sacrifice that was equal to yours."

He brought his gaze down to hers. "You were willing to give up your life for me, and I was willing to give up that which meant more than anything to me. If God allowed you to live, I promised—" He paused and swallowed hard. "I promised God I would let you go."

Sarah stood silent blinking in the moonlight, obviously trying to process his words, to understand how very much she had once meant to him.

"God brought you back, and now I must honor my pledge."

"But surely I would never have asked it of you," she said disbelievingly. "And it is not what I wish now."

"It is done," he said, "though I'd give my immortal soul to change it."

She remained defiant despite the confused look upon her face. "But what about *me*? Have I no say?"

Benton lifted his gaze, unable to look into her tortured eyes. "I fear it is out of both our hands now. It is this promise—not my will—that compels me to comply."

"What if *I* do not wish to honor this pledge?" Her voice was low and measured now.

He turned away. "You only make it harder for me."

She grabbed his arm angrily. "But God would not have brought us together if he meant for us to be apart! He would not warrant we both be unhappy!"

"I do not ask you to understand it," he said hoarsely, "only to honor it.

"So you will stand by this pledge," she said somberly. "And in so doing, deny me that which I most desire?"

He turned slowly. "You remember caring for me?"

She threw her arms around his neck and laid her head upon his chest. "I do not remember, but I *feel* it," she sobbed.

When she lifted her head, he gazed down at her pale, agonized face that spoke volumes of regret and tortured love. Slowly he bent down and tentatively pressed his lips upon hers, but it was more like a farewell kiss to a loved one than a display of deep passion. "Sarah, think of me as one whose love for you was so unbounded and unselfish that he chose to be worthy of you rather than to possess you unworthily."

She put her face in her hands and sobbed. "Oh, Doug can you not be more merciful than a bullet? This is worse than death!"

Benton's jaw tightened and he turned away. "Nothing you say can increase the blame I put upon myself. I beg of you to believe me when I say that, be your grief what it may, it can never equal mine."

When she did not respond, Benton took a deep breath and willed himself to be strong. He turned back around and tried to keep his voice from cracking. "Sarah, please know that your memory will be ever sacred to me, but..."

"But?" Her eyes glistened unnaturally in the muted light of the moon.

"But I must honor the promise...Good night."

Sarah did not speak, yet there was something exquisitely painful in her silence as she stared at him with a mournful gaze. For a long moment she did not move, though she searched his eyes as if seeking a sign that he would surrender his principles to his passion. Apparently seeing none, she sighed deeply, turned, and walked away.

For the pain in his heart, she may as well have shot him. And for the pain in his soul, he'd much rather she had. "A thousand times I would give my life to change it, Sarah," he murmured. "A thousand times!"

Chapter 28

He is no fool who gives what he cannot keep to gain that which he cannot lose.
—*Jim Elliot*

Colonel Benton stayed occupied the next couple of days and was actually glad for the outlet that planning and preparing for war provided. He'd been up most of the night with his officers discussing the upcoming move, and welcomed the weariness that now consumed him. Barely awake at this early hour, he headed to the barn.

The sun had just begun to cast a brilliant glow on the landscape, but had not yet gained sufficient strength to melt away the light snowfall that had fallen overnight. Benton wrapped both hands around his cup of coffee, the heat from the liquid doing little to penetrate the bone-chilling cold. Saluting the soldiers he passed at the doorway, he continued into the warmer confines of the barn and inhaled its rich scent.

"Good morning, Kul-nel."

Benton nodded toward the soldier who greeted him. "Good morning. Quiet night?"

"Yes sir. All quiet here."

Benton continued walking, but stopped abruptly in front of one of the stalls. "Where's Chance?" He opened the door of the stall to convince himself there was no horse inside. "Has he been turned out?" Benton had taken the horse into his stable from the beginning, but never allowed it to be ridden even in the smallest skirmish. Everyone knew that if Chance were to be killed or even wounded, the loss would be too much to bear.

"No." The soldier walked up beside him and gazed casually at the empty stall. "Miss Sarah took him with her."

"Took him where?" Benton could feel his pulse begin to throb hard against his ribcage. Before his brain could even compute what was happening, his heart had already recognized that this abrupt departure, without a word and at such a time, boded ill.

"Wherever she went, I reckon," the soldier said. "I didn't get no details on that. Figured Mrs. Ramsey would have told you. She was down here boo-hooing all morning."

The soldier lowered his gaze to Benton's cup, which had begun to slosh coffee over the sides in his shaking hand, while Benton continued to stare into the empty stall, unable to move or speak. He had wanted to take her to the stable to reunite her with her horse some weeks ago, but the surgeon had thought it better to wait and not overwhelm her with too many images of her past. In the end, Benton had agreed, not wishing to harm her recovery when she was at last beginning to recover bits and pieces of her memory.

"Funny how that horse remembered her and all." The soldier apparently decided to ignore the colonel's silence. "I think Miss Sarah might even have remembered him too."

Benton thought back to the look on her face during their last conversation when she had stared so intently at him, appearing to see images he could not see. Perhaps she *had* remembered all.

"I need to talk to Mrs. Ramsey." Benton turned and headed to the house; his body suddenly seemed so heavy that he could barely find the energy to place one foot in front of the other for the short walk to the house. Concern, despair, and a feeling of complete detachment seemed determined to pull his legs out from under him.

"Colonel Benton, have you heard?" Mrs. Ramsey came rushing out of the house with her skirts flying wildly before he had even reached the steps to the veranda.

"She's left us! Poor dear child!" She patted her eyes with a handkerchief that appeared damp enough to wring.

Benton stood rigid and silent, incapable of accepting the fact she was really gone. "Where did she go?" His voice was low as if he didn't wish anyone to overhear the conversation, despite no one being around to do so. He continued to stare in the direction of Mrs. Ramsey's voice, but could not make out her features through the blur of pain that clouded his eyes.

"I don't know! She didn't say. Or she wouldn't say. Or maybe she didn't even know." Mrs. Ramsey began sobbing again. "She just said it was time to go. Why would she do it, Colonel Benton?"

Benton had a feeling she knew as well as he did, and so he did not answer. Instead he worked hard to suppress the powerful emotions that consumed him. "The spring campaign is set to begin," he heard himself telling Mrs. Ramsey. "There is little I can do to seek her out, I'm afraid. We will be moving out in two days."

Mrs. Ramsey brought the handkerchief back to her eyes and dabbed profusely. "Oh, why would she leave now," she whimpered. "Why?"

Benton took a deep breath and let it out slowly. "She felt it was time I suppose. We cannot question, only accept."

Mrs. Ramsey grabbed his arm. "Do you think she'll come back? I barely had time to say good-bye!"

"Perhaps in good time," Benton said, almost choking on the reply because he knew it was not true. "Perhaps in good time."

Although he spoke calmly and remained casually polite in front of Mrs. Ramsey, inwardly his heart writhed and ached and moaned. Benton had known he would be leaving and that he may never see her again—but he could barely stand the thought of losing her for good. He had not expected this ending so abruptly and so soon.

Benton bowed to Mrs. Ramsey and turned back toward the barn for his horse. They were starting the spring campaign early, and he would be leaving this place of peace and tranquility in two days. He had to move forward and forget the past. There was nothing else he could do.

Surely the move would bring some sort of peace—or at least a respite from the hard ordeal of thinking about the loss. It would force him to live each day and to take each hour as it came. Planning, riding, and fighting would take all he had to give and demand even more. He would allow nothing to stop him from giving his full attention to his duties.

But as he made his way to the barn, Benton was haunted by the face that continued to rise unbidden before his eyes. The frozen ground crunched beneath his footsteps as he walked; the muted sound came as waves over him and echoed in his mind like a crushing headache. How ironic that he could have any woman he desired, yet the one thing on earth he madly craved, was the one thing he would never possess.

Benton looked heavenward and thanked God that at least he had known its value before it was lost to him forever. And though he tried to console himself that he had done the right thing, the knowledge that he had kept his promise to the Almighty provided little solace. By honoring that vow, he had failed to keep another—the one he had made to himself. No amount of hopes or wishes could repair the pain he'd caused her, and no amount of appeals or prayers could possibly make her think of him as the greatest man she had ever known.

Chapter 29

Your God shall be my God. Where you live I will live and
where you die, there will I die, and be buried by your side.
    —*From Life of General Francis Marion*

May 1865

S arah rode slowly through the bramble of the overgrown path, the low-lying mist making it impossible to see the ground. It had been more than seven months since she'd been here last, and now that the war was over, she had to come back. Necessity, not nostalgia, brought her here. After spending the last few months of the war at field hospitals and even on the field, she was exhausted and penniless. She had nowhere else to go.

Deep in the woods, the lane was little more than a trace, but then the trees opened up and revealed what lay beyond. The scene appeared just as she had imagined—just as she had tried to prepare herself for. Drawing rein, she stopped and stared for a time at the desolation of the old ground that had been debated and fought over by both armies during the conflict. Only the two stone chimneys remained of the once-glorious home built by her ancestors more than a century before. The tangle of vines and weeds that had pushed their way into every inch of the yard told the story of war and neglect and desertion.

Sarah continued to survey the old homestead, trying to assess the damage that had been done and what would be required to repair it. The picket fence around the yard was gone—used as firewood by invading soldiers most likely—but the iron gate still stood, rusty and stubborn, like a silent reminder of days gone by.

A ray of sunlight suddenly stabbed through and mingled with the mist, creating a picturesque vista despite the devastation. Sarah closed her eyes as the wafting fragrance of wild rose brought back a rush of sweet memories. She imagined the scene as it had once been, unchanged, as if time had hung motionless since the terrible conflict had begun.

But when she opened her eyes again she saw that time and war had not passed Waverly by at all. Raspberry bushes ran rampant as far as the eye could see and broken glass lay strewn like tiny prisms in the area where her flowers had once grown in rich profusion. Here and there a few blooms still flaunted their brilliant hues through the bramble, making a show of defiant splendor amid the destruction.

Sarah sat perfectly still, mesmerized. Spring had adorned the limbs of the surrounding trees in splendid robes of green, and the cheerful chirping of birds from their branches made it seem as if nothing in life had changed. Yet all had changed. The peaceful, happy days she had spent at Waverly with the sound of laughter emanating from its rooms were gone forever. That life, one of family and home, warmth and comfort, was one apparently not destined for her.

Sarah had no other choice now but to make do with what she had and to trust in God to help her through the trying times ahead. She shrugged her shoulders and took a deep breath. The war and its turmoil had dominated her life for so long that they no longer had the power to bother her—or perhaps the taunting pain and deprivation were so common that she now accepted them as normal.

Sarah watched wisps of mist move and rise as the sun's rays in the east became more pronounced. The eeriness of the scene brought to her mind other recollections of times past, and she had to suppress a shiver. She could almost feel his presence here, could recall with startling clarity every detail of the first time she had gazed upon the stalwart figure in gray, the first riveting moment when their eyes had met. Her lips quivered as she thought of how he had ridden so brazenly into her yard… into her life. The thoughts made her realize how perfectly natural it was for her to be here. The heart, after all, naturally clings to the spot where it awoke into being and yearns to return to where it spent the first days of a new and different life.

She shifted her gaze to the tree under which her brother now slept and to the bench where she had been sitting that delightful spring day. And then her eyes misted over at the thought of all that had transpired since. The tears and losses, the shattered homes and vanished dreams. In the last three years, she had lived a lifetime.

Sarah took a deep breath and dismounted. She honored him above all men for the resolution and strength of moral principle that sent her away, yet it made her own fate still harder to bear. Leading Chance around the metal gate, she paused when something caught her eye.

A figure, ghostlike as it moved through the mist, walked slowly toward the tree that had graced the once-velvet lawn. Sarah blinked, thinking she must be dreaming—or perhaps imagining something she wished to see. But the figure did not disappear as she expected it would. It knelt down near where her brother was buried and remained quietly still, apparently communing with the tree or the earth.

After a seemingly endless eternity, her heart began beating again.

Sarah walked slowly toward the image, expecting it to disappear into the mist. "General Benton?" She wasn't sure she had said the name aloud, but the figure stood slowly and turned.

Sarah watched his chest rise and fall as his breathing became labored at the sight of her—but still he said not a word. Standing there with that pained look on his face, she read each line of doubt and regret, and then of courteous indifference. Yet, he stared and blinked as if expecting her image to shimmer and melt away, as she had thought his would. They gazed at each other without speaking until a flock of birds from above rushed in to fill the silence, breaking the spell.

"We meet again." Sarah could barely draw breath, but managed to speak the words in a tone barely above a whisper. Her heart, which had earlier stopped beating altogether, now fluttered against her ribcage faster than possible to count the throbs.

"Yes, a coincidence that our paths should cross…here." Benton lifted his gaze and, looking overcome and dazed, stared blankly over her shoulder. The expression he wore was grave, and his face appeared worn with fatigue. Sarah had heard passing accounts of his hard fighting the last months of the war. The suffering he had endured and the great hardships he had confronted told plainly upon his furrowed brow and the deep crevices around his eyes. Besieged by years of service, his brown and rugged face was now lined with the weight of responsibility and obligation. His ragged uniform, dirty as the ground and nearly the same color, hung much more loosely than it once had. Yet he still possessed an image of strength that compelled admiration. This was a man whose boldness and fearlessness had won more battles than any weapon. Even to the end he had been restless and treacherous, always warring or preparing for war. Sarah could only wonder at his strength after all he'd been through.

"Perhaps not coincidence. Fate." She looked him steadily in the eye. "The hand of God."

A look of pain—not physical—crossed his face, but he mastered it quickly. "A strange God indeed that would torture me thus." He closed his eyes and pressed his lips more tightly as if he were enduring a sudden, unexpected hurt.

"Then why did you come?" Sarah's voice sounded cold and angry even to her own ears. She had hoped he had been seeking her, but now she knew he had only come to say good-bye to the memories that remained at Waverly. How strangely fate had thrown them together again, and yet he remained determined to keep his distance.

Benton sighed heavily, and his brow creased with seriousness as he seemed to ponder her question. "I don't know." His gaze moved to the landscape behind her as if following a vapor trail of memories. He shrugged and shook his head again. "I don't know."

It appeared to Sarah he was trying to keep his expression impassive, but the throbbing nerve near his temple and the desire in his eyes, revealed more than his words implied. After a moment's pause, Benton finally returned her silent stare with a look that was steady and direct. "I'm sorry we had to meet like this, Sarah. But never say I didn't try to do the right thing for once." His words were not spoken loudly, but still his voice cracked. "And never doubt it was killing me with every breath I drew."

He turned away and his chest heaved as if his large heart was beating itself to pieces for the mistakes he'd made. How solemn and grand he appeared to her; how calm and holy. "And so you intend to leave." She said the words unemotionally, as all hopes for a brighter future dried up and died in her embattled heart.

"I could not do otherwise and be truthful." Although it was obvious he was hurting, he still exuded that cool, confident soldierly demeanor that she knew so well. He looked calmly over his shoulder at her. "I believe you know my reasons."

Sarah knew what dictated his words, and it broke her heart. He believed if he failed in his promise to God, he would stain the honor he prized above all earthly treasures. That knowledge and her familiarity with his good character caused a surge of emotions to swell within her. Whether from exhaustion after the long, hard ride or the sight of her war-torn home, the feelings swept upon her like a violent wave and dropped her to her knees. She put her face in her hands and sobbed, unable to explain the pain that seemed determined to split her in two.

General Benton knelt down and took her in his arms, his somber eyes upon her. "Don't do that, Sarah. Please. Don't cry."

For his sake, she quieted her choking sobs and allowed him to lift her back to her feet. "Don't ever cry like that again," he said, holding her against him. "Ever. For anything."

Sarah felt a tremor run through him as he held her, and she almost cried anew at the thought of his tortured heart. When he grew silent, she lifted her head and saw that his gaze was curious and questioning as he observed her intently. Seeming to yield to impulse, he raised his hand to her cheek and touched away a tear. Again his hand trembled at the contact as if a great battle were taking place within him.

Studying the dampness on his finger for a moment, he raised his gaze once again to hers. "You are real then?" He stared at her still seeming to doubt his own eyes. "Not a ghost to haunt me? Not a dream?"

"I am flesh and blood," she whispered, afraid of breaking the spell.

"Sometimes I thought I had really dreamed it all," he said as if speaking to himself. His face was expressionless, but his voice trembled. "That you had never really come back from the dead."

"Don't you see?" Sarah looked up at him with imploring eyes. "God brought me back for a greater purpose. To be with you."

He heaved a deep sigh and turned away again. 'That is impossible, I'm afraid." He shook his head and clenched his fists. "All I can ask for is a merciful judgment, because you will remember that my promise was made from no want of affection for you—but rather because there was no one whom I loved better."

Sarah put her hand on his arm and spoke calmly and quietly. "General Benton, I know you promised God you would give up that which you loved more than anything at the time, and you did. But that thing was not me."

He lifted his head and slowly turned around with an inquisitive look in his eyes.

"That which you loved above all else was yourself," she said quietly. "You stand beside me now a humble man and a believer. You fulfilled your promise."

Benton's brown eyes remained locked hers, but still he did not speak. She could see he was thinking back to the days when he was flamboyant, self-righteous, and proud. It was hard to imagine those traits now in the vulnerable, virtuous man who stood before her.

"Noble you were, General Benton. And nobler you have become." Sarah felt the breeze and the warm light, but otherwise, time stood still. "The ties that brought you back to Waverly are stronger than those of reasoning or logic. The same God to whom you offered your promise has heard my prayers to return you to me."

Benton frowned, and his tired eyes looked like they had not seen laughter in years. "If only your words were a magic dust that could mend the broken pieces of time. If only it were that easy to undo that which was done in the past." His cheeks seemed to have grown even paler, though his voice was still soft and betrayed no emotion.

"Everyone makes mistakes, General Benton," Sarah said softly, but firmly. "Providence does not ask that you pay for them for the rest of your life."

To that he was silent for a moment, but she thought she saw silent acceptance begin to gleam in his eyes.

"You remember then? All?"

"Perhaps not all, but enough."

He swallowed hard, and appeared to be having trouble speaking. "And you believe you love me?"

Sarah grabbed his coat with both of her hands. "More than life, Doug. Do you not know? More than life!"

He heaved a sort of shuddering sigh and took her in his arms, tightening into a possessive hold that caused her to gasp. She felt the labor of his heart against hers, strong and rapid, a sign of the emotions that consumed him. Slowly he relaxed his embrace.

"You came into my life here." He paused and looked up at the house and the grounds, and then lowered his gaze to hers. "And you never went away." He put his hand on his heart. "Not from here anyway." The depth of feelings seemed to give added eloquence to his words.

The soft light of morning spread, flowing over them and covering them both in its magnificent splendor. For a moment they parted, and simultaneously turned toward the spot where the house had once stood. To a passerby, the grounds appeared to be in shambles, but to them, there was still the grace and charm of the meadows surrounding it—and the memories that embodied it.

Sarah felt the rough texture of Benton's hand as he clasped hers and held it by his side, just as the bright eye of the sun bore through the mists of the morning, revealing a strange and peaceful solitude that isolated them from the rest of the world. For a long moment he did not speak, as if savoring the sensation of her hand in his and the feelings it wrought.

"You asked me before why I came," he said, still staring at the pile of debris that was Waverly. "I will tell you. I left my heart here…and I came to get it back." He spoke with his usual well-mastered self-control, but she felt him trembling.

"Then you will have to stay." Sarah spoke slowly and deliberately. "Because I intend to keep it."

If Benton was surprised by the comment, he did not show it. He drew a deep breath, as if unsure of himself and his feelings. "There is no sacrifice I would not make for you, Sarah," he said sorrowfully as the slightest trace of a tear ran down his manly cheek. "But I stand here a beggar, save for the sword I wore in defense of my country."

"Riches matter little." Sarah turned to the man whose noble, fearless, magnetic, character had captured her heart. "There are other things more treasured."

For the first time, Benton's lips curved into the semblance of a smile, as he seemed to sigh with a deep relief. "You told me once to measure time, if I must, in lessons learned—not in minutes or hours or years. Do you remember?"

Sarah nodded and lifted her gaze, soaking in the scene bathed now in dazzling light. She could envision the distant sun rising on her dew-sprinkled flowers in the garden and hear the birds in the sweet-scented morning air. She knew in her heart the walls of Waverly would indeed resound with laughter once again. General Benton must have been thinking about family and laughter as well.

"I'm sure you are anxious for news. I've received a message from Lucy."

Sarah looked up at him with inquisitive—yet fearful—eyes.

"She is well and Jake is thriving."

Sarah took a deep sigh of relief at the news. "And your men?" She looked straight up into his dark, magnetic eyes. "How did they fare?"

"Most have returned home to their loved ones."

Sarah quaked at the word *most*. "Major Connelly?"

He smiled. "He is well. Reunited with his wife and making a new way—he paused for a moment—"as we all must do."

Benton grew suddenly serous and gazed into her eyes with a new thoughtfulness and softness about his face. "I love you as never man loved a woman before." He paused in an effort to control his trembling voice. "But I wonder if I can ever be worthy of you, Sarah Duvall."

Sarah wrapped her arms around him and laid her head upon his heart, at home in the great strength that encircled her. She marveled at this man who had possessed such intrepid resolution and endurance during the war, and who stood before her now with such a tender and gentle soul.

"It is I who must wonder if I'm worthy of this great privilege." She leaned back in his arms, holding his face in her hands as she gazed at him with an expression of pure devotion.

"And what privilege is that?" His brown eyes searched hers, full of adoration and affection.

"Falling in love with the greatest man I have ever known."

Visit the author:

Website: www.JessicaJamesBooks.com
Facebook: www.Facebook.com/RomanticHistoricalFiction
Twitter: @JessicaJames
Blog: www.JessicaJamesBlog.com
Pinterest: www.Pinterest.com/SouthernRomance/

6263779R00121

Made in the USA
San Bernardino, CA
05 December 2013